How it Ends

How it Ends

a novel by

Catherine Lo

HOUGHTON MIFFLIN HARCOURT

Boston   New York

For information about permission to reproduce selections from this book, write
to trade.permissions@hmhco.com or to Permissions, Houghton Mifflin Harcourt
Publishing Company, 3 Park Avenue, 19th Floor, New York, New York 10016.

www.hmhco.com

The text was set in Adobe Garamond Pro and Freeland.

Library of Congress Cataloging-in-Publication Data
Lo, Cathy, author.
How it ends / Cathy Lo.
pages cm
Summary: Jessica is a good student who hates school because she is bullied by the
"cool" girls, and she is startled and grateful when Annie, the new girl in her southern Ontario high school, seeks her out on the first day of tenth grade and defends
her from the bullying—it is a friendship that both girls need, but one based on
assumptions and misunderstandings that ultimately threaten to drive them apart.
ISBN 978-0-544-54006-4 (alk. paper)
1. Best friends—Juvenile fiction. 2. Bullying—Juvenile fiction.
3. Miscommunication—Juvenile fiction. 4. Families—Ontario—Juvenile fiction.
5. Dating (Social customs)—Juvenile fiction. 6. High schools—Ontario—
Juvenile fiction. 7. Ontario—Juvenile fiction. [1. Best friends—Fiction.
2. Friendship—Fiction. 3. Bullying—Fiction. 4. Miscommunication—Fiction.
5. Family life—Ontario—Fiction. 6. Dating (Social customs)—Fiction.
7. High schools—Fiction. 8. Schools—Fiction. 9. Ontario—Fiction.
10. Canada—Fiction.] I. Title.
PZ7.1.L6Ho 2016
[Fic]—dc23   2015007154

Manufactured in the United States of America
DOC 10 9 8 7 6 5 4 3 2 1
4500593236

For Ernie, Ethan, and Mackenzie.

ALWAYS
and
FOREVER.

How it
Ends

HOW I SPENT MY SUMMER VACATION
By Jessica Lynn Avery

1. Recuperating from the disaster that was 9th grade.

2. Working in the mailroom at my dad's law firm, because:

  a. My dad is a strong believer in learning about the real world, and

  b. My mom is a strong believer in constant parental supervision.

3. Creeping the Facebook pages of my classmates so I could torture myself with evidence of what normal people do all summer.

4. Reading everything John Green has ever written.

5. Dreading today. The last day of summer. The day before 10th grade begins.

Jessie

Here's what I wish I could say about my summer vacation:

Working in the city was every bit as glamorous and exciting as I anticipated. My dad and I bonded over executive lunches and spent our train rides to work gossiping about our coworkers. The awkwardness that usually colors our conversations fell away, and my dad was proud of how I blossomed in the workplace, leaving my *issues* behind and functioning like everyone else. Down in the mailroom, I met the kids of other lawyers, and we engaged in the types of shenanigans you would expect from a bunch of teenagers experiencing their first taste of independence. On our last day, my new friends and I exchanged tearful goodbyes and promises to keep in touch online. I left work feeling ready for the new school year, knowing that the losers who torment me at school are just unsophisticated hicks who lack the intelligence and social graces to behave like decent human beings.

Here's how it actually went:

My father and I rode the train to work in silence. He read the paper or sent emails from his phone while I played Angry Birds on mine. Each morning, we parted at the front doors, where he gave me a heartfelt pep talk along the lines of *Work hard and don't embarrass me.* While he headed up to his posh office, I headed down into the bowels of the building, where a bunch of overprivileged kids pretended to work. I was greeted on the first day with about all the instruction I received all summer: do whatever the suits tell you, look busy no matter what, and what happens in the mailroom stays in the mailroom.

After that, I pretty much spent the summer walking the fine line between working hard enough to look busy but not hard enough to make my coworkers look bad. I'd finish my duties by lunchtime and then spend the afternoon hiding in a back corner of the mailroom, reading and fantasizing about how to transform myself into an Alaska Young or Margo Roth Spiegelman.

While my dad ate fancy lunches with clients, I snuck out to buy sauerkraut-covered hot dogs, devouring them right there on the street before scurrying back to the mailroom. I don't know where the other kids went. Most of them were the children of partners, and they looked down on me because my dad is just a regular lawyer. They moved together like a flock of birds, twittering away as they passed my desk each day at lunchtime, carefully avoiding eye contact. I'd watch them go, struggling to fill my lungs with air while the weight of loneliness settled itself on my chest.

So basically, what I learned about the world of work is that it's depressingly like high school. There are still cliques, everyone does the least amount of work possible to get by, and the beautiful people are in charge.

Aren't I a ray of sunshine?

The thing is, I know there are people who have it worse than me. I don't have a terminal illness, I'm not homeless or hungry, my parents are still married after a gazillion years, and I've never had to go through losing someone I love.

I keep reminding myself that things could be worse, but there are shades of gray, you know?

I do suffer from terminal loneliness, I'm so far from popular that the light from popular would take a million years to reach me, my parents fundamentally disagree about how to parent a kid like me, and I've never experienced love, because I'm apparently invisible to boys.

But on to the current crisis: tomorrow is the first day of school. Tenth grade.

I hate school. Which is ironic because everyone thinks I love it. I'm a straight-A student (booknerd) who always tops the honor roll (loser) at Sir John A. Macdonald High School (Seventh Circle of Hell) in our quaint little Southern Ontario town (hickville) in the great country of Canada (where everything is more expensive and less cool than in America).

It's not the idea of course work that has my stomach aching and my hands shaking. I have my fellow classmates to thank for that. Tomorrow I'll be thrust back into the same space as Courtney Williams and her pack of wolves. Tomorrow I'll be Lezzie Longbottom again.

I blame *Vogue* magazine and Harry Potter. That's how it all started.

It was a Sunday in November of seventh grade, and my mom

was caught in the grip of mother-daughter bonding enthusiasm. She'd bought a stack of fashion magazines in a thinly veiled attempt to make me into someone cooler, and we were sitting at the kitchen table flipping through them and brainstorming about a makeover. That's where I found the picture of Michelle Williams and her Mia Farrow–inspired pixie cut. I was obsessed.

It took two weeks of pleading and an hour in the stylist's chair to remove my long brown hair. While my mom's hairdresser worked her magic, I sat there imagining how sleek and sophisticated I'd look, and how impressed my friends Courtney and Larissa would be when they saw my daring hairdo. But when the stylist turned the chair around for the big reveal, I looked nothing like the adorably feminine Michelle Williams. I looked like a boy with a bad haircut.

I spent that afternoon in tears, convinced I'd be the laughing-stock of my school. I finally called Courtney that night, desperate for reassurance. As I tearfully explained my predicament, I heard laughter and voices in the background. "Do you have people over?"

"I'm having a sleepover," she announced, as my heart flopped out of my chest and onto the floor.

"I didn't know," I said lamely.

I spent Sunday tugging on my hair, willing it to grow even a little bit. I practiced styling it in front of the mirror and putting barrettes in to make it seem more feminine. But no matter what I did, I looked like a pudgy little boy. A vaguely familiar-looking pudgy little boy.

Which is where Harry Potter comes in. On Monday our teacher

went home at lunchtime with a headache, and the staff rushed around trying to find a way to occupy us. Someone found the first Harry Potter movie in the back of our supply cupboard, so we settled in to watch it.

My humiliation became complete on the train ride to Hogwarts, when Neville Longbottom appeared onscreen. That's when I realized who I looked like. Sadly, the rest of the class did too.

Whispers of "Longbottom" started immediately, but it wasn't until recess that I became *Lezzie Longbottom.* It was at recess that Courtney declared me a lesbian and said that I'd cried about not being invited to her sleepover because I wanted to see them all naked.

I'll never forget the way I burned with shame on the playground. I had nowhere to go and no one to talk to. The girls turned their backs on me and whispered about how I'd looked at them like I was *interested,* while the boys chanted "Lezzie" and offered me money if I kissed Courtney before recess was over.

Even now, with hair that's grown out to shoulder length, teeth aligned through years of orthodontia, and baby fat that's melted away, I *still* see Lezzie Longbottom when I look in the mirror.

If my mother wasn't such a freak, I'd beg to be homeschooled. I know how well that would go over, though. Mom takes every little thing I tell her and blows it completely out of proportion. Like when I told her about how Courtney teased me after my haircut. Mom made a federal case out of it, and the principal hauled Courtney, her mom, and my parents in for *mediation.* What a joke. Courtney's big blue eyes filled with tears, and she told everyone that she hadn't meant anything by it—it was just a little teasing. The very next day, she dubbed me a snitch and spread the word that anyone who talked to me would become an outcast.

Is it any wonder I started having panic attacks and refused to leave my room?

When the hiding out and avoiding human contact devolved into full-on depression, my mom found her new mission in life—fixing me. She's paraded me through countless doctors' offices and counselors' workshops. She buys every parenting book she can get her hands on, and has a new strategy every other day to unlock the normal kid in me. She's tried signing me up for sports, making me join clubs, taking me for "girls' days" so we can shop our cares away, and meditation classes to quiet our minds. She throws our digestive systems into turmoil with new diets that promise that *the elimination of this* or *the addition of that* will have wondrous effects on our mental health. The only thing she really hasn't tried is actually *talking* to me about how I feel and what helps me.

So I gave up being honest with her a long time ago. I take my Prozac every day and pretend it's all working. I don't tell my mom about how I spend my days hovering around the outer edges of the outcasts, pretending to be interested in comic books and video games just so I have people to sit with at lunch. I don't tell her that I plan my route between classes painstakingly, avoiding certain hallways and coming late to the cafeteria line so I won't run into Courtney and her friends. And I don't tell her how lonely I am. Every. Single. Day.

I keep reminding myself that in three years I'll be off to university for a brand-new start, while girls like Courtney and Larissa will have the best years of their lives already behind them. There'll be plenty of time for friendship then. For now, I just need to put my head down, focus on school, and ignore everything else.

Three more years. I just have to survive for three more years.

Annie

The suburbs suck ass.

This is my mantra as I walk to school. With every step I take, I repeat it to myself. *The suburbs suck ass. The suburbs suck ass.*

I hitch up my backpack and glower at the rows of cookie-cutter houses lining the street. If life was fair, I'd be dressed in my kilt and combat boots right now, headed back to Highland Girls Academy to meet up with my friends, the Highland Heretics (or Highland Nonconformists, as we renamed ourselves once the office freaked out. Turns out private Catholic schools are a bit touchy about the word *heretic*). This was supposed to be the year I'd finally get to take the subway to school on my own. I *should* be dodging commuters and homeless people at Union Station on my way to campus instead of trekking halfway across this pathetic excuse for a town.

I get why Madge wanted to move, but I'm still pissed that Dad agreed. According to Madge, there were too many memories at the old place, and we needed a new start as a new family. But those memories are sacred to me. I don't get how Dad could just sell the only house we ever lived in with Mom like it meant nothing, just to make his new wife happy.

And our new place. Fucking Madge. Our house in the city was

more than a hundred years old. It had *heart.* Personality. Sure, the basement was full of mice and the fourth stair up from the landing was in danger of cracking open at any moment, but it was a *home.* Our new place is a plastic replica of a house. It's all glossy surfaces with nothing underneath. It doesn't even make noise. That's just messed up. There are no creaks or groans, the pipes don't rattle . . . even the dishwasher is absolutely silent. That's not a house. It's witchcraft.

My old English teacher, Mr. Berg, would appreciate the metaphorical significance of this place. A silent pseudo-house for a silent pseudo-family.

When my alarm went off at six thirty this morning, it was basically mocking me. I was up all night obsessing about what to wear today. It's crazy — I'd been dying to break free from my school uniform for years, but now that the chance was here, I was paralyzed by too many choices. Should I be Preppy Annie, with skinny jeans and ballet flats? Or Studious Annie, with horn-rimmed glasses and cardigans? What about Cool Annie, with band T-shirts and a stack of cuff bracelets up my arm? I tried on outfit after outfit at the mall this summer, but they all felt false. Like I was trying on costumes.

So this morning, fueled by the kind of manic energy that comes with lack of sleep, I settled on being Pissed-off Annie, and I dressed all in black. I even layered on the black eyeliner and mascara in protest.

I was hoping for a reaction. I thought Dad might tell me to get upstairs and scrub off the makeup, or that Madge would disapprove of my angst-ridden appearance. Alas.

When I strolled into the kitchen, Dad greeted me with a kiss and a wink. "Good morning, little raccoon. Have you seen my daughter?"

Ha.

Madge dipped her head to hide a smile, and I fantasized about tipping my plate onto her perfectly pressed suit.

I slumped down into my chair just as Sophie breezed into the room. Her eyes barely touched on me, but that didn't stop her from commenting. "Halloween isn't for more than a month, Annie," she drawled. She daintily selected an apple from the fruit bowl and then looked pointedly at the stack of pancakes on my plate.

I don't know how and when our roles got assigned, but I don't remember ever agreeing to be the messed-up stepsister while Sophie got to be the perfect one.

It doesn't help that she's so goddamned gorgeous. As if my dad didn't screw me up enough by marrying the Wicked Witch of the West . . . he had to pick a wife with a Barbie doll for a daughter.

I'm almost at the school when a car horn beeps twice and I nearly jump out of my skin. I whip around to see Sophie waving at me, her car packed with shiny-faced girls. How is it that she has a car full of friends already and I'm stuck walking to school alone? She's like some kind of social wunderkind.

I raise my arm in a halfhearted wave, but they've passed me already, tires screeching as Sophie careens into the parking lot. I stand there on the sidewalk for a moment, taking in the sight in front of me. Sir John A. Macdonald is by far the ugliest school I've ever seen. It's like a giant concrete bunker plunked in the middle of this carefully constructed suburbia.

A blight on the landscape.

Kids are swarming around the entrance like bees. My classmates. I feel lightheaded and strange. Like I'm standing on the edge of a precipice. I have the dizzying feeling that once I walk through those doors, I might never be the same again.

I give myself a little shake and pull out my phone to text Gemma, my closest friend from the Nonconformists. I snap a picture of the school and then another of the long street of identical homes. *Held captive in suburbia,* I write. *Send help.*

I stare at the screen for a few moments, hoping for a quick reply. She'll be off the subway by now, probably checking in and getting her class schedule. I fight tears as I imagine strutting through the halls at Highland with my friends instead of slinking into this new school by myself.

When no text arrives, I shove my phone into my bag and take a deep breath. There's no escaping today. I square my shoulders and head across the street to be swallowed up by the crowd entering my new school.

I'm sitting in first-period English class when Gemma's reply comes in. *Chin up, Annie-the-brave. We miss you!* She's attached a picture of the whole crew. Minus me. Gemma, Stacy, and Susanna, with their smiling faces smooshed together. Stacy's eyes are closed, like they are in every picture ever taken of her, and a little laugh escapes me before tears fill my eyes. There's this huge pit of emptiness right in the center of my chest that yawns open painfully as I look at their happy faces. I should be there.

I slump down in my seat and check out my classmates. They're all so phony.

Except.

I sit up a little straighter when I catch sight of her. Unlike the rest of our classmates, who wear their coolness like a mask, this girl is beautifully uncool. She's perched on the edge of her seat, so caught up in what Miss Donaghue is saying that she's somehow managed to scratch her cheek with the wrong end of her pen, leaving a line of blue across it. She has frizzy brown hair bursting out of a thick blue elastic, no makeup, and she's wearing a sweater that's at least two sizes too big for her. And yet she's stunning. She has these huge brown eyes and the softest features. She's so painfully real that it almost hurts to look at her.

I take a last look at the picture of my Highland friends and then turn off my phone and stash it in my bag. I have a mission now, and it makes me feel better. Today, somehow, I will get to know this beautifully uncool girl.

Jessie

When people call you Lezzie, you learn to fear the whole locker-room experience. So when I saw gym on my schedule this morning, I broke out in a cold sweat.

If not for the long line snaking out of the guidance office, I'd have dropped that class faster than you could say *Team sports give me hives*. God bless the inefficiency of our guidance counselors, though, because in the kind of plot twist that just doesn't happen to girls like me, my whole world changed inside the sweaty confines of the girls' locker room.

But I'm getting ahead of myself.

At the beginning of class, I was sitting on the gym floor feeling like the answer to one of those which-of-these-things-doesn't-belong puzzles, when the coolest girl to ever walk through the doors of our school actually came and sat next to *me*. The whole school had been talking about Annie Miller all day. She moved here from the city, and she's like some kind of exotic animal plunked into the middle of our boring lives. I'd first noticed her in English. She was dressed all in black, with thick eyeliner rimming her eyes, and I'd pegged her as a stoner before I got a good look at her. She defies categorization. Under all that black, she was luminous. With bright red hair that fell in shiny waves down her back and green eyes so bright they didn't even look real, no one could possibly confuse her with a waste case.

In gym, Annie plopped down next to me and smiled like we were old buddies. "You're in my English class, right?"

Let me just take a moment to marvel over the fact that Annie noticed *me*. I almost checked behind me to make sure she wasn't talking to someone else.

"Y-yes. I think so. Miss Donaghue?"

Annie smiled so wide I could see her back teeth. "Isn't she *great?*" She leaned toward me. "I was thinking we should sit together at lunch."

I felt like I was going to explode right out of my skin. It was one of those moments that feel so good they're almost painful. Sweat prickled my palms and my heart raced, but not in the bad I-think-I'm-going-to-die way. It was . . . *pleasurable panic.* I guess normal people would call that excitement.

We spent the rest of gym class earning detentions for our poor attitudes, and I didn't even worry about getting into trouble, which is so not like me. It all started with Annie insisting that she was the worst gym student ever. I took one look at her athletic build and called her bluff. Hilarity ensued. We fell over ourselves trying to be the most uncoordinated, and we failed miserably at hiding our laughter from our overzealous teacher, who apparently thinks she's training future Olympians rather than teaching gym to a bunch of apathetic teenagers.

By the time we headed into the locker room after class, I was so recklessly happy that I forgot to keep my head down and not attract attention. It was an oversight that did not go unpunished.

"Looks like Lezzie Longbottom has a girlfriend," Emily Watson sang.

My heart stopped. I couldn't breathe. Being humiliated was one thing, but having it happen in front of someone like Annie was unbearable.

"What did you say?"

I blinked in confusion. One second Annie was right beside me, and the next she was across the room, bearing down on Emily and her friends.

Emily patted Annie on the head like she was a little kid. "You're new here, so you don't know about our little Lezzie Longbottom yet."

If I could have tunneled through the floor to escape the scene in front of me, I would have.

"Longbottom?" Annie asked, her hands on her hips. "Like, as in Harry Potter?"

Emily faltered, and Annie looked at me with an eyebrow raised. I nodded haltingly.

"Well," Annie said with a shrug of her shoulders, "that sounds like a compliment to me."

The girls burst out laughing.

"Maybe not to a bunch of bleached-blond illiterates like you, but to those of us who *read,* we know that Neville Longbottom was the real hero of Harry Potter."

"Who are you calling illiterate?" Emily challenged.

"Well, if you'd actually read the book, you'd know that Neville is all about bravery and kindness and loyalty to his friends." Annie walked over and looped her arm through mine. "I'm pretty proud to have a friend like that."

"*Girl*friend, you mean," Emily snarled. "You're obviously a lez just like her."

Annie tossed her hair and blew Emily a kiss. "You wish, honey. You wish."

* * *

Annie's defense of me in the locker room was like battle armor, and I spent the rest of the morning feeling invincible. That is, right up until the moment when I arrived at the cafeteria doors and found no sign of her.

She'll be here, I reassured myself as long minutes ticked by. We'd agreed to meet right there, I was sure of it. I peered through the window at the chaos that is our school's cafeteria. What if she already went in without me?

"Oh. My. God." A familiar voice rang out, turning my insides to ice. "Did you see what she was *wearing?* Some people try way too hard."

Courtney.

I panicked and hunted for an escape route. I didn't want to miss Annie, but I couldn't be caught standing there, all alone.

I let my hair hang down over my face and peeked out from behind my bangs. They didn't see me yet. I slipped away from the cafeteria doors and headed down the arts hallway, fear coiling in my belly. I was going to miss meeting Annie, I just knew it. Frustrated tears prickled my eyes, and I put my head down to hide them.

I made a beeline for the safety of the stairwell and crashed headlong into someone racing toward the cafeteria.

"Sorry!" Annie yelped before recognizing me. "Jessie? What's wrong?"

"N-nothing," I forced out, blinking hard. "Just . . . the first day of school sucks."

"You read my mind." She laughed, looping her arm through mine and pulling me toward the cafeteria. "Sorry I was so late. I got caught up talking to my art teacher." She held up her phone. "I'd have texted you, but I forgot to ask for your digits."

I rattled off my cell number, my heart thumping. "I should get yours, too," I said, fumbling with my bag.

"No need. Texting you right. . . . now."

I felt my whole body relax. Who was this girl? I'd never felt so immediately comfortable around anyone in my life. "C'mon," I said, "I'll show you where to buy the worst food you've ever tasted."

We waded into the lineup, and I watched in wonder as Annie shamelessly heaped fries, chocolate milk, and two enormous cookies onto her tray. By the time we strolled out to look for a table, I felt giddy, my earlier panic forgotten. For the first time ever, I walked through the cafeteria with my head held high, feeling like a new person with Annie by my side.

"Who do you usually sit with?" she asked innocently, peering around at the crowded tables.

My heart lurched, and I snuck a glance at my fellow outcasts at the back table. Charlie and Kevin were sitting with a girl I didn't recognize. They were all hunched over their laptops, most likely playing an online game over the school's WiFi.

I couldn't take Annie over there. She thought I was cooler than that. "I don't see the people I sat with last year," I lied, angling my body away from them and dropping my tray onto the nearest empty table. "Let's sit here."

"Okay . . ." Annie said, looking puzzled. "But . . . isn't that guy over there waving at you?"

I looked up to find Charlie flailing his arms like he was about to take flight. *Oh, good Lord.* I waved back and smiled shyly at Annie. "He's just someone I know from class."

"Should we go sit with them?"

"Maybe another time," I said, not wanting to share her.

"I think he likes you," Annie declared, sitting at the table and popping a fry in her mouth.

"You're insane."

"What? He looks totally bummed we didn't go over."

I looked back at Charlie. He definitely looked disappointed, and I could guess why.

"Trust me," I told Annie. "I hung out with them for a while last year, and he never gave me a second glance. If he's disappointed, it's because he didn't get a chance to meet the hot new redhead at school."

Annie

Holy shit.

"Are you kidding me?" I whirl around and glare at Jessie. "You're crazy, you know that? Certifiable."

"You hate it," Jess says, like a complete idiot.

"I *love* it! I cannot believe *this* is the room you were afraid to show me. I'm so stinking jealous that if I didn't like you so much, I'd hate you."

Jess's face melts into a relieved smile. She's such a freak. I swear to God, she worries about the most random shit. She obsessed all the way home from school, telling me over and over that she hasn't redone her room since she was a kid, and that she's never put much thought into it. I was expecting *Dora the Explorer* and Barbies, the way she was freaking out.

I drop my backpack by the door and rush into the room. "Would you look at all this *space?*" I say, twirling around with arms spread wide. "I could do cartwheels in here."

Jessie inches into the room and I grab her by the hands, twirling with her until we both fall, dizzy and laughing, onto carpet so thick I feel like it's hugging me.

"It's like nerdvana in here," I tell her, surveying the room.

Her face falls. "That's me." She sighs. "Nerd extraordinaire."

"Nerds are sexy," I say, pulling on her ponytail before getting up to check out her books. No joke, Jess has an *entire wall* of bookshelves, filled with the most kick-ass collection of books I've ever seen. I run my fingers along the spines, feeling like I'm looking into her brain. There's something of everything in here, from Judy Blume to A. S. King, to Maya Angelou to Charles Bukowski. There must be thousands of dollars of books on these shelves. This isn't a bedroom—it's a library.

And there's more.

She has a fucking reading area. And I'm not just talking about a beanbag chair in the corner. This girl has a full-on leather armchair, with a wooden table and a fancy reading lamp, like something out of a magazine.

And her bed. My God.

When I was a kid, I remember clearly the bed I wanted more than life itself. It was pink and girly and had a canopy. I shit you not, it was the exact bed Jessie has in her room.

If you paid a Hollywood stylist to design the perfect room to suit Jess's personality, she couldn't have come up with anything more perfect.

"Your room is probably way cooler," Jess says, picking at the carpet and eyeing me nervously.

"Are you crazy? My room is four blank walls and a bunch of unpacked boxes. I just never know what to *do* with my room, you know? I don't know how to make it mine, like you have."

I wander over to the far wall, where Jess has posted a collection of quotes.

"Let me guess which is your favorite," I say, running my fingers over the papers before stopping on one that makes me smile. "This one?"

It's "The problem with the world is that the intelligent people are full of doubts, while the stupid ones are full of confidence."

Jessie laughs and shakes her head. "That's a good one, but I love this one more." She points to a quote from a *Calvin and Hobbes* comic strip: "Reality continues to ruin my life."

I stop in front of a page marked *Alice in Wonderland* and feel the air rush out of my lungs. It reads, "I can't go back to yesterday because I was a different person then."

"That's a good one too." She pulls the page off the wall and hands it to me. "For your room. It's time you started decorating it."

I could kiss her.

Instead, I grab my sketchbook out of my bag and head for her bookshelf. "Let's find some new ones to add to the wall."

We sprawl on the carpet, flipping through books and sharing the quotes we find. Jess scribbles her favorites into a journal she pulled off the bookshelf, and I copy mine into my sketchbook before adding drawings and embellishments.

I'm finishing my fifth or sixth sketch when I look up and realize that more than an hour has passed in silence. I sneak a look at Jess. She's sitting cross-legged with a book in her lap, chewing on a piece of hair that's come loose from her ponytail. I stop sketching quotes and start drawing her instead. There's something so intense about watching someone when they don't know anyone's looking. All the *stuff* they carry around with them falls away, and you can catch the quickest glimpse of who they really are, underneath everything.

I'm drawing Jessie's eyes and marveling at how the little line that's usually between them smooths out when she reads, and at that moment she looks up and catches me watching her.

"What?" she asks, swiping at her cheeks. "Do I have something on my face?"

I shake my head and stop sketching. The little line is back on her forehead. "I was drawing you," I tell her, holding up the page so she can see.

"Oh my gosh," Jessie breathes. "That's amazing." She comes over and sits beside me. "I didn't know you could draw like that."

I shrug. "Drawing is easy. It just takes practice."

"Clearly you've never seen my impressive collection of stick figures."

I look down at the drawing in my lap. I've messed up the eyes, I realize. And the shape of the face isn't quite right. I flip back to a book-quote page. I don't usually show my sketches to anyone, and I'm not sure what possessed me to share a half-finished one.

"Any new quotes?" I ask, gesturing at her notebook.

She picks it up and reads a few to me. She's come up with: "I am haunted by humans"(Markus Zusak), "Sometimes people just want to be happy, even if it's not real" (Veronica Roth), and "Never trust anyone who has not brought a book with them" (Lemony Snicket).

She looks over at my sketchbook, open to "It does not do well to dwell on dreams and forget to live," and groans. "No Harry Potter."

I blink at her in surprise and then remember the locker room. "Don't be stupid. You can't let a bunch of idiots turn you off of Harry Potter. You're a reader!" She looks like she's about to cry. "Besides," I add, "you are *so* Hermione Granger."

She laughs through her tears. "It's the hair, isn't it?"

"Kinda," I admit. "But mostly 'cause you're bookish and smart."

She points at my sketchbook. "What else have you got in there?"

I flip through the pages, stopping at a quote I memorized from *The Bell Jar*. "This one's my favorite: 'I felt sorry when I came to the last page. I wanted to crawl in between those black lines of print the way you crawl through a fence.'"

"I've felt like that," she whispers.

I nod, and flip through the other quotes I've sketched out. She stops me at "There will come a time when you believe everything is finished; that will be the beginning."

"I love that," she says, surprised. "I've never seen it before. Where'd you find it?"

"I actually don't know where it's from. My dad says it all the time, and it just popped into my head." I pull the page out of my sketchbook and hand it to her. "From me. This'll be my contribution to your wall."

"Our wall," she corrects, taping the page to the empty space where the *Alice in Wonderland* quote used to be.

"Yes," I agree, feeling at home for the first time since we moved out here.

Our wall.

Jessie

Annie is the geekiest cool girl ever. She's like a rebellious supermodel who's secretly a complete nerd underneath.

I mean, really, how many girls with true popularity potential would opt to join the Avery Family Games Night willingly? I thought I was going to die on Monday when my mom told Annie all about our Friday night ritual of tacos and board games, but Annie practically begged for an invitation.

She's been over at my house nearly every day since school started, but never for one of our goofy family dinners. I was a complete basket case before she came over tonight, and my mother's antics certainly didn't help.

"Look what I found," Mom singsonged about half an hour before Annie was due to arrive. She held up the most enormous sombrero I'd ever seen. It was green and yellow, with little white balls hanging off the rim. "Can you believe I found one for Annie?"

"Oh my God, Mom. Please, please, please put that away. Can we *not* do the sombreros tonight?" The thought of Annie wearing that straw monstrosity was more than I could bear.

"What in the world are you talking about, Jessica? Of course we're doing the sombreros. We do the sombreros every Friday. It's *tradition.*"

"A tradition I think we should most definitely keep in the family. *Exclusively* in the family."

"You're being ridiculous," my mom scolded, pulling the other three sombreros out of the pantry while I broke into a cold sweat. "Annie is excited about taco night. She's going to love this."

My heart banged against the inside of my chest, and I debated telling my mom that she was coming dangerously close to giving me an anxiety attack. With my luck, though, she'd have an ambulance here in five minutes, and Annie would arrive to sombreros *and* paramedics.

"Mom, maybe we should set down some ground rules before tonight," I said, trying not to sound shrill. "Let's not scare Annie away forever with our craziness, okay?"

"What's gotten into you? This is hardly the first time Annie has been over here. What are you so nervous about?"

I opened my mouth to explain, but words failed me. How do you tell your mother that she gets embarrassing when she hits the tequila on taco night? Or that cutthroat Monopoly might not be cute to an outsider?

Before I could translate my panicked thoughts into words, the doorbell rang and Avery Family Games Night began.

Of course, as usual, I'd worried far too much. Annie embraced my family's craziness like she was born into it. She wore her sombrero with pride and devoured a whopping seven tacos, beating my dad out for the title of biggest eater and forever earning his respect. She also convinced me that we should speak Spanish all throughout dinner, which proved hilarious given that our only exposure to the language had been *Dora the Explorer* episodes and Taco Bell commercials.

"Hola, soy Annie."

"Un taco, por favor."

"Cuidado, amigo."

"Vamanos!"

Later on, while my dad was destroying us all in Monopoly, Annie masterminded a strategy in which the three of us conspired to bring him down. I watched with a mixture of amusement and reverence as my parents laughed their way through the bending and warping of the rules. Only Annie could get away with messing up Monopoly during games night.

When my parents busted open the tequila, Annie and I escaped to my room.

"Thanks for tonight," I told her, my voice breaking.

"What are you thanking *me* for? I'm the one who invaded your family night."

I rolled my eyes. *"Endured* my family night, you mean."

"No," she said, suddenly serious. "You're really lucky, Jess."

"I take it your family doesn't do games night?"

"You know I have a stepmom and stepsister, right?"

I nodded. "You mentioned."

"My mom died in a car crash six years ago," she said flatly. "I haven't had much of a family life since then."

My stomach started to hurt. "I'm sorry."

She shrugged. "It is what it is. Now my dad's remarried to a total bitch and I'm the freak of my family."

I reached out and put my hand on her arm, feeling awkward. I had no idea what to say.

She swiped at her eyes and flashed me a too-bright smile. "Think your parents would adopt me?"

"In a heartbeat."

"Then I'll be an honorary Avery," she declared. "And we'll be sisters."

"We can speak Spanish and eat tacos together forever," I confirmed.

The conversation moved on, but I felt unsettled, like I'd left something unfinished.

It wasn't until hours after she'd gone home that I finally thought of all the things I *should* have said. I considered calling, but I didn't want to drag her mind back to that sad place.

I sent a text instead: *"Friendship is its own kind of family."*
—*Jessica Avery*

Her reply was almost instantaneous: *"Yo quiero Taco Bell."*
—*Chihuahua*

Annie

Sketchbooks, graphite pencils, modeling clay, canvas, brushes, acrylics . . . Charcoals! I forgot charcoals.

I yank a pencil from the bun on top of my head and add yet another item to the list I've been compiling since third period, when my art teacher announced our independent study project.

It *must* be almost seven o'clock by now, I figure. But when I check my clock, it's only 5:09. *Crap.* So far, I've cleaned my room, organized my desk, finished my science homework, and revised my list of art supplies . . . and there are still nearly two hours till my dad gets home.

I'm seriously losing my shit over this art assignment.

I had a full-on out-of-body experience in class today when Mr. Belachuk explained how we'll be creating a portfolio of work that expresses who we are as artists. One minute I was sitting there looking over the assignment sheet, and the next I could see my mother's paint-flecked hands and smell the solvents she used to clean her brushes. There was this ache in the middle of my chest, and I just knew that the only way to fix it was to *create* something.

That's when I started making my list and fantasizing about

shopping for supplies. I want to do it all—sculpture, paintings, sketches. I want to take the mess inside me and transform it into one beautiful thing after another.

Two hours.

I let my head fall forward onto my desk. We'll never make it to the store tonight. Even if we eat right at seven o'clock, when Dad gets home, he'll still want to check in with Madge and get changed and watch the news. The sign in the window of Morton's Art Supply will flip to CLOSED and I'll still be stuck here, crawling out of my skin.

I groan and pull out my sketchbook in an effort to distract myself. Of course, it just happens to fall open to the drawing I started at Jessie's house the other day, ratcheting my frustration level up even further. It's driving me crazy that I can't get this sketch right. Portraits are usually my specialty. There's this point when I'm drawing a face where everything comes together and the essence of the person shines through. It's like magic, the way it happens. One minute it's a simple drawing, and then, with just the right line here or bit of shading there, it suddenly springs to life. I can't seem to get there with Jessie, though. No matter what I do, the sketch stays lifeless.

I throw my pencil down. I have *got* to get out of here.

There is one option. The absolute last-resort, can-barely-even-stand-to-think-about-it option. Madge. If I swallow my pride and suck up just a little bit, she might cave and give me some cash so I can take the bus across town and start shopping.

I close my eyes and let myself imagine the feeling of wandering the aisles at Morton's with no one to rush me or complain when I spend twenty minutes marveling over the rainbow of colors in the acrylics section or admiring the shelves of blank canvases just waiting to be transformed.

Before I can think twice about it, I'm suddenly in the kitchen, clutching my list like a talisman.

"Smells great, Madeleine," I say, cringing at my own false sincerity. "Need any help?"

Madge's eyes narrow in suspicion, and a smile tugs at the corners of her mouth. "You can set the table," she says. "And then fill me in on whatever it is you want."

I grip the page tighter. "I have an art project coming up," I tell her, "and I really want to buy some new supplies."

My heart starts thumping as her lips press into a straight line.

"You don't have to drive me or anything," I blurt. "I'm totally cool with the bus. I just need some money, and I don't want to wait till Dad gets home." The words are flying out of my mouth and I want to snatch them up and stuff them back in there. I *never* beg Madge for anything.

The balloon of excitement that's been keeping me afloat all day hardens into a heavy weight as she gets that *look* on her face. The one that says I'm an inconvenience.

"Have you been through the boxes downstairs yet?" she asks with a sigh. "We paid the movers a fortune to haul everything here, and I remember at least four or five boxes from your room labeled

Art Supplies. There's also Sophie's old art kit, and I'm sure my water-colors are down there too. It would be such a waste not to use what we already have."

Yeah, right. First off, I'm pretty sure Sophie's old "art kit" has Crayola written on it. And second, Madge hasn't picked up a paint-brush in all the time I've known her, so whatever *watercolors* she's talking about are ancient.

Her mouth keeps moving but I tune her out. I know this lec-ture already. Madge loves words like *wasteful* and *responsibility* and *sacrifice*. I've heard every combination of them imaginable. *Don't let her get to you,* I remind myself, stuffing my list into my back pocket. Madge doesn't matter. My dad will understand. I'll just wait and ask him.

✳ ✳ ✳

By seven o'clock I have a solid plan. I'll wait until dessert. Dad's always in a better mood after he eats. I'll tell him all about art class and show him my sketchbook so he knows how serious I am. My school sketchbook, that is. Not the one I keep under my bed titled *101 Ways to Make Madge Disappear.*

I manage to choke down two whole bites of dinner before realiz-ing that I'll never last till dessert. My heart is pounding and my knee is bouncing and everything tastes like cardboard. I run my fingers over the list perched on my lap right before I explode.

"I need new art supplies for a project, and I made a list!" I prac-tically shout, waving the page like I'm performing a magic trick.

Everyone jumps in surprise, and Sophie looks at me like I've sprouted another head.

My dad recovers first. "Art supplies? For school?"

"Yeah," I say, feeling my cheeks go hot. "We have this big independent study project where we have to make an artistic statement using different media."

"Well, now," Dad says, sitting back in his chair and looking at me closely. "It's good to see you excited about something again." My heart throbs. Dad's always rushing from one thing to the next. I can't remember the last time he stopped and gave me his full attention.

All the hard edges around my father disappear for a moment, and he suddenly looks just the way I remember from when I was a little kid. Before Mom died. Before Madge. There's a warmth in his eyes that I haven't seen in forever. I want to race to my room and grab my sketchbook to capture him just like this.

"A portfolio," he says wistfully. "You sound just like your mother right now."

Dad hardly ever mentions Mom anymore, and never around Madge. I think on some level, he knows that hearing about my mom is too much for her. It's not like my parents got divorced or broke up or anything. Mom died. And a piece of him died with her. This happiness Madge fights so hard to protect is a pale shadow of the happiness he used to know.

I beam at him and then, without even meaning to, sneak a look at Madge. All the color has drained from her face. My heart skips a beat, and I have a confusing moment of pity for her before my anger flares up. *I should be able to talk about my mom in my own house.*

My dad obviously notices her too. "You know, Madeleine is quite creative, just like you, Annie," he says.

I raise my eyebrows and fight the impulse to laugh out loud. Madge is the opposite of creative. The first thing she did when she moved in with us was take down all my mother's paintings and replace them with hokey prints of kittens and sunsets.

"I know nothing about the art world," my dad goes on, turning to Madge. "You'd be the perfect person to take Annie shopping and help her pick out supplies."

"Oh, I don't think Annie would be interested in that," Madge sniffs. "We already discussed this earlier, but apparently she didn't like the plan *I* proposed."

My dad looks back and forth between us, his brow furrowed. "Plan?"

"I *told* Annie that if she went through the boxes of supplies downstairs and made a list of things we don't already own, then I'd take her shopping for what she needs."

I gape at her. "Um . . . no, you did not!"

"Pardon me?" she says. "Did I not tell you specifically to check the supplies downstairs?"

"Yes, but you *never* said you'd take me shopping. You said I should use whatever leftovers were down there."

Madge sighs and gives my father a pointed look. "This is exactly what I've been talking about, Martin. I'm just trying to put some basic rules in place, but she has no respect for my authority. When she doesn't like what I have to say, she just runs to you for a different answer."

Dad rubs his hands over his face. "All right. Annie, I didn't realize you already had an arrangement with Madeleine."

"She's lying! She just doesn't want to spend the money on my supplies, and it's totally unfair. How come Sophie gets to spend two hundred dollars on a pair of jeans and I can't buy new supplies *for school?*"

"Whoa!" Sophie says. "Don't drag me into this mess. Besides, I have an interview at the mall next week anyway. I can pay my own way, thank you very much."

"But Sophie, your schoolwork!" Madge cries.

"Relax, Mother, it's a part-time job, not a career choice."

"I'll get a job too, then," I say, turning to face my dad. "I'll pay you back every penny, but I really want new supplies. This is *important* to me." I widen my eyes at him, willing him to understand. Art is sacred to me. It's what ties me to my mom. I don't want to use Madge's cast-off leftovers for this project. I don't want Madge involved at all.

"Enough with the job talk," Madge snaps, slapping her hand down on the table. "This isn't about jobs *or* money. It's about entitlement, Annie. We all know you've had to make adjustments, but just because your life is hard, that doesn't mean you get to do whatever you want and get whatever you ask for."

I grip the edge of my chair to prevent myself from launching across the table and slapping the smug expression off her face. I can't believe she's calling *me* entitled.

"Dad," I say, ignoring her, "you *know* I never ask for anything. I'm not being unreasonable here. I'm asking for stuff for school."

"You girls are killing me," my dad groans. "You know that, don't you?"

Madge and I both sit on the edge of our seats, waiting to see whose side he'll take.

"Of course you can have the supplies you need, Annie. We are not in such dire financial straits that we can't afford materials for school."

I beam at him.

"However," he says ominously, "Madeleine does bring up an important point. You can't just ignore everything she asks you to do. We're a family now, and you need to show Madeleine the appropriate respect. It's not fair to her that you don't follow the rules she sets out."

I can feel Madge's gloating eyes on me, and I refuse to give her the satisfaction of a reaction.

"The plan she's proposing seems perfectly reasonable to me," he goes on. "No one is forcing you to use old materials that don't meet your needs, but it's only logical that you should at least look through what we have to see if there's anything worth saving . . ."

"Fine," I say, knowing I won't find anything useful.

"And I want to see you put a genuine effort into reusing anything that might work," Madge lectures, unable to hold back. "In fact, I plan to compare your shopping list to what's down there to make sure you're keeping up your end of the bargain."

I glare at her before turning to my dad. "Are we done here? I'd like to be excused."

Dad looks to Madge for approval, making my blood boil.

"She hasn't finished her dinner," Madge says disapprovingly, "but I suppose if she clears her space and agrees to make more of an effort . . ."

I stand up before she can finish her sentence and gather my dishes with a clatter. *Make more of an effort.* What a bitch. Madge hardly even *talks* to me, except to order me around and remind me that she's in charge. She slobbers all over Sophie, giving her every little thing she asks for, and then ignores me ninety percent of the time.

Back in my room, I flop onto my bed and fumble with my headphones, pushing them into my ears and cranking up the volume on my iPod until the music is punishingly loud. Three Days Grace's "I Hate Everything About You" slams into my brain, obliterating the image of my dad letting Madge crap all over everything important to me.

I burrow under my covers and let the music wash over me until there's no more Madge or Dad or Sophie or me. Until my heart stops pounding and my brain stops screaming. *Goddamn* that art class, making me feel all inspired. I know better than to get my hopes up like that. *Stupid stupid stupid.*

A Nine Inch Nails song is pulsing to an end when I finally crawl out from under the covers. I turn the music down to a less earsplitting level and switch from my angry playlist ("Madge Sucks") to my relaxing playlist ("A World Without Madge"). Paramore's "The Only Exception" washes over me as I reach for my secret sketchbook and flip through the series I've been working on, detailing the many and varied ways Madge might meet an untimely end. Right after #41, *Abducted by sadistic aliens with a penchant for medical experimentation*, I start in on sketch #42: *Buried alive beneath an avalanche of second-rate art supplies.*

Jessie

"I know!" Annie shouted, shattering my concentration for the millionth time. "A werewolf who secretly does good deeds . . . like fighting crime. A werewolf superhero."

"You mean, when he's not morphing into a cold-blooded killer?"

"Exactly. To make amends for his sins." Annie pecked away at her laptop and then frowned at the screen. "That's cheesy, isn't it? I can't do cheesy."

"A werewolf with a heart of gold? Definite cheese potential."

Annie groaned and pushed her laptop away. "What have *you* got?"

I held up my brainstorming page for her to see. So far, all it contained was the word *Brainstorming* underlined twice.

Our assignment was to write a short story that turned an idea on its head. "Give me the unexpected," Miss Donaghue had enthused. "Make me see the world in a whole new way."

It had sounded exciting in English class. But trapped here in my room on a Saturday afternoon, it was becoming a nightmare.

I pulled out my laptop and opened my documents folder, scanning its contents for inspiration. I've started dozens of stories in the last year. *Started* being the operative word. I can't seem to finish any.

I stared hard at the long list of half-written documents lined up accusingly on my screen. I can't figure it out. Every teacher I've ever had has raved about my writing. I can *start* stories all day long, and they all begin with such promise. I get high off the potential of it all. There always comes a point, though, where everything falls apart and I'm powerless to put it back together.

Basically, I suck at endings.

No. That's not quite right. I'm *incapable* of endings.

"You know what we need?" Annie asked, pulling me away from my gloomy thoughts. "Retail therapy."

I snorted and turned back to my laptop. "Yeah, right."

"I'm serious. We need to get out of this room and clear our heads."

I felt my shoulders tensing up. "I can't go anywhere," I said. "This assignment is due *Monday*. That's the day after tomorrow."

"Thank you for the days-of-the-week lesson, Einstein. We still have tonight and all day tomorrow to finish. And you have to admit, we're just wasting time in here. We've been working for two hours, and all we have to show for it is a shitty werewolf idea and a blank brainstorming page."

Annie grabbed her bag off the floor. "C'mon. Live a little! Come out of your room and step into the real world. Inspiration might be waiting for us at the mall."

"The mall is the least inspiring place in the world," I squeaked out unconvincingly. "And I planned to have this finished by to-night."

"It's not due till Monday, freakshow. You need to calm your shit down. There are no bonus points for finishing a day early."

My stomach started to churn. I don't do last-minute. I always have my assignments finished, printed, and stapled together in the front pocket of my binder at least the day before they're due.

I looked at the clock and did some quick calculations. It was two o'clock. If we left right away and made it back by four, I could still put in at least a few hours of work before bed. "You're really not worried about this at all?" I asked her.

She shrugged. "I'll pull an all-nighter if I have to. I do my best work under pressure."

"An all-nighter?"

"You're kidding me, right? Are you telling me you've never stayed up all night to finish an assignment?"

I blinked at her, feeling the full weight of my uncoolness.

"You haven't! My God. Okay. This will be your challenge . . ."

I started shaking my head before she could even finish her sentence.

Annie put her hands on my shoulders and gave me a little shake. "Breathe," she told me. "You're starting to wig out, and I haven't even given you your mission yet."

"I don't want a mission."

"Oh yes you do. It's my duty as your best friend to introduce you to the joys of the slacker lifestyle. It's not like I'm making you hand in the assignment *late* or anything."

I could feel my eyes bugging out of my head, and Annie burst out laughing. "This'll be good for you," she said, handing me my bag. "We're going to go buy makeup we don't need, eat fried food on a stick, and then, if you're really lucky, we'll hit the bookstore."

That perked me up. "Really?"

"Absolutely," she said, slinging an arm around my shoulder. "But the catch is, no homework for the rest of the day. I don't care if you start your assignment at the buttcrack of dawn tomorrow, but you have to promise me you won't type a single word today."

"I will not type a single word," I promised, smiling brightly.

"Correction. You will not *write* a single word."

"*Ugh.* Fine. You win. But I'm calling you tomorrow when I'm in tears because I've left it till too late."

"Yeah, yeah." She propelled me toward the door.

"And you'll explain it to my mom if I get an incomplete because I don't finish on time."

"Mmmhmmm."

"And—"

"Shut it, Jess."

"Right."

Two hours later we were at a sticky food-court table, polishing off a disgustingly fantastic bowl of cheese fries and taking quizzes from the magazines Annie bought at the pharmacy. So far, we'd learned that Annie's ideal boyfriend is a rebel, she was born to be an artist, and she's destined to live in New York City. I, on the other hand, have a geek as an ideal man, was born to be a writer, and am destined to live out my days in my hometown. I can't believe they paid someone to come up with that stuff. Although . . . it might make a good fallback plan if I flunk out of school for not finishing my homework.

I held up a limp fry coated in fluorescent-orange cheese sauce. "You know, this is the first time I've ever eaten these."

"Shut up!"

"No, really. My mom is convinced that artificial cheese will kill brain cells or something."

"That explains my science mark, then. I practically live on these things."

"Let the record show that *you* are the one who brought up school on slacker day," I pointed out.

Annie rolled her eyes. "You are a true inspiration to slackers everywhere. Clearly, the cheese sauce is doing its job."

She picked up our tray and headed for the garbage cans. "C'mon, rebel. Let's go hit the bookstore."

I jumped up and skipped along after her. "This is the best day *ever.*"

Or it *was.* Until we rounded the corner and I saw Courtney and Larissa sitting on a bench outside the bookstore.

I stopped in my tracks and pulled on the strap of Annie's bag. "Never mind. I . . . Let's just go."

"Go where? What's wrong?" She followed my gaze to the benches and sighed. "Come on," she said. "We're *going* to the bookstore."

I put my head down and followed Annie, my heart thundering in my chest. *Please please please don't notice us.*

"Hey," Courtney called out as we passed.

"Hey," Annie answered, slowing to a stop and smiling at Courtney. My anxiety reared up like a frightened animal, clawing away at my insides.

"You're in my science class," Courtney said, getting up and walking slowly toward us. "The infamous Annie Miller. Tough girl from the city, right?"

Annie crossed her arms over her chest and stuck her chin up in the air. "And you're the infamous Courtney Williams. Queen Bee of suburbia. Right?"

My heart liquefied and my brain screamed at me to *run*. Courtney would blame me for the Queen Bee comment, I just knew it. Who else would have planted that idea in Annie's head?

Before I could make a break for the bookstore, though, Courtney *laughed*. And not a mean, mocking laugh. It was a real, genuine, appreciative laugh. "I like you," she told Annie before turning around and heading back to the bench.

"Lucky me," Annie muttered, looping her arm through mine and steering us into the bookstore.

I made it to the middle of the store before the dizziness hit. "Hang on," I said, trying to sound casual. I leaned against the closest shelf and took slow, even breaths.

"What's wrong?" Annie asked, narrowing her eyes at me. "Are you freaking out?"

"No," I scoffed, grabbing a random book off the shelf. "I just wanted to check out this book."

"I see," Annie said in a mock-serious voice, one side of her mouth twisting into a smile. She plucked the book from my hands and turned the cover to face me. "We're reading erotica now, are we?"

I could feel the heat radiating off my face. "I just . . . those girls don't . . . we don't get along."

"They're just girls, Jess. You don't have to be scared of them."

I nodded, blinking back tears. "I know."

"But you were going to miss out on book shopping just to avoid them."

I shrugged, willing her to stop talking about it.

"Don't do that, okay?" she said gently. "Please don't do that. You're amazing. Don't let anyone make you feel like you're not."

I forced a smile onto my face. "I won't," I said, wanting to believe it.

I love how Annie didn't back away from Courtney. I'd give anything to be that kind of girl, but I'm not. Whatever protective shielding girls like Annie and Courtney have, I was born without it.

Annie

I stop halfway down the stairs and hold my breath, listening hard. Nothing. The house is that kind of intense quiet that almost seems loud.

I creep down the rest of the stairs and ease into the dining room. It's two thirty in the morning and I should be asleep. That's not why I'm sneaking around the house like a criminal, though. I'm on a mission, and I don't feel like explaining myself to anyone.

I sit cross-legged on the floor and pop open the bottom door of the china cabinet. I know it's in here. A big black memory box all about me. My dad stores everything in there—school photos, report cards, drawings, and souvenirs.

My fingers close around it, and I pull it onto my lap. It's so heavy. The weight of my fifteen years.

I hear footsteps upstairs, and then the click of the bathroom door closing. I'd like to stay down here and spread everything out on the floor, but I don't want to get busted studying pictures of myself in the dead of night. I'm pretty sure that trips some kind of weirdness alarm.

Back in my room, I set aside the report cards and newspaper clippings. It's the pictures I'm after.

I'm obsessed with old photos.

It started with the book about Sylvia Plath that Miss Donaghue lent me. She'd read my essay about *The Bell Jar* and thought I might like to learn more about the author. I inhaled the book in a day and then bought my own copy, mainly because of the photos in the middle. There's this one picture of Plath that I can't stop staring at. As stupid as this sounds, I'd never really thought of her as a real person before. It's like . . . it's like she was too much to be contained in such a simple-looking package. The picture in the book looks like someone you might see at the bus stop or in the mall. No matter how long I stare into her eyes, I can't see any sign of the tormented genius who wrote *The Bell Jar*. I can't see the person who decided to kill herself. She doesn't look like a ticking time bomb to me. She looks like a regular person.

So I started thinking about pictures of me. How do I look to other people?

I lay my school pictures out on my bed, sorting them by grade before scanning through them. I'm looking for some essence of me. Something that shines through from an early age. But if it's there, I can't see it, because all I *can* see when I look at those pictures of me is my mom.

When I had a mother, my hair was always done in a special way for picture day. Mom would put curlers in sometimes, or get up super early to put in French braids. I loved those mornings. When I look at the pictures from kindergarten, grade one, and grade two, I see a smiling Annie who looks happy in her skin. And that had everything to do with my mom. It's the third-grade picture that gets me the most, though.

The memory of third-grade picture day is so vivid I can almost touch it. That morning Mom set the alarm for seven thirty to give us lots of time. She woke me up giggling, and when I look at the picture, I can feel my heart beating fast, just the way it did that morning. Seeing my mom happy was like staring into the sun . . . it was almost too much to take.

She washed my hair under the bathtub faucet while I bent over the tub. She always remembered to put a towel over the edge so it wouldn't be cold and hard against my skin. That morning, she used her special shampoo on me. It smelled like the salon where she got her hair cut, and I remember feeling very grown up. Then she towel-dried my hair and sang silly songs while she wove two French braids on either side of my head.

The best part, though, was that once she finished my hair and helped me into my new dress, she knelt beside me and pressed her cheek against mine while I looked in the mirror. "You're so beautiful, Annie," she told me. "I'm so proud of you."

I wish she were here now. I can't see myself the way she saw me anymore. I don't know who I am without her.

Jessie

I am in love with Scott Hutchins.

In a staggering sign that the universe is not really as against me as I thought, Scott is my new lab partner in science class. I started the semester as Annie's partner, but Mr. Donaldson separated us last week. Apparently our constant chatter was getting in the way of our academic success. Annie lost out in the deal. She's now stuck next to Courtney, while I get to share space with Scott. Or perhaps I lost out, because she got an A on her plant cells quiz while I failed miserably. My first failure ever in school. I don't even remember answering any of the questions. I spent the whole quiz fighting the temptation to write my name down as Jessica Hutchins.

It's pretty much impossible to concentrate on Mr. Donaldson's voice with Scott sitting beside me every day. I keep catching myself contemplating the muscles in his forearms when I should be thinking about chloroplasts.

Scott is basically the hero from every book I've ever read. It's almost funny—like the gods took all my thoughts about what makes the perfect guy and combined them to form Scott Hutchins. He's tall and built, with arms that make my stomach swoop. He's one of those naturally athletic guys who live for sports. He walks in these great loping strides and has wavy brown hair that flops across his eyes in a way that makes you want to smooth it back for him. Add that he wants to be a veterinarian and that he famously cried during an animal cruelty video in class last year, and I could die from how perfect he is.

Up until today, I was pretty sure he was merely tolerating my presence as his lab partner, so I've been doing my best to keep my drooling over him as discreet as possible. Today, though . . .

I was trying to copy notes off the board while pretending that Scott's arm wasn't inches from mine, when he leaned over and whispered into my ear, "Do you get any of this stuff?"

All I could think of was the bag of Doritos I'd devoured before class. The heroine is supposed to have sweet-smelling breath, not smell like nacho cheese when her Romeo finally leans in.

He pulled back and looked straight into my eyes. He's so unbelievably beautiful. He has the kind of eyelashes a girl would kill for. I smiled at him and leaned over to aim my whisper at his ear, hoping that if my breath was bad, it would blow past his face and he wouldn't notice.

"I failed the plant cells quiz miserably. I need a serious study session," I said.

"Me too! Want to study together?"

Yes, it's true. The one and only Scott Hutchins asked *me* to study with him. Let me say that again because I can hardly believe it's true: Scott Hutchins wants to spend time with me. Outside of class.

Of course I right away went and did something stupid to humiliate myself.

As I was sitting there, no doubt smiling the world's goofiest happy smile, Mr. Donaldson tragically caught sight of me. "Miss Avery," he boomed. "Would you like to define the term *biology* for the class?"

My textbook was miraculously open to that page, so for a split second I was convinced the universe really *did* love me. "Biology is the study of living orgasms."

Oh. My. God.

The laughter was swift and punishing. I have never wanted to die so badly in my life. Scott's shoulders were shaking, and even Mr. Donaldson was fighting a losing battle with a smile.

And then the emotional roller coaster continued, because as I was sitting there willing myself not to cry, Scott leaned over and said (in the lowest, sexiest voice you can imagine), "Hey, don't be upset, Jess . . . It was funny."

I nodded, looking down at my lap to hide my tears.

He reached across me for my notebook and then pulled it over between us.

Don't be embarrassed, he wrote. *It was a great joke!*

It was the perfect solution to my I-can't-talk-to-hot-Scott-Hutchins problem.

I wish I could say I did that on purpose, but it turns out I'm just a dork. As soon as I wrote that, I freaked out that it was all wrong. Did it look like I was begging for compliments?

I need your dorky brain to rub off on me. If I flunk this class, I'm off the basketball team.

So we're on for that study session?

Yeah! Library at lunch?
Sounds good!
Thanks, Jess.

I'm going to laminate that page. I'll tack it to my wall so I can marvel at its beauty. Hell, I'll sleep with it under my pillow.

By the time the bell rang, I felt weightless. It hardly even bothered me that I needed to wait for Courtney to finish whispering a story to Annie before we could leave class together.

Annie knows me so well. The second she saw my face, she knew something was up. She raised her eyebrows at me and commanded, "Spill it! What's going on?"

"Nothing . . . I just made some lunch plans with my lab partner. I hope you don't mind if I take off after we eat."

She stopped dead in her tracks. "Are you shitting me?"

"It's not a big deal," I assured her. "We're just both really behind, so we're going to meet in the library to go over some stuff together."

"You *like* him."

"Of course I *like* him. He's my lab partner."

"Yeah, right. I mean, you *like* like him."

"Are we really having this conversation?"

"Don't get all pissy with me! I can tell you like him!"

We turned the corner into the arts corridor, where the crowds were thinner. "Annie. Seriously. I don't *like* like him. I just think he's nice, and I want to do better in science. Plus, he's Scott *freakin'* Hutchins. I wouldn't stand a chance even if I *did* like him. Which I don't! Please don't make a bigger deal of this than it is, or I'll feel all awkward and nervous."

I don't know why I lied to her. I know Annie wouldn't make fun of me. She'd be happy. But I can't admit that this might be the beginning of something. Guys like Scott do not fall for girls like me without the assistance of a full-on makeover or a fairy god-mother.

"Ooookay. I believe you, but if *anything* happens, you need to tell me. Right away. Got it?"

I put a hand on my heart and the other in the air. "I swear to you, Annie Miller, that if I develop a crush on my lab partner, you will be the first to know."

"Good."

"Now . . . what's up with you and bitchface?"

Annie looked puzzled for a minute and then realized who I was talking about. "She's not that bad, Jess."

"Yeah, right. Courtney Williams is a real sweetheart."

Annie looked ready to say something, but she stopped herself. The second bell rang, and we stood there awkwardly for a second before heading off to class.

I watched her walk away, memories of Courtney haunting the edges of my brain. *Stop it, Jess,* I told myself. *Things are different now.* I have Annie. She'd never turn on me like Courtney and Larissa did. Our friendship is stronger than that.

"You are *such* a liar," Annie accused at lunch, leaning back in her chair and shaking her head at me.

I dragged my eyes away from my science textbook and tried to focus on her. I was due in the library in ten minutes, and I was trying to cram as much knowledge into my brain as possible before meeting Scott.

"What are you talking about?" I asked, rubbing my sweaty hands on my jeans.

"If you're really not hot for Scott, why are you so nervous? And *don't* tell me you're not, because you normally scarf down twice the amount of food that's on your plate right now, and you've barely even eaten a bite of what's there."

"Of course I'm nervous," I told her. "I've never studied with anyone but you. And this is one of the most popular guys in school. I'm not nervous because I want something with him . . . I'm nervous because I don't want to make a fool of myself in front of him."

The temptation to tell her the whole truth was strong, but the need to avoid utter humiliation was stronger. I mean, let's face it, I'm pretty much the most socially challenged person alive. The odds were good that I was misreading the whole situation.

Annie's smile was blinding. "Is that it? *That's* what you're nervous about? Jessie! You're the smartest girl I know. You couldn't look dumb if you tried. He's gonna be blown away by your tutoring ability." Annie peeled the lid off her container of yogurt and dug in. "You had me really worried there."

"Worried?"

"Yeah . . . you know. You're my best friend." She gave me a playful kick under the table. "I don't want to see you get hurt."

My mouth was suddenly dry. "Wh-why would I get hurt?" My voice came out so squeaky it made me cringe.

She shrugged. "You know . . . if you liked him or whatever and he wasn't interested."

A rush of feelings hit me so hard I couldn't sort them out. I was embarrassed and hurt and angry all at once. Annie could not imagine a situation in which Scott would be interested in me. That bothered me much more than it should have, given that I could barely imagine such a scenario myself. But Annie is supposed to be my best friend.

I swallowed hard and fought to keep the quiver out of my voice. "Obviously he wouldn't be interested. I'm not delusional, Annie."

"That's not what I meant," she protested. But it *was* what she meant, and we both knew it.

✳ ✳ ✳

By the time I walked into the library, I was a mess. And it didn't help that Scott wasn't there. I was just starting to panic when I felt a tug on my backpack. I turned and flashed him a beaming smile . . . only to find Charlie standing where Scott should have been.

"Wow," he said, rubbing a hand on the back of his neck. "It's good to see you looking so . . . happy. We miss you at lunch."

I looked at him sideways. "Really? I figured I was kind of annoying, always hanging around last year."

"You were never annoying."

"Kevin *told* me I was annoying. Daily."

Charlie's face broke into a lopsided grin. "Kevin finds everyone annoying. I thought you were great."

His smile was contagious, and I laughed, remembering how exasperated Kevin used to get.

"Anyway," Charlie said, clearing his throat, "I just wanted to give you this." He slipped a thin booklet out of his binder and held it up.

"A comic book?" I raised an eyebrow at him. "I don't read those, remember?"

"Oh, I remember your stubbornness, Ms. Snobby Reader. But do you remember how I said one good comic would change your mind about that? Besides, this isn't just any old comic. I wrote this one."

"Seriously?" I asked, taking it from him. "It looks so professional."

I flipped it open to take a look, but his hand shot out and settled over mine. "Don't read it now. I mean . . . save it for later. When you have time. We can, uh, talk about it later."

I nodded and slipped the book into my bag, rattled by the feeling of his hand and the intensity of his voice. "You look different," I blurted.

He shrugged. "I grew my hair out a bit," he admitted.

"And got some new clothes," I said, like a complete moron. "I mean . . . not that there was anything wrong with your old clothes . . ."

Charlie gave a low chuckle that made me blush. "You're as smooth as ever, Jess," he teased. "But you do have a point." He leaned in closer and looked around before whispering, "Don't tell anyone, but my mom picked out my clothes last year. I decided it was about time for that to stop."

"Much better," I choked out, trying not to notice the way his T-shirt stretched across muscles that had definitely not been there last year. What the heck was wrong with me?

"I have to admit that I did have help. Have you met Jody yet?"

I shook my head as Scott walked through the library doors. I felt like my heart was going to implode.

"She's new this year, and she decided that Kev and I needed fashion interventions. You should come hang out with us again — I think you'd really like her."

I opened my mouth to reply just as Scott stepped between us. "Hey, Jess," he said, completely ignoring Charlie. "You ready?"

I nodded and shot an apologetic look at Charlie, who was blinking at us in confusion. *No worries,* I said to him in my head. *I can hardly believe it myself.*

Scott put a hand on the small of my back and propelled me toward the tables in the far corner of the library. "Let's sit back here where we can talk without Adamson kicking us out."

I walked ahead of Scott, consumed by the warmth of his hand. When we reached the back desks, he pulled it away, leaving my whole body feeling cold and abandoned. I perched on the chair next to him and fumbled with the zipper on my bag. "Where should we start?"

"Can we go back to the first unit and go over that test? I totally bombed it."

I smiled up at him and got lost in his eyes for a second. *Mental note: Do not make direct eye contact.* I pulled out my textbook and started talking, and everything else fell away. No lie, I was on fire. I started explaining about the differences between plant and animal cells, and it was like I was channeling Bill Nye the Science Guy. I just couldn't stop talking, and it was all *good.*

When I finally came up for air, there were just minutes left in the period. We'd been working steadily for more than forty-five minutes, and we both looked a little dazed.

"Thank you so much, Jess," he said in a voice so sincere it almost made me cry. "You're really, *really* smart."

And the best part? He wants to do it again!

The entire day felt so completely surreal that I probably shouldn't have been as shocked as I was to find Larissa Riley waiting for me at my locker at the end of the day. It was like falling down the rabbit hole.

I've known Larissa since second grade. We bonded in Saturday morning figure-skating class, where we endured the harsh criticism of Coach Grant and consoled each other over hot chocolate after class. We had sleepovers every weekend, sat beside each other at school, and spent every recess wandering the playground, making plans for the future. Larissa had dreams of becoming a famous actress, and I planned to be a writer.

When Courtney moved to town in sixth grade, we had long, serious discussions about welcoming her into our group. We sat at my kitchen table with a huge piece of chart paper and listed the pros and cons. Courtney was magnetic, with long blond hair and a razor-sharp sense of humor. She had quickly become the class clown and prom queen all rolled into one. Those were all pros. We'd been a team of two for a very long time, though, and that was a powerful con. Eventually we decided to invite Courtney to a sleepover, and we officially became a group of three.

I've often wondered about that day at the kitchen table. If we'd decided not to befriend Courtney, would my life have turned out differently? Would Larissa and Courtney still have become best friends, leaving me behind? And would Larissa still have turned her back on me and laughed along with the others when Courtney declared me an outcast?

"Hi, Jess!" The present and past folded over each other dizzyingly as Larissa tucked a strand of jet-black hair behind her ear and beamed at me, looking disturbingly like her second-grade self.

"Hi . . ." I reached out for my lock, only to realize a second too late that she was standing right in front of it. I let my hand drop and looked at a spot just over her left shoulder. No matter how much time passes, I still feel that same knife of betrayal in my stomach every time I see Larissa.

"I was just wondering . . . I mean, I'm having a party, and I thought you and Annie might want to come."

I had this weird sensation that I was on one of those prank TV shows where they film you with a secret camera. "Oh! . . . Um . . . When is it?" I didn't want to go. I couldn't think of any reason why Larissa would invite me over except as some cruel joke.

"A week from Friday. It's not, like, a huge deal or anything. My parents will be there. But I thought it would be fun. I was sort of hoping we could all be friends again. You know, move on from the past?"

I forced my face to look puzzled, as though I didn't know what she was talking about. As though it had escaped my notice that she'd dumped me as a friend as soon as Courtney declared me uncool, and as though the whole Lezzie Longbottom thing had never happened. "Sure! That would be great! But Annie and I have plans that day. This totally sucks, but my parents are having this thing, and —"

"Larissa!" Annie came bounding up at the exact wrong time.

"Hi, Annie!" Larissa's smile was genuine, and I could feel things slipping away from me.

"Courtney told me all about the party!" Annie said, linking her arm through mine. "We'll be there for sure. I'm so ready for a party."

"Jess said —"

"It's that Friday two weeks before Halloween," I interrupted with exaggerated dismay. "We can't make it, *remember?*"

Annie wrinkled her forehead in confusion. "Why not?"

"My parents are having that *thing*."

"Whatever," she said with a dismissive wave of her hand. "Your mom is totally chill. She'll be fine with us going to a party instead." Annie turned to Larissa. "Don't worry — I'll talk to Mrs. Avery. We'll be there for sure."

On the way home from school, I tried to make a joke out of the whole misunderstanding. I wasn't ready to believe that Annie might actually *want* to go to Larissa's.

"I so cannot believe you didn't get my signals about the party."

"What are you talking about — signals?"

"The *signals!* You know, my parents' plans . . . I was trying to give us an out."

Annie stopped walking. "Why would we need an out?"

"You're playing with me, right? This is Larissa Riley we're talking about. The girl who's been tormenting me since middle school and has never so much as said hello to you before today. Do you actually believe anything good could come out of this invitation?"

Annie put her hands on her hips and raised an eyebrow at me mockingly. She looked far too much like my mother at that moment. "You're paranoid," she declared.

"You're delusional."

Annie adjusted her backpack and started walking, not even checking to see if I was following. "I don't know why you have to be like this, Jessie," she lectured. "You're always so damn suspicious. If you just stopped being such a pessimist, maybe you'd find that there are lots of people at school who actually want to be your friend."

I snorted and immediately wished I could take it back. Annie just picked up her pace. I had to run to catch up to her. "I just don't understand why you would want to go to a party with a bunch of people who you yourself have called phony."

"That was before I got to know them."

"Since when do you know them?"

Annie stopped abruptly and I nearly crashed into her. "I keep thinking about how we've both complained that no one at school looks beyond appearances—that people just judge before they get to know anyone. That's been our biggest complaint about Courtney and her friends, right?" I shrugged my shoulders noncommittally.

"Well, don't you think we've been doing the same thing? We've talked shit about Courtney and Larissa all year, laughing at their Facebook pages and making fun of them. But when you think about it, we were totally judging them without getting to know them."

"Maybe for you, but I've known them long enough to—"

"Come on, Jess! You're judging people by things they did back in *middle* school. That's not fair!"

I wanted to tell her that what's not fair is being mocked every day. What's not fair is girls writing nasty things in your notebook when the teacher isn't looking and crank calling your house after school. What's not fair is being laughed at for everything from your weight to the clothes you wear. But Annie was looking at me like I was a stubborn child, and I could sense the futility of trying to make her understand. Annie has never been bullied. She has always belonged.

"I just think you're going to be disappointed when you find out the truth about them."

"Then let me be disappointed. But don't be mad at me for making friends with people."

"I'm not mad, Annie. I just don't want to go to the party."

"And that's fine. But I *do*. Will you be upset if I go without you?"

"I guess not," I mumbled, blinking back tears.

She grabbed my hands, her voice pleading. "We're two separate people, Jessie. It's okay that we don't do *everything* together."

Her words were knives raked along my skin. I could hear the goodbye in every syllable. I knew the day would come when Annie would ditch me for more popular girls. It was Larissa all over again.

I pasted a smile on my face. "You're right, Annie. I'm wrong."

She let out a yelp, her arms spread and her eyes to the sky, as though looking for divine guidance on how to deal with me. "I'm not being *mean* here, Jess. Normal people have lots of friends. They hang out with all sorts of people. You can be my *best* friend without being my *only* friend."

I know she's right. I know I shouldn't feel threatened just because she wants other friends. But I can't help myself. I've known all along that Annie could be doing cool things with cool people instead of wasting her time with me. I can't shake the terrible feeling that this is how it will end.

Annie

I turn to the side and check out my reflection. *Disaster.*

I've always had a love-hate relationship with clothes. I can't seem to find a style that's all my own, and I hate the feeling of pretending to be someone I'm not. The best I've done here is my all-black angry-teenager look—a look that pretty much summed up how I felt at the beginning of the year, when I was mourning my old life. But those clothes feel wrong now. Like they're not a reflection of *me* anymore.

Which is why I'm standing here in the only nonblack outfit I own that still fits—a rather tragic floral skirt and matching sweater. I look like something out of the preteen fashion section of a Target flyer.

I'm fighting back tears and contemplating skipping Larissa's party when Sophie materializes in my doorway. "Martin says be ready in twenty minutes." Her eyes barely touch on me as she delivers the message.

The minute she steps out of the doorway, I realize that I need her. "Sophie?"

There's a long pause before her face reappears, her eyes narrowed in suspicion. "Ye-es?"

"Can you . . . help me?"

"Help you do what, exactly?"

I almost tell her to forget it. Sophie and I will never be friends, and asking her for help is downright painful. But I have to admit that Sophie has *style*.

"I'm going to a party tonight, and I have no idea what to wear," I blurt out, gesturing at my outfit and gritting my teeth against her slow smile.

"So you're finally ready to abandon your doom-and-gloom angsty look, are you? This will be fun, giving you a makeover." She crosses her arms over her chest and cocks her head to the side. "A few questions first."

"Okay."

"House party or other?"

"House."

"Grade level of host?"

"Tenth."

"Coed?"

"Of course. Would I care about all this if it wasn't?"

"Good point. Parents home or away?"

"Home."

"Drag. Okay. Come with me."

"But . . ." I gesture toward my closet.

"Listen, Annie—I can't believe I'm doing this, but I'm pretty stoked you asked me for help. So, for this one night only, I'm opening my closet door to you."

My jaw drops.

"I know. But we're almost like sisters . . . technically. Plus, I want you to go out and have a blast so you'll take that stick out of your ass and be human around here."

Sophie heads off to her room, leaving me staring after her. She turns at her door and looks at her watch. "I'd hurry up if I were you."

I race to her room, already envisioning myself in her clothes.

When my dad calls upstairs for me twenty minutes later, Sophie's still hard at work. "Hold on, Martin," she yells down the stairs. "I'm not done with her yet."

"Done with . . . "

"I'm making Annie gorgeous."

I close my eyes, my stomach fluttering. Patience isn't one of my dad's best qualities. I'm expecting him to start nagging that it's time to go, or threatening me with no ride if I don't hurry up. He must be as shocked as I am at Sophie's sudden friendliness, though, because he doesn't say a word.

Sophie works her magic for almost another hour, and still, my dad stays silent.

Finally she steps back and smiles. "Turn around."

I look up at her, and it's suddenly hard to breathe. There's a softness in Sophie's eyes that reminds me of my mother. I feel dizzy, as if I'm in the present and the past at the same time. I swallow hard around the lump in my throat, terrified that I might break down in front of her. Then I turn and catch sight of myself, and all those thoughts scatter.

I can't believe the girl in the mirror is me. I look *hot*. My usual heavy eyeliner and mascara are gone. With far less makeup than I normally use, Sophie's managed to give me a natural look that makes me seem more sophisticated and less like a kid playing dress-up. She's blown out my hair, lent me a pair of low-rise jeans that make me look at least two years older, and finished off the outfit with a black tank top that's just this side of acceptable for parental viewing.

"Sophie," I breathe. "You're a miracle worker."

"I know, right?" She laughs at the expression on my face. "It wasn't that hard. You're very pretty."

A blush creeps up my cheeks. *Why's she being so nice to me?*

Sophie races down the stairs ahead of me, calling for Madge and my dad to come see.

"Annie," my dad thunders as I ease down the stairs on Sophie's heels. "You're gorgeous!"

Madge actually *smiles* at me. "You look beautiful," she says before turning to Sophie. "I'm so proud of you, darling. Are those your clothes Annie's wearing?"

Sophie shrugs. "I always wanted a sister to trade clothes with."

For a moment, I have a flash of how things could be around here. Maybe if I try harder, Sophie and I could be friends. Maybe I could feel more at home here instead of always needing to be at Jessie's house. Maybe I could have my own home.

"Let's get going," Dad says, jingling his car keys.

"Actually," Sophie says, "can I drive her?"

"You want to drive Annie to her party?"

"Yeah . . . and maybe I can borrow the car to go out tonight, too?" Her hopeful eyes are on Madge now. "I'll just be at Margot's house. I'll leave in time to pick up Annie from the party and get her home before her curfew."

My dad's smile is huge. "Well, what do you think of this, Madeleine? We'll have the place all to ourselves." He waggles his eyebrows at her, turning our stomachs.

"We're out of here," Sophie announces, snatching the keys from Dad's hand. "You two behave while we're gone."

"So gross!" I squeal as we run for the car. Sophie's cheeks are flushed and her smile is real. I feel like I'm flying.

"So where is this party?"

I give directions as we drive, settling into the seat and committing this night to memory. Sophie changes the radio station—something forbidden in Dad's car—and we race along into the night with dance music blaring.

✱ ✱ ✱

Larissa's house is even nicer than I expected. Judging from her wardrobe, I figured she had money, but nothing prepared me for her house. The entranceway alone is more than twice the size of my bedroom.

Her father answers the door, a glass of wine in his hand. "Welcome!" he booms. "Head on down to the basement. The party's in full swing down there." He gestures toward a door at the end of the hall, and I can hear the dull thud of music coming up through the floor.

I fight off panic as I slip down the stairs. *What if I have no one to talk to?* As I round the corner at the bottom of the staircase, a squeal startles me. Larissa races up and grabs onto my arm like we're long-lost pals.

"Annie! I'm so glad you came."

I look around the dimly lit room. There are at least forty people down here, huddled in groups.

Larissa pulls me over to a corner. "Guess who's been asking about you tonight?"

"Um . . . I don't know. Who?"

"Scott!"

"Scott Hutchins?"

"Of *course* Scott Hutchins. You know, the absolute cutest guy in our grade!"

If she's so smitten with Scott, why's she excited that he's asking about me? "I don't know. I kind of think Jonathan's hotter."

Larissa gives me a playful push, laughing so hard she snorts. "Well, duh, but since he's my *boyfriend,* don't get any ideas!"

"Ha. Yeah. Just kidding!" *Since when are they dating?* I make a mental note to befriend some people who are better at gossiping than Jess.

"Anyway, Scott is Jon's best friend, and they were talking about hot girls in our grade and Scott totally said that he thinks you're cute."

My mind swerves to keep up with this. "But I thought he liked Jessie."

Again with the snorting laughter. "Jessie? Be serious. She's just tutoring him in science. Jessie's hardly his type."

I feel a swell of protectiveness for Jess before remembering that she ditched me here to fend for myself.

"So, can I tell Jon to tell Scott that you like him?"

"Huh? I mean . . . I'm not sure. Maybe let's just wait and see what happens."

"Come on!" She grabs me by the arm and drags me into a corner of the room. "Look who's here!" she announces as we stumble into Jon and Scott.

I smile, staring somewhere between the two of them. It feels like everyone in the room is watching us.

"I'm glad you came, Annie," Scott says, handing me a red plastic cup of something. "Did Jess come with you?" *I knew it!*

"Nah. She had other plans."

"I'm kind of glad," he says, leaning over so he doesn't have to shout over the music. "That means I get you all to myself tonight."

A little thrill snakes its way up my spine. I take a sip from the cup and sputter at the taste. His eyes are sparkly. "It's got rum in it," he explains. *Rum?* I suddenly see my dad's disapproving face in my mind. I haven't drunk anything since last September, when my friends and I smuggled wine coolers into school and got wasted in the girls' bathroom. I ended up with a three-day suspension and a massive guilt trip from Dad. He made me promise I wouldn't touch alcohol again until I'm nineteen. Rum. I grip the plastic cup hard, debating. It would be easy enough to set the cup down someplace and forget about it. Or I could just pretend to drink. I sneak another look at Scott, though, and think *Fuck it.*

I gulp my drink and feel it blaze a trail all the way down to my stomach. Booze and Scott Hutchins. This is going to be an interesting night.

I lose track of how many times Scott refills my drink. I'm having a moral crisis, and the rum helps take the edge off. I know Jessie likes Scott, even though she swears that she doesn't. So the whole time I'm flirting with him, I keep a running tally of pros and cons in my head.

Basically the situation is this: Do I take Jessie at her word, or do I put my friend first and follow my instincts? I keep going back and forth. I love Jessie, but I'm pissed at her. I know she's not being honest with me, and I'm mad that she refused to come with me tonight. She *should* have come just to be a good friend. She stayed home because she's afraid of Courtney, but she won't listen to me when I tell her that Court's changed. And she's mad that I won't sacrifice my social life to join her in hiding, but I have just as much of a right to be mad that she's not trying to overcome her fears to spend time with me.

So when Scott leads me over to a couch in the far corner of the basement and starts looking at me like I'm dessert, I think, *What the hell?* I like him and he likes me. So what if Jessie has a secret crush on him? She's not here and not going after what she wants. I shouldn't have to sacrifice what I want . . .

I close my eyes and let him kiss me. My God. His lips are so soft and my heart's beating so fast and all I can think is, *This is what it feels like to have someone care about you.*

I never, ever want this feeling to end. I want to crawl inside Scott's skin and never come out.

His hand slips under my shirt at the exact same time my cell phone buzzes in my pocket. I don't know which makes me jump more. Scott looks somewhere between puzzled and annoyed until I pull out the phone and hold it up by way of explanation. He smiles awkwardly while I squint at the screen. "My stepsister's outside," I apologize. He groans.

When I get up to make my way to the door, I sway unexpectedly, and he's there to support me. "I must have drunk more'n I thought," I say.

Sophie's eyes are wide when Scott opens the door to her car and folds me inside. "I'm Scott," he introduces himself, shaking her hand.

We pull away while he waves from the driveway. Sophie gets all the way to the end of the street before she speaks. "Well, well, well."

"Did you have a good time tonight?" I ask, hoping to distract her from my current predicament.

"Not as good as you, apparently! Now, talk! Who's the hottie, and why do you smell like a bar?"

"Wha—"

"Don't even try to hide it." She pulls over and swivels to face me. "You're totally drunk. And you apparently have great taste in guys. Now, spill it, sister!"

"Okay. I drank something with rum in it all night and we made out and he's really cute and I like him a lot."

Sophie's laugh bounces around the inside of the car. "Good for you! Now let's get you home and into bed before my mom and your dad see you."

"Why are you being so nice to me?" I mean for the question to come out in a joking way, but it's absolutely stark in its seriousness.

Sophie goes still, her laughter gone. "I know this all sucks for you. I know my mom can be a bitch sometimes and that I've been kinda rough on you. I just . . . I get so frustrated with you for always making such a huge deal out of everything and picking fights every two minutes. But after you and Mom fought about the art supplies, your dad sat me down and told me the whole story about the night your mom died and how hard it was for you afterward. I guess I kind of get now why you're always so angry and sad."

It's the nicest thing she's ever said to me. Sadly, maybe even the nicest thing anyone has said since my mom died. I open my mouth to thank her, but a sob comes out instead.

"Good God, Annie! Don't turn into one of those pathetic girls who get overly emotional when they drink." She shoots me a sly smile. "I recommend you dry those tears before we get home. The less you have to talk to anyone on our way in, the greater the chances you'll make it through this undetected."

At home, Sophie sneaks me into my room and then brings me a glass of water and an Advil. "Drink the whole thing," she commands, and watches while I drain the glass.

"Thanks, Sophie," I mutter as I drift off to sleep.

The next thing I know, I'm jolting awake, heart pounding. Madge's face is inches from mine, and she's screeching my father's name. I leap out of bed, bumping into her and knocking the clothes I'd borrowed from Sophie out of her arms.

My dad skids into the doorway, his glasses askew.

"She's *drunk*," Madge accuses.

"Madeleine! I thought someone was hurt!" Dad puts his arm out to prop himself up against the door and clutches at his chest.

I fall back on the bed, watching them through eyelids that are too heavy to keep open. "Can we talk about this in the morning?" I mumble, rolling over.

Madge is clearly not impressed. She slams my bedroom door behind her, ranting about irresponsible behavior. I know there's a massive grounding on the horizon, but I don't even care. I curl up under the covers, my cheeks sore from smiling.

Hickville is definitely starting to get interesting.

Jessie

Why didn't I go to that stupid party on Friday? Everything would be different if I hadn't been such a loser about it. I let fear win again.

I knew something big had happened when I didn't hear from Annie all weekend. I sent her message after message, and they all went unanswered. I was convinced that Courtney had gotten to her and turned her against me. I was sick with the thought of Annie ignoring me in the halls on Monday and laughing about me with my old friends.

Turns out that Annie got drunk at the party and her stepmom busted her. She was grounded all weekend with no phone and no screen time, which is why I didn't see her at all until last night, when she came by under the pretense of borrowing a textbook.

As soon as she walked into my room, I could tell she had news. She looked nervous and excited and *jumpy*. I should've seen it coming a mile away because the first thing she did was ask me for the millionth time if I liked Scott, telling me she needed to hear the absolute truth. Not having any idea of what she was about to say, I swore to her I didn't like him. And then she hit me with the news: they kissed, and she's pretty sure they're going out now.

My room started to spin around me, and I could barely focus my eyes. I had that feeling you get in your stomach when a roller coaster goes over the crest of a hill and then plummets toward the ground. I did my best to keep my face calm, worried that Annie would notice that I was in freefall. She just chattered on and on, though, oblivious to what was happening inside me. She was so *happy;* it made me sick.

I stayed up half the night with that feeling eating away at my insides. I kept trying to imagine the scene Annie had described — the two of them sitting on a couch kissing — and I couldn't do it. My mind refused to accept the idea of Annie and Scott together.

Just before I finally drifted off to sleep, around four a.m., I decided that things might not be as bad as they seemed. They were drunk; Annie had said that. Maybe it was just a drunken party thing. Maybe nothing would come of it.

My psychiatrist would call that a defense mechanism — my brain's attempt to soften the blow of difficult news by rationalizing it. After today, I just call it stupid.

Today.

I was running late this morning, so I had to send Annie on ahead and then bum a ride with my dad. By the time I raced through the front doors at school, the first bell had already rung, and I still had to get to the second floor to get my books from my locker.

Which is why I got stuck in a stairwell during the national anthem.

Which is why I saw it.

I was just inside the upper stairwell doors, peering out into the hall beyond, when I caught sight of Annie. I was smiling to myself, thinking we'd both be late together, when I saw an arm loop around her waist and someone lean in to kiss her on the neck. I swear my brain froze. I felt like I was in the middle of some awful nightmare. My brain was wailing *No, no, no,* but there it was. Scott— *my* Scott—was sneaking kisses with Annie each time the hallway monitor looked the other way.

My nose was practically pressed to the glass, so there was no mistaking what happened next. As the announcements ended, Scott gave her what looked to be the softest, tenderest kiss and then pulled back to look into her eyes. Since her back was to me, I had a front-row seat to the expression on his face. There was no explaining away the way he looked at her. I just stood there in the stairwell for the longest time. I didn't feel like going to class. I didn't feel like doing *anything.*

I'd love to say that I'm the sort of friend who can put her feelings aside and be happy for Annie. But it turns out I'm not. I wish I could turn back time and be honest with her. If I'd told her about my feelings for Scott, would she have stayed away from him? If I'd gone to the party, would he have kissed me instead?

I didn't realize it until today, but sometime during the last month, my days started to revolve around thoughts of Scott. When my mind wanders, it wanders to him. When I fall asleep at night, I think about his smile, and when I wake up in the morning, I count the hours till I get to see him. I choose my clothes more carefully, do my hair, and even put on makeup thinking of him.

And now what?

What do I do with my feelings for him now that the hope is gone? What do I look forward to? And how am I supposed to watch Annie live out everything I ever hoped for?

Annie

Jessie's talking, but I'm not really listening. I keep craning my neck to catch a glimpse of Scott. He has math first period, down the next hallway, and if Jess would hurry up at her locker, we could swing past there and run into him accidentally on purpose.

I've been a hormonal mess all week, and I keep worrying that Scott is going to come to his senses and realize that he could do so much better than a head case like me. One minute I'll be smiling uncontrollably, thinking about Scott, and the next I'll be sobbing, thinking about the anniversary of my mom's death coming up.

"Let's go," I say, turning to Jessie. She's fixing her hair in front of a little magnetic mirror stuck to her locker door. Wait . . . *what?*

"Since when do you have a mirror in your locker?"

She jumps like I've caught her doing something wrong, and slams the door shut. "My mom gave it to me. It's no big deal."

That's when I see the highlights in her hair. Seriously. Jessie. With highlights. This is the girl who started the year without even brushing her hair some mornings. And the closer I look at her, the more I see. She's wearing all new clothes from head to foot.

"Are those new jeans?"

"This is what happens when my mom notices I'm feeling down," she says, striking a pose. "I was having a rough couple of days, so she took me shopping and gave me a little makeover to cheer me up." She looks down at herself. "Do I look okay?"

A mixture of sadness and jealousy churns in my stomach. "So *that's* why you couldn't do anything yesterday? Why you didn't answer your phone when I called?" There's a tiny little part of my brain telling me to shut the hell up, but Jessie doesn't even notice how hysterical I'm getting.

"Yeah. I didn't mention it before, because I had no idea it was going to happen. Out of the blue, Mom just told me to get in the car for a surprise." Jessie starts walking, not even noticing that I'm not following. I watch her go, trying to push away the rush of feelings turning my insides to fire. Then I turn and walk away.

I blink back tears as I push open the front doors of the school, half expecting a teacher to jump out and force me back to class. But no one notices me leave, which makes me feel even worse. I shiver and bundle my hands inside the arms of my thin sweater, thinking of my nice warm jacket back in my locker. I can't go back, though. I don't want to go back.

By the time I get to my front porch, I'm sobbing hysterically and shivering violently. I just want to get inside and curl up on my bed and forget this day ever existed. I reach for my pocket to get my key, and my stomach clenches so hard I think I might throw up. My fucking key is in my jacket pocket. Fuck fuck fuck fuck *fuck*. I throw my bag against the side of the house and slump down on the icy steps.

I'm going to have to go back to school. What else can I do? I'll freeze here on these steps, and no one will be home for hours. I bury my face in my hands, sick at the thought of trekking back to school in the freezing cold.

Just when I think things can't get any worse, I hear a car pull up to the curb. God, I hate the suburbs. In the city, you can have an emotional breakdown right on the street and people will step right over you, minding their own business. Here in the boonies, though, people love to get *involved*. I say a little prayer that whoever it is will just keep on moving, but the sound of a car door opening shatters that hope. *Goddamn it.* I'm about to say that I'm just waiting for someone when I hear Mrs. Avery's voice.

"Annie? Sweetheart, where is your coat? And why are you home from school?" Before I can string together enough thoughts to form a response, she's out of her car and racing toward me, concern etched on her face. "Are you sick?"

All the years of pretending to be okay evaporate in the face of her kindness.

"Are you locked out, hon? You can come home with me . . ."

I nod my head and pick up my bag, my whole body numb from the cold.

Mrs. Avery settles me in the car and then pauses before shutting the door. I look up at her, and she does the most unbelievable thing. She takes off her coat and wraps it around me before sprinting over to her door and jumping into the car.

"How you managed to get here all the way from school without freezing to death is beyond me." Her shivering fingers crank the heat up to high, and I move to give her back her coat. "Don't even think about it," she commands, swinging the car around to head back to her house.

Tears prickle in my eyes. Mrs. Avery has known me for only a few months and she's kinder to me than my own family.

She pulls up to a stop sign and sneaks a look at me, taking in my tearstained cheeks. "I have an idea," she says. "What would you say to the two of us playing hooky from everything and heading to the coffee shop for a warm drink and some treats? I think you need some girl time."

My throat constricts, and I'm suddenly weak with want. Most of the time I feel tough and independent, but today I *need* a mother to take care of me.

At the coffee shop, Mrs. Avery makes a big deal out of introducing me to the lady behind the counter, telling her that it's a special occasion. I order a hot chocolate and a brownie, and they put extra whipped cream in my drink.

We find a tiny little table tucked away at the back and sit down. As soon as it's just the two of us, though, I'm all awkward and nervous. I'm not sure what to say.

"Thank you for all this, Mrs. Avery," I start. "My stepsister will be home later and I can be out of your hair."

"No trouble at all. Something very upsetting must have happened to make you run out of school without a coat."

"Just a bad day, I guess."

"It must have been . . . you left less than an hour into the school day."

A smile tugs at the corners of my mouth. "I never even made it to first period."

"That *is* a bad day. Want to talk about it?"

What can I say? That I'm jealous of her relationship with her daughter? That seeing Jessie happy makes me sad? What kind of friend would think that way? "I miss my mom."

Mrs. Avery's face softens, and she takes my hands in hers. Something inside me cracks, and words start tumbling out of my mouth before I can stop them. "She died six years ago on Halloween. I miss her so much, and I feel like I'm the only one who even remembers her. My dad got remarried to this horrible woman with a perfect daughter, and it's like they want to start over with a brand-new family and I'm an ugly reminder of the past."

Mrs. Avery is quiet for a few minutes, and I start to feel like a total idiot. This woman is so kind to me. She doesn't need me dumping all my problems on her.

"That sounds like a lonely way to live. Have you talked to your father about how you feel?"

I snort. "He knows I don't like Madge . . . that's my stepmother . . . but he doesn't get why. Every time I complain about her, he just figures I'm being difficult and that I won't give her a chance because she's not my mom. He's not really around enough to see how bad it is."

"Does he travel?"

"A bit. But mostly he just works long hours. I feel like he doesn't want to be home anymore."

"Sometimes when people are sad, they immerse themselves in

other things. Maybe your dad works so much because he's trying to distract himself from missing your mom."

"I doubt it. I feel like he forgets all about her. He *never* talks about her. And he got married so fast . . ."

"How long have he and . . . Madge . . . been married?"

"Her name is Madeleine, but I call her Madge because she hates it." That makes Mrs. Avery laugh. "They met about four years after Mom died. Six months later, they got married in our backyard, and she and her daughter moved in. So it's been about a year and a half now."

"That's all still pretty new. It takes a while to adjust to these things."

"I don't want to adjust. I want my mom back. Or at least to feel like we're still remembering her."

Mrs. Avery nods. "What do you remember about your mother?"

The question is a bright, shiny gift. "She was beautiful and smart and kind. She was an artist and always had paintbrushes sticking out of her pockets and shoved in her hair." Tears overflow and run down my cheeks, but I don't want to stop talking. "She made me feel like I was the best thing that ever happened to her. She used to come up with all these little adventures we'd go on. Like, this one time she bought a map of the city and designed a scavenger hunt for us. We rode the subway all afternoon, checking items off her list, like getting a picture of a pigeon, picking up five pieces of litter, and finding a street performer who played the harmonica."

"She sounds very special."

"She was. Now I feel like someone has pressed the Pause button on my life. No one in my family even notices me anymore, let alone makes me feel important. I feel like the best part of my life died with my mom."

Mrs. Avery crosses her arms on the table in front of her. Our drinks have gone cold. "Why don't I talk to your dad?" She holds up a finger when I start to protest. "Not to tell him what you've told me. That's just between us. But to see if he'd be okay with you spending some extra time with us. I'd be happy to do some of the things that you're missing a mother for—like shopping and talking about school and boys. And if you'd like to trust me with those things, you're welcome to join Jess and me. What do you think?"

I'm worried that Dad won't react well to Mrs. Avery telling him I miss my mom, but what the hell, it's the truth. "Okay," I say finally.

Jess has no idea how lucky she is. I wish I could trade places with her for just one day. Her mother is fucking unreal.

Jessie

This week was a complete disaster, and it's left me feeling like the slightest thing might break me.

I skipped science on Monday after seeing Annie and Scott kiss. I just couldn't face sitting next to him, knowing there was no hope. I'd skip the whole rest of the semester if I could, but my geeky heart hurt from missing class, and I was paranoid that the school would call home. So I gathered my courage and walked into class on Tuesday with as much dignity as I could muster.

I was prepared for Scott to be awkward with me. Or maybe even a little distant. I wasn't prepared for him to act as if nothing had changed.

"Jess!" He greeted me with a smile that made his eyes sparkle. "Thank God you're back. There's a test next Monday. Can we study later this week?"

I will fully confess that I forgot all about Annie in that moment. One look in those deep brown eyes and I had to fight the impulse to crawl into his lap.

"Sure!" I practically yelped, feeling the stirrings of possibility.

"Great. I already asked Annie, and she can make it too," he said, turning to face Mr. Donaldson as though he hadn't just ripped my heart out and stomped on it.

On Wednesday, he called me a "good friend" before asking me nine questions about Annie within the first twenty minutes of class. *What's her favorite movie? What kind of music does she listen to? Does she ever talk about me?*

On Thursday, Annie went home sick, and Scott put his arm around me and said he loved me before asking what kind of flowers he should send her. Okay, so his exact words were something along the lines of *You're the best, Jess! I love how smart you are,* but I got fixated on the *love* word for so long that I didn't hear a word Mr. Donaldson said all period.

And then Friday. Friday we ate lunch together, like the messed-up little love triangle we are, and then hit the library to study. Or, rather, I hit the library to study, while Scott and Annie snuck flirty little looks at each other and found about a million reasons to touch. I wanted to stab myself in the eye with my pencil.

I blame the tension from having to deal with them all week for what happened tonight.

Annie and I were playing Would You Rather while we settled in to sleep in my room.

"Would you rather kiss Mr. Donaldson or Miss Donaghue?" Annie asked, laughing.

"Easy. Donaghue." I dodged the pillow she threw at me.

My turn. "Would you rather wear the exact same clothes to school all week or make out with Andrew Larson?" Andrew Larson has a hideous case of what Annie calls summer teeth—summ'er here, summ'er there.

"Ugh!" Annie groaned. "Good one. Would I have to wear the same underwear too?"

"Yep."

"How long would we have to make out?"

"Twenty minutes. With tongue."

"Same clothes all week. No question."

"Gross!" I teased. She laughed softly and then yawned. I felt so deliciously happy. It was a perfect moment in time plucked out of a hectic and unsettling week. I should have just luxuriated in that moment and fallen asleep content. But I am me, and it seems that I am incapable of just enjoying life.

"One more," I said, my brain screaming at me to shut up. "Would you rather be best friends with me or with Courtney?"

I don't know where that came from. I'd intended to say Scott's name, but Courtney came out instead.

"Jess," Annie groaned. "Don't get all weird about Courtney again."

"Again? When have I been weird about Courtney?"

"Oh. Hmmm . . . let me see . . . how about *every day?*"

She rolled over so she was facing away from me, and I lay back on my pillow, stewing. *Let it go. Let it go. Let it go.* I took a few deep breaths and tried the relaxation exercises my therapist showed me years ago. All to no avail. I could feel the sweat beading around my hairline. I dug my fingernails into my palms and tried to hold back the compulsion to continue the conversation. All the words I knew I shouldn't say were tearing through my brain, howling for escape. It was useless trying to fight it. I knew I'd be up all night if we didn't talk right then.

"Annie? . . . Annie?"

"Mmmhmmm . . ." Her voice was drowsy.

"Why'd you choose me?"

"For wha—" She was on the verge of sleep, and part of me knew I should leave her alone. But a bigger part needed to know the answer to that question.

"To be friends with . . . on the first day of school . . ." I cringed when I heard the words come out of my mouth, and I half hoped that she was too asleep to have heard me.

Annie sat up on the bed and crossed her legs, pushing her hair off her face. "What do you mean, I chose you? You're the one who talked to me first."

She was wrong, though. I remember that day clearly. "No," I told her. "You talked to me first. You asked if I was in your English class."

"You're crazy, Jess. I thought you looked really nice and that you'd make a good friend, but it was you who asked about English class."

I started to get frustrated. Annie should know me better than that. Admittedly, I've never told her about my anxiety, but she's supposed to be my best friend. She should *understand* me. She should know that there's no way I'd ever be able to initiate that kind of conversation.

"Whatever. Why me?"

"Why you—what? Why did I think you looked nice?"

"I guess so . . ."

She narrowed her eyes. "We've talked about this before. I liked how genuine you were."

"But you could have been friends with anyone. With someone more popular. Why are you hanging out with me?"

"I thought we were friends . . ."

"Yeah, but—"

Annie flicked on the light and looked at me like I was crazy. "What the fuck, Jess. Do you want to be my friend or not?"

I shrank back from her anger. Why was she getting so upset? I was paying her a compliment and telling her how popular she could be. "Of course I want to be your friend. You're my very best friend ever."

"Then why are you pushing me away?"

"I'm n-not!" I dug my nails into my palms, but I couldn't stop the sob from rising up. I felt like such a baby and wished I'd just kept my mouth shut.

Annie looked shocked. "Are you crying? What's the matter with you?"

I don't know. "I just . . ."

She sighed like a reluctant child being forced to make nice. "Jessie. You're my best friend. I don't know why. It doesn't matter why. Why do you have to overthink everything?"

"You're right." I nodded my head and fought to keep my voice casual. "I'm just tired, I think. You're my best friend too."

She smiled at me and reached over to turn out the light. "Go to sleep, you big loser." Her tone was teasing, but the words stung.

The thing is, I know I'm a loser. That's kind of the whole point. I've let Annie into my world little by little since the first day of school, and I've gotten comfortable showing her the real me. The *me* I normally keep hidden. I have this horrible feeling that she's going to get tired of me soon. Tired of all the *stuff* that happens in my head and the limited confines of my room.

I know I'm spiraling right now. I know my therapist would tell me that I'm *disaster planning* and *perseverating*. But I can't stop. Annie was my insurance policy against the loneliness and the worrying. She made me feel *normal*. What'll I do if I lose her now?

Annie

"Are you sure you're okay?" Jessie asks for the millionth time.

I lie back on my pillow, pressing my cell phone against my ear and silently screaming at her to just leave it alone.

"I'm fine, Jess. Really. I appreciate the call, but I just want to be alone tonight."

"Okay. If you change your mind, I'm home. You can always come over."

"You're a good friend," I tell her before ending the call.

And she is. A good friend, that is. The only one of my friends who remembered about today.

It's the sixth anniversary of my mom's accident.

I check my messages again and sigh. Not one of my old friends from the Nonconformists remembered. No texts, Facebook messages, emails, or missed calls. That cuts me so deep I can barely breathe. Some of those girls *knew* my mom. I can't believe they forgot.

I fucking hate Halloween.

Tonight Madge and Sophie are dressed in lame costumes, get-ting ready to hand out candy together. My dad is hiding in his office, pretending to work. And I'm here in my room, huddled under the covers.

I can hear the shouts and laughter of kids all up and down the street, and it's like fingernails on a chalkboard. Even though I know it's irrational, it offends me that people can celebrate on the night my mom died.

My phone rings again and I check the screen. Scott. I swallow hard and shove the phone under my pillow. He and Larissa have been calling all night, trying to convince me to go over to Jon's with them. He's having a "party." A party only six people are invited to. Which basically means his parents are out of town and he's inviting people to come drink and hook up in his basement.

Don't get me wrong . . . I love making out with Scott. But not tonight. Not with my mom watching over me.

The ringing stops and seconds later, my phone dings with an incoming text. I squeeze my eyes shut in frustration. *Fucking take the hint.* I haven't told any of them about my mom, so it's not like they're being total assholes, but *come on.* I told them I couldn't go out tonight. Just leave it alone.

My phone dings again, and I pull the covers up over my head.

Ding.

Ding.

Ding.

Seriously? I whip the covers back and yank the phone out from under my pillow. I'll just turn it off. None of my old friends are going to call anyway.

Ding.

I wipe away tears of frustration and try to focus on the screen.

Five text messages . . . now six. All from Courtney:

Look outside.

I brought you a treat!

I hate Halloween too.

Pick up the phone!

Jon's party is lame-ass.

Scott & Liss are idiots. Come chill with me.

A smile tugs at the corners of my mouth. Courtney. I creep over to the window and peer outside. She's leaning against a tree, holding up a six-pack of Heineken and a duffle bag full of God knows what.

I inch open the window. "You're crazy," I whisper-yell. "How am I going to get down there?"

She pulls out her phone and sends another text.

You could use the front door . . . but that's so boring. Sneak out that window, you rebel.

I look back at my comfortable bed and reconsider my plan to lie around all night feeling sorry for myself.

Screw that.

I stuff a bunch of clothes under my covers so it looks like I'm asleep and then turn out my lights. I grab a thick sweater and hoist a leg over the windowsill. It's a short jump into the tree next to my house, so I gather my courage and leap, earning a whoop of surprise from Courtney.

"You're badass!" she yelps, maneuvering under the tree to help me slide down. "I thought you'd just shimmy down the drainpipe."

I turn around and look where she's pointing. "Huh. I've never snuck out before," I admit with a smile.

"I'm honored to be your first time," she deadpans, handing me a beer and hoisting her bag over her shoulder. "Follow me."

"Dare I ask where we're going?"

"It's a surprise."

I follow Courtney out to the street, pulling the sleeve of my sweater down over my beer to conceal it. Courtney takes no such precautions. I watch with wonder as she struts right through the groups of parents and trick-or-treaters, drinking openly from her can of beer.

"You know that's a three-hundred-dollar ticket," I say, gesturing at her open drink.

"Don't be such a goody-goody," Courtney teases. "It's part of my Halloween costume. I'm being a rebellious teenager, doncha know?"

I laugh and feel my shoulders relaxing. Courtney is like no one I've ever met before. She does what she wants, when she wants, with no explaining herself or apologizing.

✷ ✷ ✷

"You've got to be kidding me," I say when it becomes obvious where we're headed. "You didn't get enough of this place all day?"

"This is different. You're gonna love this," she says, skirting around the back of our school to where a fire escape leads up to the roof.

I shake my head as Courtney scales the ladder and disappears from view. This girl is going to get me arrested.

By the time I heave myself over the ledge and onto the roof, Courtney is wrestling two camping chairs from a stack stashed in a corner. "You come prepared," I joke.

"A bunch of us hang out here sometimes," she explains, nodding toward the edge of the roof. "Check it out. The neighborhood looks totally different from up here."

I peer over the side and feel dizzy. Courtney's right. The neighborhood seems bigger somehow. Less claustrophobic.

She pops open our chairs and digs two blankets out of her duffle bag. We wrap ourselves up and then sit, looking out over the streets of the town.

"I've lived here most of my life," Court says, raising her beer in a sweeping arc over the streets below. "And I've never, not even for one day, felt like I belong here."

I raise an eyebrow at her.

"Oh, not in an 'I'm an outcast' way. More like in an 'I was born for bigger things than suburbia' way."

I shrug. "I can see that, I guess. I'm not a big fan myself."

"See, that's how I knew we'd be friends. You don't belong in this shitty town any more than I do. The only difference is, you've actually gotten to live in the city, and I've been stuck here forever."

"Your mom really loves it here that much?"

Courtney snorts. "She can't stand it. I begged her to move after my dad left. I figured we could go anywhere, you know? Make a brand-new start somewhere different. But she wouldn't leave. It's pathetic, but I think she's still waiting for my dad to come back. She's afraid to leave in case he changes his mind and can't find us."

I sneak a sideways look at her as she cracks open another beer and hands it to me. "I'm sorry," I tell her. "That sucks."

She shrugs and grabs another drink for herself. "So explain the Halloween thing to me, city girl. I mean, I know why *I* turned down the invite to Jon's booty-call party, but I'm not sure why you did."

I shrug and take a sip of the beer. "Bad memories."

"We've got all night," she says, clinking her can against mine.

I look over at Courtney and think about her mom waiting in a house she hates, hoping that her deadbeat ex-husband will come back for her. If anyone understands heartache and loss, it's got to be Court.

"My mom died on Halloween night six years ago," I tell her. God, I remember it so clearly. It was two weeks after picture day and the Friday before a spelling test. Mom had driven out to some small-town gallery that wanted to display her paintings. She normally worked from home, and I remember being mad that they'd chosen Halloween, of all days, for their meeting.

"It was pissing down rain that night, and the streets were slippery." I blink back tears as I tell her how Dad and I waited for Mom to pull into the driveway. Even though she hadn't said anything, we knew she'd have take-out. McDonald's, maybe. Or Wendy's. Dad and I were both starving, but she'd trained us well, and we knew not to snack before she made it home.

I was sitting at the front window, watching the way my breath made little circles of fog against the glass, when Dad came through the kitchen and spotted me. "Hey, monkey," he said. "Don't worry. She'll be home soon. Traffic is probably a nightmare."

His voice was light, but I saw him look down the street and frown as he came up beside me. Mom had called to say she was on her way almost two hours earlier.

Dad perched on the edge of an armchair beside me. It was nearly five o'clock and starting to get dark outside. In my mind's eye, I saw kids in houses all up and down the street finishing their dinners and starting to get into their costumes. Mom had promised to be home in time to curl my hair and help me into my princess costume. I was getting mad.

"Where *is* she?"

Dad's hand was warm on my shoulder. "She'll be here, hon. I'm sure she's going as fast as she can. Everyone's rushing home in time for trick-or-treating. I'll bet she's stuck in the drive-thru of that slow McDonald's." He was trying to joke, but I could tell he was freaked out.

At five thirty I found him in the kitchen, trying Mom's cell over and over again. He hung up when he saw me, and suggested that we eat some sandwiches to tide us over in case we needed to start trick-or-treating before she made it home.

"But Daaaad!" I can still remember the way I whined, and it makes me feel so ashamed. "You don't know how to curl hair like Mom does, and she has my tiara in the trunk of her car!"

I felt like Halloween was ruined.

"It's raining, anyway," he reasoned, a sharp edge in his voice.

"Curling your hair would be a bit of a waste when it's going to get wet."

I stomped up the stairs and he followed. My dress was on the back of my door, and I grudgingly let him help me into it. It was pink and sparkly and had a little crinoline and hoop underneath that made it fall in a bell shape. I felt gorgeous.

"I have an idea," Dad said. He slipped out of my room and came back with Mom's pearls. "I don't think she'd mind, as long as you're careful."

I felt my grumpiness fall away as he fastened the pearls around my neck. I'd never worn anything so beautiful. Dad brushed my hair till it shone and pulled the sides back with a sparkly barrette. I remember hugging him in thanks as we heard a knock at the door.

"Mom!" We must have left the door locked, I realized as we raced each other down the steps. I couldn't wait for my mom to see me looking so beautiful. I knew she'd squeal and clap her hands and hug and kiss me. And I knew I'd wiggle away and pretend to be embarrassed.

But when Dad opened the door, there was a dripping policeman standing there with his hat in his hands. *This guy is way too old for trick-or-treating*, I thought. I reached for the second-rate candy we gave to the older teenagers in pathetic costumes. I stopped, though, when I heard a moaning sound coming from my dad. I looked beside me and saw that he had sunk to his knees with his hands over his face.

"Sir," the police officer began. "I need a moment of your time.

In private, if possible." He was trying to get rid of me, that much I understood.

My dad seemed to jolt awake with the realization that I was still there. "Go upstairs." It was not his regular voice.

I stayed where I was. I wasn't being disobedient . . . I was mesmerized. I felt as if the pieces of a puzzle were sliding around in my mind but hadn't yet fallen into place. I didn't want to leave.

"Upstairs, Annie." His voice was harsh. I blinked back tears.

The officer stepped in. "Annie? Is it Annie?" he asked. Funny, the things you remember. He had the kindest eyes and a voice straight out of a Disney movie. I nodded my head at him. I wanted him to like me.

"I need you to go upstairs so I can talk with your dad for a bit. He's not in any trouble, and neither are you. I'll call you back down when we're done, okay?"

I nodded again and walked upstairs like a good little girl. I waited in my room for a few minutes till I was sure they weren't going to check on me. Then I went to the landing and listened to every word.

"That's how I learned that my mother had died," I tell Courtney. "I was sitting in a sparkly pink dress, wearing her pearls and waiting for Chicken McNuggets with fries. I heard the policeman tell my dad about the six-car pileup on the freeway. I heard him say her car had flipped over several times and that they had done all they could. I heard him give his condolences and leave. Then I waited for my dad to come get me."

Courtney reaches across the space between our two chairs and takes hold of my hand. "I'm sorry," she says, and I can tell she means it.

We sit in silence, and I feel peaceful in a way I haven't in a very long time. "I've never told anyone that story before."

She winks at me. "I figured it had to be something pretty major to keep you from making out with loverboy at Jon's party."

I swat at her shoulder and nearly drop my beer. "He *is* a pretty great kisser," I admit.

"I know," Court says. "He's my ex."

My whole body goes cold. "Wh-what?"

She laughs and waves her hand at me. "Relax. It was ages ago."

I grip my beer and try to read her expression. "Why didn't Larissa say anything? She practically threw me at him at her party."

"Like I said, it was years ago. A stupid eighth-grade thing she's probably forgotten about. We've hooked up a few times since but kept it a secret, so she really had no idea."

Hooked up a few times since? I have a million questions I want to ask her, but I have the feeling I'm treading across a minefield. "And you're okay with us going out?"

"Don't look so nervous," she says. "I'm not my mom—I don't go backwards, and I'm not waiting around for some guy to come back to me. Scott and I are done."

I let out a sigh of relief. "Thank God."

"Just . . . be careful, okay? Scott's great, but he's a bit of a player."

The beer sours in my stomach. "A player?"

"I'm not saying he doesn't like you or that he's gonna ditch you or anything. I just . . . if I were you, I'd take things slow and keep it casual, you know? Just have fun."

I nod, as if my heart isn't cracking into a million pieces. "We're totally casual," I assure her, lying through my teeth. "There's no way I'd get serious about anyone right now."

Jessie

When we walked into English class today, Miss Donaghue was handing back our short story assignments. Finally.

From the moment I handed mine in, I couldn't wait to get it back. I've never poured so much of myself into anything before. I got inspired the day after my mall adventure with Annie, and I stayed up until the wee hours of the morning polishing it. It's the best thing I've ever written, and my first short story to get a proper ending.

"Annie," Miss Donaghue said when she caught sight of us. "You continue to surprise me. I truly did not expect the werewolf Good Samaritan story."

I stopped in my tracks, gaping at Annie. "You didn't!"

"What? It turned out great, right, Miss D?"

"Surprisingly so." She laughed. "There's some good character development in here, which is difficult to pull off in a short story, and you made excellent use of humor to offset the horror elements."

I raised my eyebrows at Annie, impressed. So much for the slacker lifestyle.

"And Jessica," she said. "Excellent writing as usual. I really enjoyed the way you played with the conventions of fairy tales."

"I'm so glad you liked it," I said breathlessly, my heart leaping.

"I must admit, though, that I was hoping for a different ending."

I blinked at her in surprise. The ending was the best part. "I . . . I wanted to turn the damsel in distress story on its head," I explained, thinking perhaps she'd missed the point. "Instead of the princess being rescued by a prince's true love, she's rescued by friendship."

I could feel Annie's eyes on me, and my face flamed with embarrassment. It sounded so cheesy here in the classroom, but it was different in the story.

"I see that, and I enjoyed it very much," Miss Donaghue assured me. "But I couldn't help hoping along the way that the princess might find that she didn't need rescuing at all. It seemed as if that's where the story was going, and then the friendship solution came in at the last minute and ran off with the ending."

I reached out to take my paper from Miss Donaghue, but she held on to it and made sure I was paying attention before she continued. "Just because that's the ending *I* wanted doesn't mean it's the way it should end, though. Do you understand what I mean?"

I shrugged. I wanted her to stop talking. I felt like the whole class was overhearing my story get ripped to shreds.

"I want to give you something to think about in case you feel like working on this story some more. Right now, the ending feels tacked on, but if this is the ending you like, there are ways of building up to it so it flows more naturally."

I nodded, afraid to say anything. Her words were careening around inside my head, and I was having trouble piecing them together. I just wanted to escape to my desk and catch my breath.

"Come see me if you'd like some help developing this," she said, letting go of my paper. "I think that with a little work, it could be something really special."

"Sure," I said, knowing I'd never touch the story again. I folded the pages and pushed them down into the bottom of my bag.

I swung into my desk and dropped my bag on the floor, ignoring the looks Annie was giving me.

My cell phone vibrated with a text from Annie: *Don't pout. She said great things!*

I turned and nodded at her, faking a smile to show I was fine. I wasn't, though. I was dangerously close to a panic attack.

I took deep breaths while Miss Donaghue handed back the rest of the assignments. In through my nose and out through my mouth. *You can do this,* I told myself, just like my therapist taught me. *Imagine breathing in the calm and breathing out the panic.*

By the time Miss Donaghue started passing around copies of Shakespeare's *Twelfth Night,* I was feeling better. I even managed to roll my eyes at Annie when our loser classmates started groaning about the play.

"You're going to *love* this story," Miss Donaghue said. "In fact, some of you might already be familiar with it." She held up a DVD case. "Who's seen *She's the Man?*"

A few hands went up.

"Isn't that the one where the chick dresses up like a guy?" Marcus Jones asked from the back of the classroom. *Great.* Whispers of *Lezzie Longbottom* echoed around the edges of my brain, shattering my calm and inviting the panic back in.

I focused on Miss Donaghue's voice and pushed back the memories. "Yes," she said, ignoring the laughter that ensued. "The role of gender and sexual identity is fascinating in this play, and we'll be discussing that in depth. We'll also explore love, ambition, disguises, and mistaken identity. All is not what it seems in the kingdom of Illyria. Or at Illyria High School, as we'll see in this movie."

Excited chatter broke out as Miss Donaghue got ready to play the movie.

"Hey, Miss D," someone behind me said, "isn't the girl in this movie the one who went mental?"

And that was it.

Miss Donaghue kept talking. Something about Amanda Bynes. But I couldn't hear a word over the roaring in my head. My throat had closed up and I couldn't get air into my lungs.

Not now, my brain screamed. I hadn't had an anxiety attack in more than six months, and I'd never had one in the middle of a class.

I could feel the sweat beading on my face. I had to escape. I had to get out of there.

I was sure all eyes were on me, but I couldn't stop to explain. I grabbed my bag and ran for the door, holding my hand over my mouth like I was going to be sick. Miss Donaghue could draw her own conclusions.

I heard her shouting after me, but I burst through the classroom door and ran down the hallway. I had no idea where to go. I just knew I needed to be away from everyone. I had an Ativan in my bag. The emergency pill my mother lets me carry. I just needed a private space and the magic pill, and I'd be okay.

I ran down the stairs and out onto the field. Under the bleachers was perfect. No one would find me there. I skidded into a far corner and wrenched open my bag. I knew the pill container was tucked away in there somewhere.

I dumped everything out onto the dirt. My binders, wallet, text-books, tampons . . . everything lay jumbled among the candy wrappers and cigarette butts that littered the ground. No pill container. Crying in great, heaving gasps, I shook my bag and heard the reassuring sound of the little pill rattling. My fingers found the zipper to an inside pocket and yanked it open. *Thank God.*

I wrenched the top off the bottle, and the pill flew out.

"Fuck!" I screamed so loud I'm sure they must have heard me back at school. I groped around in the dirt and found the tiny pill under a gum wrapper. I snatched it up and pushed it under my tongue before I could think about the disgustingness it had been sitting in. Then I sank to my knees and waited, trying hard to take breaths as deep as I could muster.

It took about twenty minutes, but eventually my heart slowed down and my sobs subsided. I had the lingering feeling that I might throw up, but the panic was gone.

I looked around drowsily, fresh tears in my eyes. Why was I so messed up? How did I go from sitting in English class to sobbing under the bleachers, eating a pill out of the dirt?

God, I hate being me.

Annie

I'm packing up to head to Jessie's house when Larissa's text comes in:

911. Meet at Court's in 1 hour.

I squint and double-check the message. 911? I really hope she's exaggerating.

I fire off a text to Courtney. *Plans tonight. What's L's emergency?*

I've been looking forward to sleeping over at Jess's house all week. We have a hardcore movie night planned—chick flicks from dusk till dawn. We're in competition to see who can choose the cheesiest romantic comedy ever made, and I'm pretty sure I've got this locked down after raiding Madge's stash of old DVDs. My overnight bag is packed full of junk food and fashion magazines, and Jess has promised a full-on girly spa experience, with mud masks and manicures. Our goal is to have the world's most stereotypical slumber party.

No clue, Courtney writes back. *But she was crying when she called to come over.*

I toss my phone onto the bed and pace my room. I can't just cancel on Jess. She's expecting me any minute. But this isn't like Larissa. God, what if Jon broke up with her? My stomach clenches thinking about how heartbroken she'd be.

If we meet at Courtney's at seven, I could probably stay till eight or eight thirty and still make it to Jessie's before nine o'clock.

I text Courtney back. *I'll be there, but I can't stay long.*

L's sleeping over. Stay as long as you can.

I take a deep breath and pull up Jessie's number, then freak out before dialing. I hate lying, but there's no way I can tell her that I'm going over to Courtney's. She'll never understand the reasons why. I send a text instead: *Family crap here and I'm stuck for a bit. Be there by 9?*

My hands sweat while I wait for her reply.

Everything ok? she asks.

I am the worst friend in the world. *Yeah. Just annoying. I'll be there as soon as I can.*

Admit it . . . you're just having trouble coming up with cheesy movies and you know you're gonna LOSE.

I laugh. *No way, Avery. You're going DOWN.*

I look up and down Courtney's street while I wait for her to answer the door. I'm terrified that Jess will spot me somehow. She lives only a few blocks away.

Courtney whips open the door, and I can hear Larissa's sobs all the way down the hallway.

"Oh, thank God," Court says, spotting my overnight bag. "I'm so glad you decided to sleep over. She's a wreck."

Shit.

"This?" I ask, sizing up my bag and stalling for time. "I just . . . it's for just in case."

"Yeah, well, this is officially the 'just in case' situation. Larissa's slobbering all over me, and I can't get her to calm down enough to tell me what's wrong. I don't do this emotional shit. You need to get back there *now.*"

It takes us twenty minutes and two rum and Cokes to calm Larissa down. I'm watching the clock and freaking out, murmuring encouraging words out loud while screaming in my head.

"What happened, Liss?" I ask, rubbing her back and praying it doesn't set off another round of sobbing.

She hiccups and swipes at her tearstained cheeks. "It's . . . it's . . . my mom."

She sits up straighter and takes a long sip from her drink.

"You know how my mom's been working a lot, right?"

Courtney nods her head in response. They've obviously had this discussion before.

"Well, I wanted to Google showtimes for the movies tonight and her phone was on the coffee table, so I figured I'd just use it instead of hunting for mine." A tear rolls down her cheek. "There was a text sitting there from a guy named Josh. I just had this feeling, you know? So I opened her messages, and there were a ton from him. You guys, she's having an affair. For real."

I can't think of a single thing to say. I just sit there blinking at Larissa in shock. Luckily, Courtney is as unfazed as ever. "What do you mean *for real?* Are you absolutely positive?"

"Um, yeah. I'm gonna need therapy for the stuff I saw on there."

"Like sex talk?"

"And pictures." Larissa shudders.

"All right, Mrs. Riley!" Courtney jokes, bumping her shoulder against Larissa's. "Is this Josh guy hot?"

Larissa laughs through her tears. "Not funny, Court! This is my *mom* we're talking about. What do I *do?* Do I tell my dad? Confront my mom? Pretend like nothing's wrong?"

"You do nothing," Courtney says, like it's obvious. "It sucks you saw that, but you have a good thing going with your parents still together. You don't want to mess with that."

"So I just ignore the fact that my mom is *cheating* and pretend everything is fine?"

Courtney shrugs. "The worst thing that ever happened to me was my dad leaving. I haven't seen him in years. It fucked everything up—for me *and* for my mom. You don't want to go through that, Liss. I say you just let things play out between your parents and stay out of it."

"What would you do, Annie?" Larissa asks.

"I don't know," I say honestly. "I mean, if it was my stepmother, I'd happily tell my dad. I'd *love* to find a reason to break them up. But if it was my *mom,* it'd be another story. I'd feel like she cheated on me, too. Like she'd cheated on our whole family."

"Exactly!" Larissa cries. "That's exactly how I feel."

I go on, feeling like I'm helping. "Maybe tell your mom you found the texts and see what she says. Maybe things aren't as bad as they seem."

"Maybe . . ." she says doubtfully. "My mom's not the sit-down-and-talk-about-it type, you know?" She takes a deep breath and forces a smile onto her face. "Sorry for bumming you guys out. You probably both had plans for tonight. It means a lot to me that you dropped everything to be here."

She gives us each a sloppy hug, and the bottom drops out of my stomach. I check the clock: eight thirty. I can still make this work. We just have to keep her calm until all that rum hits her. I've seen Larissa drunk often enough to know that she'll pass out on the couch, and then I'll be able to make a break for it, guilt-free.

"You're not bumming us out," I assure her. "It's actually kind of a relief to know that my family's not the only messed-up one."

"Your stepmother sucks, huh?" Courtney says.

"Pretty much. She kind of swooped in on her broom and took over the family."

"Bitch," Courtney pronounces, clinking her glass against mine. I look down at my untouched rum and Coke and check the clock again. Maybe just one drink before Jessie's. The stress of trying to keep everyone happy is killing me tonight.

"What's Sophie like?" Larissa asks. "She's so *ridiculously* gorgeous. Don't you just hate her?"

"Sometimes." My mind wanders back to the night of the party. "But sometimes she surprises me, you know? I wish we were closer. It's just weird becoming insta-sisters. There are all these expectations about how we *should* be, and we're not like that at all."

I settle back on the couch and pull my feet up. It feels good to talk about this stuff.

We chat about Sophie for a while, then about how creepy Court-ney thinks her mom's new boyfriend is, and then about the coun-seling sessions Larissa's little brother has to attend for anger manage-ment. I feel the pressure in my chest loosening as I listen to them bitch about their family dramas. It's such a relief to talk with people who get dysfunction. Jessie's fairy-tale home life makes me feel like shit sometimes. *Jessie.*

Oh my God.

I root around in my bag, hunting for my phone. "Oh shit! Oh shit! Oh shit!"

It's 10:13, and there are five texts from Jessie.

You still coming?

It's getting late.

You ok?

Where are you?

Text me back—I'm worried about you!

I let out a low moan that makes Larissa giggle. Clearly we should have cut her off several drinks ago.

"I have to go," I tell them, scrambling to get my stuff together.

"What's wrong?" Courtney asks, eyes narrowed. "You're not ditching us to go out with Scott, are you?"

"What? No! I was supposed to . . ." I consider making up a lie, but I'm so damn tired of lying. "I was supposed to sleep over at Jessie's tonight, but I came over here first to make sure Larissa was okay, and now I'm so late and she's gonna be pissed."

I text Jess back while I talk. *SO SO SO sorry. Things are dragging on longer than I thought. Can you forgive me?*

Larissa looks like she's going to start crying again. "Why didn't you tell us?"

I shrug and check my phone. Nothing from Jess.

"Okay," Courtney says, putting her drink down and leaning forward. "This is going to make me sound like a total bitch, but I *have* to ask: What's the deal with you and Jessie?"

"What do you mean?" I ask absently, staring at my phone and willing a response to come up. *Please please please.*

"Why are you freaking out? So you came over here to hang out with friends and got caught up. Who cares?" Courtney gathers up our glasses and heads for the kitchen.

I send another text. *Jess? You there?*

"Sorry, Liss," I say, giving her a hug. "I really have to go."

"Don't worry about it. I'm glad you came."

Courtney comes back in just as I'm hoisting my bag onto my shoulder. She has three fresh drinks in her hands, and she rolls her eyes when she sees me getting up to leave. "Just text her back and tell her you can't come," she says. "It's so fucked up that she has you on such a short leash."

I blink in surprise at the nastiness of her tone. "I'm not on a short leash," I say as my phone dings. "I had *plans* with her. I wouldn't ditch you or Liss, so why should I ditch her?"

I check my phone for Jessie's reply. *Sorry! Dozed off. Everything ok?*

Tears well in my eyes. *Everything's fine. I can come now if you want.*

Everyone's asleep here. Things ok at home?

Yeah. Feel terrible about tonight.

Just glad you're ok. Talk tomorrow?

Love you, I write, choking on a sob. Jess is the most purely good person I've ever met, and I'm a total shithead for tonight.

Love you too.

"Seriously?" Courtney snaps, looking over my shoulder.

I throw my phone down, suddenly furious. "Why do you hate her so much?"

"Whoa!" Courtney says, putting her hands up in defense. "Who said I hated her? I'm just pissed because this is the shit she *always* pulls. We've known Jess a lot longer than you. She even used to be friends with us a million years ago, did she tell you?"

"That's not the way she remembers it. She said you guys bullied her back in middle school."

Courtney groans. "Of course she did. She's so melodramatic. Do you want to hear what *really* happened?"

I flop down on the couch, my heart throbbing. I don't really want to sit here and listen to Courtney badmouth Jess, but I do want to fix what's broken between them. This all seems so stupid, hanging on to petty shit from years ago. I just want everyone to get along so I don't need to sneak around anymore.

"Look," Courtney says, offering me a drink as a peace offering, "I know Jessie's your friend. I get that. She's nice, and she means well."

I take the drink and nod at her to continue.

"She's just not my kind of person. I find her really annoying and clingy, and I can see her getting that way with you and it bugs the shit out of me."

I raise an eyebrow at her, but she continues before I can object.

"You have to admit that she doesn't fit in with us," Courtney says. "She's too . . . *sensitive*. She gets offended by the tiniest things, and she blows everything out of proportion. We *tried* being friends with her in middle school, but she was just such a drag all the time. She used to make us feel guilty about everything. So we started hanging out without her and giving her signs that we didn't want her around. She wouldn't take the hint, though, and would still tag along no matter what. So we started to get more and more obvious to push her away."

"It wasn't nice, some of it," Larissa said. "I still regret that. But at the time it seemed like the only way to get through to her."

"I'm not saying we handled it in the most mature way," Courtney says with a laugh. "But at the time it seemed nicer than just saying 'Get lost, we don't want to be friends with you.' When she finally clued in, though, she went nuts. She told her mother we were bullying her, and I got hauled into the office with my mom. It was awful. Mom was still depressed about my dad leaving, and she totally lost it on me. I wanted to smack Jess, I was so mad."

Courtney sets her drink down and gives me a searching look. "I don't want to be a bitch about someone you like, but I can't stand her. I haven't liked her since that day in seventh grade, and I don't like her now."

I rub my hands over my face. "You guys are killing me with this drama."

Courtney shrugs. "I just thought you should hear both sides of the story."

"I'm not saying you're wrong or that Jessie's right. You're both hurt and pissed off for legit reasons. But people change, Court. Maybe it's time you gave her another chance."

Larissa nods, but Courtney shakes her head.

"Just hear me out. I love Jess. Yes, she can be needy and she's not into some of the things we're into, like parties or hanging out at the mall—"

"Or basically *anything* fun," Courtney interrupts.

I shoot her a look. "But she's a great friend. She's loyal and smart and so, so funny."

I look at their dubious faces. "Listen, I really like you guys *and* I really like Jess. Life would be a hell of a lot less awkward if you could all try to like each other. You don't have to be her best friend, or even invite her to parties or anything, but it would mean a lot to me if we could all eat lunch together and play nice."

Larissa bites her lip and looks at Courtney. "What do you think?"

"Please, Court?" I say. "Give her a chance. Things are different now. It's not seventh grade anymore."

"Oh, fine," Courtney huffs. "I'll play nice with Jess. But I'm doing this for you, Annie. I don't like her, but I can be *pleasant.*"

"Yes!" I squeal as Courtney shoots me an exasperated look.

I settle back on the couch, feeling infinitely better. Maybe tonight worked out for the best. Yes, I missed the sleepover at Jess's, but I managed to smooth things over with Courtney. Now I just have to work on Jess, but that should be a walk in the park.

Jessie

All I wanted was two more pills. Just two. I didn't even plan on using them. I just needed to know I had them.

I waited until after dinner to sneak into my parents' room. Mom was doing dishes, and Dad was on the phone in his home office.

Mom keeps my prescriptions locked in the medicine chest in their bathroom, but I know exactly where she keeps the key.

I tiptoed over to her jewelry box, listening to the noises in the kitchen that told me I was still safe. In the bottom drawer, the lining pulls away, and that's where she hides the key. I noticed her putting it away months ago and stored the memory away in case I ever needed it.

I stole into their bathroom and slipped the key into the lock. I hadn't realized how tense I was until the key turned with a little click and relief flooded through my body. *Just two pills,* I decided. *Mom will never notice two pills.*

There was a jumble of prescription bottles on the top shelf— mine, my mom's, and my dad's. I fumbled through them as quickly as I could, nervous that I'd be caught before I could find the Ativan. My fingers closed around the bottle when—

"What are you doing in here? Oh my God! I knew it! I knew

those pills were a bad idea!" Mom's shriek was like an explosion in the tiny bathroom. You'd think she'd caught me shooting up heroin, the way she was freaking out.

"It's not what you think, Mom," I said, holding up the bottle and backing away from her. "I just need another one or two for my emergency pill bottle."

"Why? Why would you need more? You had an anxiety attack, didn't you? Why didn't you tell me?" She was getting hysterical, and my heart started to pound.

"Stop it, Mom! You're freaking me out!"

"I'm freaking *you* out? I catch you in here breaking into the drugs you *know* you're not supposed to take without supervision and *I'm* freaking *you* out?"

I sat down on the side of the bathtub, trying to breathe slowly. Two attacks in two days was more than I could handle. I looked at the bottle in my hand and wondered how ballistic my mother would go if I popped a pill right in front of her.

"Stephen!" she screamed, dropping to her knees in front of me. "Are you okay, honey? Are you having an attack? Do you need an ambulance?"

"No!" I whisper-screamed. "This is *nothing*, Mom. Just leave me alone for two seconds."

The thought of my dad coming made my heart clench alarmingly in my chest. I needed to be alone, but I was afraid that if I ran off, my mom would call 911 or something equally ridiculous.

My dad sauntered into the bathroom. He knows my mother

and her hysteria too well to get worked up until he sees the sight of blood. "Meredith, I swear to God! I was on a conference call. What is the problem?"

"Look at her!" my mother screeched, pointing at me as though I was at death's door. "She's having an anxiety attack and she's sneaking pills."

"Jesus Christ," my dad muttered, snatching the pills out of my hand and reading the bottle. "This is her own medication, Meredith. If a doctor prescribed it, she can take it. Do you need one?" he asked me.

I nearly snapped out of the attack from sheer surprise. My dad does not believe in anxiety. He thinks my *issues* are all in my head and that I need to toughen up instead of making excuses and hiding behind imaginary problems.

I shook my head at him. "I'm okay."

"Good girl." He turned to my mom. "You. Out!"

"I don't think you understand what's happening here . . ."

"We'll discuss it *in the other room.*"

My dad rarely yells, but when he does, we listen. Mom pursed her lips and looked at me disapprovingly, then relocked her medicine cabinet before following my dad out of the room.

I put my head between my knees and took deep breaths. I could hear Mom and Dad fighting in the next room.

"She's having a *panic attack*. We can't just leave her in there alone."

"She's having a *panic attack* because you're panicking her. You were so hysterical that I'm pretty sure the neighbors have called the police by now. You need to calm yourself down. Jessica is just fine until you start freaking out."

"She was sneaking pills, Stephen. Those pills are supposed to be given only under supervision."

"And did you *ask* her why she was sneaking them?"

"It's because she had a panic attack! I need to find out the details."

I heard my dad sigh and then I heard the squeak of their mattress as he sat down. "Meredith, I'm going to be very clear about this, and it's something you're not going to want to hear. Jessica is just fine. She's a shy, nervous teenager, not a deranged lunatic. You're turning her into a bundle of nerves with your overreactions. This is a crisis entirely invented by *you.* You're the one who dragged her to the doctor and had her put on medication, and now you're freaking out that she's taking it. *You* are the one with the issues here, not Jessica."

"You have *never* been supportive of Jessie's mental health issues."

"Because she *doesn't have any mental health issues!*" Dad roared. "This is getting ridiculous. I have never, not once, seen Jessie out of control. I have, however, seen you out of control when it comes to her. I think *you* are the one who needs a visit to the doctor. Now, I don't want to hear another word about this nonsense. And if you don't stop pathologizing our daughter, I'm going to drive you to the therapist myself. Deal with your own shit, Meredith, and stop dumping it on Jess."

The door slammed, and I could hear Dad storming down the stairs.

My heart was hammering, but not in an anxiety-attack way. I found that I could breathe deeply, and that my brain was strangely quiet. *My dad thinks this is all my mother's fault.* It was a confusing and depressing thought. Do I blame my mom? That was a question that hurt my heart to ask. So instead I cleared my mind and waited for my mom to come back in.

It took ages.

When she finally walked into the bathroom, her eyes were rimmed in red. She pasted a smile on her face as she picked up the Ativan bottle Dad had left on the countertop. "I'll make an appointment with Dr. Morgan on Monday," she said brightly. "I think it will work out best if we discuss this with him."

I nodded, blinking back tears.

Mom kissed me on the forehead. "I'm sorry I got so worked up. I just worry about you." She brushed her fingers through my hair and looked me hard in the eyes. "Why don't you splash some water on your face and brush your hair. Annie came to the door a few minutes ago, and I told her she could wait in your room."

My heart wrenched as she walked out of the bathroom. I wanted to talk about what happened — about the things my dad said — but my mom would never do that. She pretends my dad's opinions don't matter, but they do.

I stumbled out of the bathroom, wishing Annie wasn't waiting for me. I was sure she would see the crisis all over my face. I gave her a halfhearted smile as I walked in, waiting for her to ask what was wrong. Instead, she came running up and gave me a huge hug. "I have the *best* news for you. But first I have to tell you something that's gonna piss you off."

Great.

I blinked at her as she barreled ahead, oblivious to the fact that I'd just had a complete meltdown two rooms away.

"I didn't have a family thing last night," she confessed. "I spent the night at Courtney's house."

I felt myself give up. It was the strangest sensation. I'd feared Annie abandoning me for Courtney for so long, and now that it was happening, I couldn't muster the energy to care. All the fight had left me.

I walked over and sat on my bed, looking at Annie through tears of resignation.

"I knew you'd be pissed. I should have just told you the truth. But here's the thing: Courtney and Larissa feel bad about everything that happened in the past, and they agreed to try again."

Her words made no sense. "Try what again?"

"Being friends. Getting over the past. I know a lot of shitty stuff happened, but I want us all to be friends—to spend time together."

"And they agreed to that?" I had a feeling Annie wasn't telling the whole story.

She smiled hard. "Yes! That's my great news. We can all eat together and hang out."

I looked at Annie's bright eyes and wished I could be more like her. In Annie's world, people like me can be friends with people like

Courtney. I knew she was wrong. But like I said, I had no more fight left in me.

I'm like one of those bouncy rubber balls I used to get out of the gumball machine at the supermarket. I'm hurtling out of control, bouncing off other people, with no ability to control my own direction.

"I'll think about it," I said, to buy myself some time. I don't know why I bothered putting her off, though. I already know that I'll follow Annie in her misguided attempts at fixing my social life, just like I'll follow my mother to the doctor's while she tries to fix what's wrong in my head.

I'll bounce along between them, even though I know it's pointless. There are some things that can't be fixed.

Annie

I write "x = −1" and then flip to the back of my textbook to check the answer key.

"Goddamn it," I mutter.

Scott looks up from across the table and gives me a crooked smile. "Problem?"

"There's something wrong with this answer key," I say, erasing my work so viciously that the paper tears. "I'm usually great at math."

"You're sexy when you're mad," he says, pressing his leg against mine under the table. "Your eyes get brighter."

"You're an idiot," I joke, heat rising in my cheeks. "And this is all your fault. I can't concentrate on math with you sitting across from me."

He props a textbook up between us, slouching behind it so I can't see him. "Pretend I'm not here, then."

I roll my eyes and start in on the problem again. I refuse to be bested by this stupid equation.

Two lines into my solution, I can feel his eyes on me again. "Let's get out of here," he practically growls, and I snap my textbook shut.

We scurry out of the public library and into the street, where Scott pulls me in for a kiss that makes my knees buckle.

I drop my bag on the sidewalk and wind my arms around his neck as his tongue darts into my mouth. I can't get enough of him, and it scares the shit out of me. Courtney's words dance through my brain. *Scott's great, but he's a bit of a player.*

I didn't mean to get this serious, but I can't help feeling like this.

Scott thinks everything I do is amazing. He likes to just sit and watch me sometimes. I'll look up to find him staring at me, and when I ask him what he's looking at, he says stuff like "Your hair looks like it's on fire when the sun hits it" or "I'm counting your freckles." Stuff that makes my heart beat fast and my skin flame.

Scott looks at me and sees *me*. I feel special and important and beautiful. I feel like I *matter.*

He rests his forehead against mine, and I smile at the look in his eyes. I want to capture it on paper so I can see it whenever I want. So I can keep this feeling with me even when he's not around.

"I have an idea," I say excitedly, and he raises his eyebrows in expectation. "Let me draw you."

"Ah," he says, nodding. "You want me to be your nude model."

I laugh. "No! I want to draw your portrait. Will you pose for me?"

"Sounds hot," he says, looping an arm around my waist. "Your place or mine?"

Down in his basement, I sit cross-legged on the couch and wonder how someone with so much personality can be such a lifeless model.

Scott's sitting across from me like a mannequin, his face completely expressionless.

"Relax," I tell him, earning a tight smile.

I uncross my legs and nudge him with my foot. I want that heated look in his eyes. I want to capture his wanting.

"Imagine I'm naked," I whisper, praying that his mother isn't eavesdropping.

His eyes snap onto mine and it's perfect. My pencil flies across the page.

"Don't move!" I laugh as he lunges for me. "I need to get this right."

He groans and sits back, looking at me as if he wants to devour me. I've almost got the eyes exactly right when he runs his hands up my legs and makes me forget to breathe. "Just one second more," I manage, just as the eyes on the page match up perfectly with the eyes staring me down.

I toss the sketchbook aside and feel myself spiral into him.

We've made out down here a million times, but this is different. Things get heated so fast. I feel like I can't possibly get close enough to him. His clothes make me angry.

I can see from his eyes that he feels the same way. There's this crazy moment where he pulls back and looks at me, and it's so intense I can't even breathe.

When we start kissing again, he puts his hand up my shirt and unhooks my bra. He's done that before, and I've always scooted away to do it back up, shaking a finger playfully at him. But this time it feels right. He pauses for a minute to see if I'll protest. When

I don't, he lifts my shirt so slowly and carefully that I think I might explode. My breath catches in my throat and he breaks my gaze to look down at me. He lets out a low moan, and a blush creeps up all the way from my toes.

He kisses my belly button and then trails little kisses up to my chest. I stop breathing. In my head I'm begging him to touch me and terrified that he will all at once. His lips close around my nipple and his tongue darts against it and I moan. Loudly.

That breaks the spell in a hurry. Our eyes meet in a panic. Scott's mother is the fun police. She's on constant patrol when I'm over, on high alert lest I corrupt her angelic son.

"Yes, honey?" she calls from the top of the stairs.

We scramble in slow motion, frantically rearranging ourselves while trying not to sound frantic.

"Yeah, Mom?" He tosses me a blanket and moves over to the chair.

"I thought I heard you call me." She comes down the stairs so fast that she must be taking them two at a time. Her eyes take in the scene in front of her, and she zeroes in on me sprawled on the couch. "Are you cold, Annie?"

I pull the blanket up a little higher. I didn't have time to fix my bra. "A little, Mrs. Hutchins. But Scott found me a blanket, so I'm good now."

"I can make you kids some hot chocolate," she suggests, her eyes never leaving me.

"That'd be great, Mom. We're about to put in a movie."

Her eyes flick over to the television, where MTV is on low

volume. "You haven't started the movie yet? What have you two been doing down here all this time?" There's a hard edge to her voice, and I look at Scott in a panic.

He's so smooth, though. "We were *talking*, Mom."

She smiles hard, overcompensating. "Of course! Of course! I didn't mean anything by that. I'll get you hot chocolate and a snack, and you can settle in for the movie." She rushes up the stairs, probably eager to get back as soon as possible and reevaluate the situation.

We stifle our laughter behind our hands as she clears the top step. "That was close!" I reach behind me to do up my bra, embarrassed that Scott's watching me.

"Annie . . ."

"Mmmhmm?"

He goes quiet and I start to get nervous. I meet his eyes, and he looks more serious than I've ever seen him. "I love you."

My mouth drops open, and there are no words in me. I feel tears tracking down my face. I haven't heard those words from anyone in such a very long time. Scott's suddenly beside me on the couch, drying my tears with his shirtsleeve. "What's wrong?"

"I . . . I just . . ."

He looks down. "I shouldn't have said that."

"No! I mean . . . I love you too." I'd hesitated to say the words, not sure if I meant them. But as they pass my lips, I feel the truth of them. "I do," I repeat, more confident now. "I love you."

He puts his arms around me, and we sit back on the couch, nestled together. I close my eyes and see the pieces of my life falling together. All the loneliness. All the sadness. It doesn't matter any-more because I have someone who loves me.

I jump when I hear his mother come back down the stairs, but Scott just holds me tighter and ignores her startled look.

She clears her throat loudly. "Here are your snacks." She holds out the tray, waiting for Scott to get up and take it from her.

"Thanks, Mom. Can you put it on the coffee table?"

She sniffs and sets the tray down. "Are you planning on watching the movie?"

"I think so."

"Well, why don't you come on over to the chair, Scott?" she sug-gests. "That way Annie can stretch out on the sofa."

"No, thanks, Mom. I'm comfortable here."

"Well, then. What movie are you watching?"

"We haven't decided yet."

"Why don't I join you? I haven't watched a movie in so long!"

"Maybe another time, Mom. I was hoping for some time with Annie."

It's almost painful, holding my smile back. I want to shout from the rooftops that I love him. I want to break into song and dance around the basement. Instead, I fix my gaze on MTV and try hard to ignore the waves of suspicion rolling off of his mother.

"I'll be down to check on you soon," she warns.

"I'm sure you will," Scott says with a laugh. He tightens his arm around me, and I feel my whole life beginning.

Jessie

I could kiss Dr. Morgan. I have a bottle of Ativan in my bag, a refill of my antidepressants, and a mother who's been put in her place.

To be honest, I've never really had much faith in Dr. Morgan's ability to relate to a girl my age. He has messy black hair shot through with gray, a pair of half-glasses that rest on the tip of his nose, and a white jacket that's usually buttoned wrong. After today, though, I'm quite sure he's a genius.

He looked at me over the top of his glasses and said, "You've looked better, Jess. What seems to be the trouble today?"

My mom jumped in. "Jess has been having panic attacks, and I caught her sneaking Ativan on Saturday night."

I crossed my arms over my chest and prepared for a lecture, but Dr. Morgan surprised me by ignoring my mom entirely. "Why don't you tell me what brings you here today, Jess?"

"Ummm. Well, my mom brought me in because of the other night."

"And what happened?"

I took a deep breath and angled my body away from my mother. "I had a panic attack in English class the other day, and I had to take

an Ativan to stop it. My mom only gives me one pill at a time, so
I snuck in to get more pills in case I had another attack at school."

"How often have you been having anxiety attacks?"

"I haven't. At least, not full-blown ones. This was my first real
attack since last school year."

"That's excellent news. It sounds like the medication we prescribed is helping you manage your anxiety well—"

"Dr. Morgan," my mother interrupted, "I'm concerned about
the—"

Dr. Morgan put up a finger to silence my mom, never looking
away from me. "I'll speak to your concerns shortly, Mrs. Avery. For
right now, I'd like to get more information directly from Jessica."

I bit back a smile and continued. "It was a bad one, the attack in
English class. It really scared me." It felt good to admit that.

Dr. Morgan tapped his pen against his chin. "Sometimes when
people experience a panic attack in a setting like school or work, it's
exacerbated by worries about other people seeing. It could be that
the severity would have been quite different if it had happened at
home."

I thought back to how easily I'd managed the panic in my parents' bathroom. "I think that's a big part of it," I admitted. "I don't
want people at school finding out about my anxiety."

"Have you talked to any of your friends about it?"

"No. I don't want anyone to know."

He nodded slowly. "I understand how you feel, but you might
want to think about confiding in a trusted friend. It might help you

manage your anxiety if you know there's someone you can turn to at school. Knowing you have a safety net can actually decrease your anxiety levels."

"I'll think about it—" I said.

My mom jumped in. "What about Annie? I know she'd support you."

I shook my head. "Not yet."

"But I really think—"

"This is a decision Jessie needs to feel comfortable with," Dr. Morgan said. "It's very important that she has control over this information. It's not a choice that should be taken away from her."

I could have kissed him.

"Now, let's talk about the Ativan."

I blushed and looked down at the floor.

"I'm not upset with you that you're using the Ativan, Jessica. I prescribed it to you for a reason. I'm more upset that you don't have access to it, to be honest," he said, giving my mother a stern look.

"But you said she shouldn't have free access to it."

"No, Mrs. Avery. I said it should be monitored. I don't want Jessica becoming reliant on Ativan as an escape from anxiety attacks, but it shouldn't be withheld from her. That just increases her anxiety and causes feelings of guilt and insecurity."

My mother bristled. "I wasn't *withholding* it. Jessie had a pill on her at all times. She never told me she needed more, so I assumed she wasn't taking any."

Dr. Morgan turned to me. "Why didn't you just ask for the medication?"

I sighed, debating. "I didn't want this to become a big *thing*."

He nodded at me to continue.

"My mom gets all worked up about my anxiety, and it makes things worse for me. She freaks out about every mood I have. Whenever I'm feeling tired or upset, she assumes I'm depressed or that I'm having an anxiety attack."

"I do *not* always assume the worst, Jessica. You're putting words in my mouth."

Dr. Morgan held up a hand. "Some of these concerns would be best addressed with your therapist, Dr. Richards, and I would recommend you two do some sessions around this. But let's stay focused on the issue of medication. I propose we give Jessie some freedom to manage her anxiety. That includes refraining from always checking in about it or attributing behaviors or reactions to anxiety. It also includes allowing her to have free access to her Ativan as a means of getting relief from anxiety attacks."

My mom nodded hesitantly.

"Now, Jessie. With these freedoms comes responsibility. You'll need to monitor yourself for escalating symptoms of anxiety or depression and take the initiative to seek out help when you need it. Do you think you're mature enough to handle that responsibility?"

"Yes," I said eagerly.

"I'm only giving you twenty pills for now, with a stern lecture. Get ready."

I smiled at him, feeling the stirrings of excitement in my chest.

"I'm prescribing Ativan as an escape route from an anxiety attack, not as a treatment for your anxiety. Think of it like taking

Tylenol to relieve back pain. The Tylenol masks the pain, but doesn't fix whatever is causing it. One of the risks of using Ativan in this way is that sometimes people come to rely on the easy fix instead of using strategies for managing anxiety. I don't want to see you fall into that trap."

"I promise I'll only use it for emergencies." It took everything I had not to bounce up and down in my seat.

Dr. Morgan nodded. "I also want to know that you're going to keep doing the hard work of getting control of your anxiety. That means admitting when you need help, booking appointments with me or your therapist, and challenging yourself to face your anxiety rather than avoiding situations that make you feel anxious."

I felt a little twinge in the back of my mind. Avoidance works for me. Avoidance is my friend. "I promise," I said, with more conviction than I felt.

"And just because your mother is going to take a step back doesn't mean she's going to stop monitoring you. She's still your mother, and it's her job to keep you safe. Mrs. Avery, if you notice her consistently avoiding social situations or exhibiting extreme symptoms of anxiety or depression, I want you to drag her back in here, even if she's kicking and screaming."

My mother smiled for the first time. "You know I will."

"This is an experiment in seeing how well you can manage yourself at this stage, Jessie. I want you to take it very seriously." He handed me my prescription. "If you find that you're taking an Ativan daily or if you feel like you *need* it to face certain situations, you need to come back in so we can adjust your primary medications. Agreed?"

"Agreed."

The minute we got home, I packed the Ativan in my bag. I love the way the pills rattle together reassuringly. It's like I have a bottle of confidence stashed away. I feel like I can tackle anything.

I texted Annie straightaway: *Let's do lunch with Courtney and Larissa tomorrow. I'm ready.*

Her reply was almost instantaneous. *You are THE BEST.*

Yes. Yes, I am.

Annie

Jess is at her locker. Perfect.

I race up alongside her and wait for her to notice I'm different.

"Holy crap, you scared me," she breathes, pushing her hair back from her face before resuming her struggle to free a book from the stack in her locker.

I roll up onto my toes, willing her to take a closer look.

She stumbles backwards as the book finally comes loose, then stows it in her bag. "Did you study for the science quiz?" she asks.

Seriously?

I shake my head and widen my eyes at her.

"Why are you being all weird?" she says, examining me closely.

I shrug. "I'm just . . . happy," I tell her, wanting her to ask me why.

"Well, cut it out, it's creepy."

I frown at her, and she laughs. "I'm just teasing," she says lightly, handing me her science notebook. "Quiz me before class?"

This isn't how it's supposed to go. I'm supposed to saunter up to her locker, and she's supposed to take one look at me and say—

"You look different."

I turn around to find Courtney strolling up to us. *Finally. Someone who's not completely blind to the fact that everything's changed.*

"You noticed," I gush.

Courtney looks confused. "I meant you, Jessie," she says. "Nice jeans."

Jess's eyes widen. "Th-thanks," she stutters. "They're new."

Courtney gives me a pointed look. One that says, *See, I can be nice to Jessie.*

My shoulders slump. It's not that I expected my friends to be able to see that I'm not a virgin anymore, but I did expect them to notice that I'm *different.* It's like someone's flipped on a light switch inside me, scattering the darkness.

I fall into step between Courtney and Jess as they head off toward class. I'm dying to tell them, but I feel weird bringing it up. It would be one thing if they noticed and convinced me to spill, but it's completely different to bring it up out of the blue. What am I gonna say? *Hey guys, guess what! Scott and I did the nasty, and it was freakin' awesome.* A giggle escapes me as I imagine the look on Jessie's face.

"What the hell?" Courtney asks, watching me crack up over nothing. "Are you even listening to me?"

"Sorry, Court," I say, catching sight of Scott up ahead. "I was thinking of something else."

She follows my gaze and heaves a sigh. "You're so boring since you hooked up with him." She taps a perfectly manicured fingernail against my forehead and says, "Lunchtime, bitch. You and me. I have stories, and I want your undivided attention."

I'm dimly aware of her sauntering away while Jessie starts in on how rude she is, but it's all background noise, because Scott looks up and our eyes connect and it's like an electric current is running down the hallway between us.

Every little detail comes back to me in a rush, and I feel all lit up inside.

I read a gazillion things about sex before saying yes. I checked out so many novels about people losing their virginity that I was sure the librarian would phone home. I scoured the Internet . . . I even bought an issue of *CosmoGirl* that had the article "How to Know When You're Ready" advertised on the cover. So I was pretty much prepared for my first time to be disappointing. And painful. But it was neither of those things. The only ridiculous thing was that I started crying afterward because I was so overwhelmed. And then I felt like a total loser because really, who cries during sex? Not to mention that I had to spend a good half hour reassuring Scott that it was wonderful and that I had no regrets and that I didn't feel pressured. Tears after a debut performance turn out to be stressful for a guy.

Since that first time, we can't seem to stop. I'm almost embarrassed about how many times we did it this weekend. Almost. We've now had sex in Scott's basement, in my garage, in the dugout at the park, and in the men's bathroom at the library. We can't spend more than five minutes together without wanting to get naked. And I'm incapable of stopping at just kissing anymore. Once we start fooling around, it's an inevitability that we'll end up having sex. If Mrs. Hutchins ever catches us, she'll kill me.

I look at Jess and make a decision. If I don't talk about this, I'll explode.

"Can I tell you a secret?" I ask, leaning in close to her.

"You know I love secrets," she says, nodding her head excitedly before noticing something behind me. Her eyes go wide, and I turn to see what's wrong.

Some random guy has appeared, and he's shuffling his feet, waiting to talk to us.

"Yes?" I ask impatiently, annoyed at having my big revelation interrupted.

He peers up at Jess, and she smiles awkwardly. "Hi, Jessie," he says, fidgeting with the strap of his backpack. "I was just wondering if you had a chance to look at the comic I gave you."

She blushes so hard she almost starts to glow. "Yeah . . . I mean, a little bit." She looks down, and I can tell she's lying.

"Well . . ." he says softly. "What did you think?"

"It's . . . interesting —"

He nods his head slowly, as if he's trying to decode her answer. I look back and forth between them. What the hell is going on here? How have I never heard of this guy before?

"Hi," I interrupt, holding out my hand. "My name's Annie."

"Charlie," he says, shaking my hand. Then he turns back to Jessie and opens his mouth to say something else, but he's interrupted by the bell.

"I have a science test," she blurts just as he says, "Martins will lock me out if I'm late for math." They both laugh, and I decide that I'm either in the Twilight Zone or I've been living under a rock.

"Who was *that?*" I ask as we make our way to science.

Jess shrugs and stuffs her notes into her bag. "Just some guy I know from last year."

"You mean, just some guy who's totally in love with you."

She looks at me like I'm nuts. "Bless you for even *thinking* a guy would be interested in me, but you're so incredibly wrong that it's not even funny."

"Are you *blind?* He was practically falling all over you."

Jess gets a weird look on her face and shakes her head. "I think he's just one of those guys who look like they're flirting when they're just being friendly." She mutters something that sounds a lot like, *That's the only kind of guy I seem to meet.*

"What?" I ask.

"Nothing. Besides, I'm pretty sure he has a girlfriend. I've seen them eating together at lunch." She gives her head a little shake and stops walking right outside the science room. "Didn't you have some big secret you wanted to tell me?"

"Yeah," I say, my heart sinking as Donaldson appears in the doorway. "But it'll have to wait till later."

Jessie

Annie should've tried out for the track team, I thought as I trailed her through the cafeteria in my new pair of high-heeled boots.

We arrived at Courtney's table, and I eased my tray down before collapsing into a chair. The boots are only one of the ways I'm off balance these days. I've officially graduated to the cool table in the cafeteria. Well, technically, Annie is the one who graduated, but Courtney has tolerated my presence for a full two weeks now. Being tolerated is a heck of a lot better than being tormented, so I'm doing my best to stay positive.

Which brings me to confession time: I've been cheating. There was no way I could've pulled off the first few days at Courtney's table without pharmaceutical support. My mother's head would explode if she knew, but I've taken an Ativan every day before lunch for the past two weeks.

I know, I know. I'm doing all that crap I'm not supposed to do. I'm letting down Dr. Morgan, I'm deceiving my mother, and blah blah blah.

But it's not like I'm planning on making a habit out of this or anything. It's been a temporary measure to get me settled in with

Courtney and Larissa. I'm already starting to feel more comfortable, and that's all I needed. Starting tomorrow, I'm going back to my *No Ativan* rule and no one will be the wiser.

I still have ten pills left. That's enough for ten anxiety attacks, and there's no way I'll have ten anxiety attacks at school this year.

Plus, the way I figure it is, I can only realistically work on one major goal at a time. Dr. Morgan said I should stop avoiding situations that make me anxious, and I've made *major* progress on that goal this week.

The first day I sat at Courtney's table, I was a nervous wreck. My hands shook so hard that I spilled my Coke, and I was sweating so much that Larissa took one look at me and said, "Ew," before turning back to Annie and ignoring me for the rest of the lunch period.

I went home in tears and decided it was too hard. There was no way I could go back to sitting with Courtney and Larissa. But I didn't give up. With the magic of Ativan, I calmed my panic enough to come back a second day, and then a third . . . and now here I am two weeks later, still braving the lion's den every single day.

"Are you high?" Courtney screeched, shocking me out of my reverie. My heart thudded, and I looked down at myself to see what my latest offense might be. Finding nothing, I peeked in her direction and found with relief that she was tearing into a freshman, and not into me.

Courtney put her fingertips to her temples as though the poor girl's presence was causing her physical pain. "Where's the rest of the decorating committee? Get them here *now.*" The terrified girl scampered off, and Courtney threw her folder full of decorating ideas down on the table in disgust. "Am I the only person with taste in this school?"

I looked away, but not before she caught sight of my horrified expression. "What?" she demanded. "You think I'm being *mean?*"

I shook my head so fast I made myself dizzy. Proximity to Courtney has not lessened the degree to which she terrifies me.

"Oh, shut up, Court. You *are* being a bitch," Larissa said, giving me a little wink.

"I'm not *being* a bitch, I *am* a bitch. And without me, there would be no Winter Formal, so quit your complaining." She turned and pointed a long fingernail at me. "Bitches get stuff done. Remember that. You can put that up on your little geek wall."

I startled and looked at Annie. *She told Courtney about my wall of quotes?*

The decorating committee arrived, and Courtney spread them out at a nearby table, firing instructions at them while tapping away on her phone, recruiting an unsuspecting minion into completing her math homework, and flirting with what seemed to be the entire first string of the basketball team.

I had to admit, Courtney got stuff *done.* She ran that cafeteria table like it was the flight deck of the starship *Enterprise.*

"Earth to Jessie," Annie said, waving a hand in front of my face.

"Sorry. I was caught up in the madness."

She laughed, looking at Courtney in a way that made my insides clench. "It's incredible, isn't it?"

"She's a real force of nature," I said wryly.

If Annie detected sarcasm, she chose to ignore it. "Like a tornado. Or a hurricane."

"In terms of destructive potential, yes," I said, bracing myself. This was where Annie would disagree and extol Courtney's many virtues.

Except she stayed quiet. I tore my eyes away from the Courtney show to find Annie sneaking glances at Scott's table. I stabbed at my pasta salad and sank down into my chair. I wish I could say that Scott's involvement with Annie has diminished my feelings for him, but I'd be lying.

I snuck a glance at my old table from last year and thought about how little things have actually changed. I used to hover around the outskirts of the geeks, pretending to be interested in the differences between the Marvel and DC universes, and now I hover around the popular girls, pretending to care about the theme for the Winter Formal.

I turned my attention back to Annie and watched as she and Scott pretended to be oblivious to each other. And thus began the dance. It plays out the same way every day. Scott can't come over to our table for at least five minutes without opening himself up to the taunts of his fellow Neanderthals, so he pretends to be completely disinterested in our table until then. If it takes too long, Annie texts him under the table, pretending not to care that he hasn't come to talk to her yet. He gets the message, rolls his eyes, and then uses it as an excuse to come talk.

Who says my new lifestyle is without its entertainments?

Thank God for Ativan.

Annie

It's been six days, fifteen hours, and forty-five minutes since I last saw Scott. I slump down on the couch and check my phone for the millionth time this morning. I texted him a *Merry Christmas* as soon as I woke up, but he has yet to respond.

"Put your phones away, girls," Madge says, sweeping into the room wearing a Santa hat. "It's Christmas!"

"It's seven o'clock in the morning," Sophie grumbles, stashing her phone in the pocket of her robe. "Why are we up so early?"

"Because Santa was here," Madge trills, handing my dad a cup of coffee and taking her seat beside the tree. "Time for presents."

I slide my phone under my leg, knowing I'll feel it vibrate if Scott texts. He's in Florida for the holidays, visiting family friends. His mom made a point of telling me all about how perfect their sixteen-year-old daughter is before they left. I'm pretty sure she's planned their wedding already.

"This one's for you, Annie," Madge says, dropping a heavy box onto my lap. "At least *try* to look happy."

I stretch my mouth into the widest smile I can manage, and Madge shakes her head at me before handing Sophie a tiny square box wrapped in gold paper. I steel myself for disappointment. Dad lets Madge do all the shopping, so Christmas morning is basically me pretending to like the junk she picks out for me while overlooking the fact that Sophie's gifts are about a million times nicer.

Sure enough, Sophie unwraps a delicate pair of earrings that are so *her,* while I unwrap a fully stocked makeup kit that is so *not* me.

"Do you like it?" Madge asks. "You looked so pretty the night Sophie did your makeup, so I thought you'd like some of your own. To replace all that black eyeliner."

I'm searching for the words to respond when my phone vibrates under my leg, bringing a smile to my face and saving the day. "It's great," I say with real feeling.

Madge blinks in shock, and my dad pats her affectionately on the knee.

I jump up, concealing my phone against my leg. "I just have to use the bathroom," I say. "Be right back."

I rush into the bathroom and swipe my thumb across the phone screen. *1 new picture/video message.* My knees go weak.

Merry Christmas! Celebrating with breakfast on the beach. I scroll down to find a photo someone has taken of him at the breakfast table. That someone undoubtedly being his mother, because she's taken great care to include the gorgeous brunette sitting next to him. I zoom in to get a better look. Who wears a bikini to the breakfast table? And why is she sitting so close to him?

I swallow my panic and text back, *Miss you xox,* even though what I want to write is *Who's the chick?*

The rest of the gift opening is a blur. I can't get the picture out of my head, and all I want to do is go back to bed and hide under the covers, with loud music blaring.

As soon as Madge finishes opening her last gift from my dad, I jump up to head for my room.

"Annie," she calls after me. "You need to help clean up here."

I feel like my head's about to explode, but I head back into the room, nearly crashing into my dad in the doorway. "Actually, everyone," he announces, "there's one more gift. Go sit down."

Dad comes back with a huge box wrapped in bright red paper, and Madge starts bouncing in her chair and clapping her hands like a little kid. I'm about to barf from the corniness of it all when Dad says, "This one's for you, Annie."

"What a surprise," Madge says, no longer bouncing. "I didn't know you bought something extra for Annie."

The box is enormous. It comes up to my waist and is just as wide. I unwrap it to find . . . another wrapped box. Inside that one is another, smaller box. This keeps going for six boxes, and my dad and I are laughing our heads off by the time I get to the last one. But the laughter dies on my lips when I open it. Inside is a velvet box containing my mother's diamond necklace.

"Is it . . . it's Mom's, right?" I don't really have to ask, though. This necklace is engraved in my memory. Mom had it from before I was even born, and she never, ever took it off. My father gave it to her on their wedding day, and it was her most prized possession. I thought it was lost when she died.

My dad turns to Madge. "Would you ladies mind giving us a moment alone?"

Her eyes are shooting daggers at him, and Sophie seems reluctant to leave, but they get up and give us our space.

"When the officer came that night, he asked me to identify your mother's body. I was so scared to go. I dropped you off at your grandmother's house, do you remember?"

I nod my head. I miss Grandma so much. She died a year after my mother.

"After I said my goodbyes to your mom, a nurse handed me a plastic bag with your mother's purse in it and a few things recovered from the accident site. One of the things was that necklace. The chain was broken, but the diamond was still there. I made a silent promise to your mother that when you were old enough to handle the responsibility of such a valuable necklace, I would pass it on to you."

Dad takes the necklace out of its box and fastens it around my neck. The pendant is cold at first, but it quickly warms against my skin. I suddenly feel my mom all around me. "I'm so proud of you and the young lady you've become," he tells me. "Your mother would be so proud too."

I blink back tears and look at him — really look at him — for the first time in forever.

"Thanks, Dad," I breathe, all thoughts of Scott and his mother and the brunette fading into the background. "This is the best Christmas ever."

Jessie

Back to school tomorrow. I just packed my bag, and the news is not good. I only have three pills left in my Ativan bottle.

I'm screwed. There's no way I can get my prescription renewed. Even if I went back begging Dr. Morgan for more, he wouldn't trust me with Ativan again. Not after I burned through seventeen pills in a month.

It started out so small. I only needed them for lunches with Courtney and Larissa. I wanted so badly to be relaxed and fun. I wanted so badly to be someone different than who I am.

And it worked. Sort of . . .

It didn't make me the life of the party, but it did quiet my brain enough that I could sit through lunch without my thoughts racing around, reminding me of how unworthy I am.

It's not like I took a pill every day. But on days that made me nervous, I'd sneak one to calm myself down. The day Scott begged me to help him and Annie study for an upcoming science test over lunch, for example, and the time I got matched up with Larissa for a presentation.

I've been braver and more outgoing this past month than ever before.

With a few tradeoffs.

I'd hoped the side effects would lessen with time, but each time I take the Ativan, I feel foggy and sluggish. No one has really commented on it, but it's reflected in my grades. It's not a huge dip, but it's enough to bother me. I'm not as mentally sharp on the medication as I am normally, and I'm so sleepy at night that I don't always finish my homework.

Three more pills.

I know what I'm *supposed* to do. I'm supposed to talk to my mom, get my antidepressant meds adjusted, and probably go back to counseling. But the thing is, I don't *want* to do all that. I know the Ativan wasn't supposed to be a treatment for anxiety. But it *worked* for me. I could function when I had those pills. I could get through the day without feeling horrible, and I could walk around feeling confident that I wouldn't suddenly lose it.

If I ask for help now, I'll have to go back to square one with my mom. She's just started relaxing around the whole anxiety issue.

The fact of it is that as well-meaning as they are, my mom and Dr. Morgan, and even my therapist Dr. Richards, don't really understand my anxiety. They've read about it, and they know all the facts, but they don't know what it's like to walk around feeling anxious. I feel *uncomfortable* nearly every minute of every day. There's a tightness in my chest and a buzzing in my head, and I feel so *keyed up,* with no relief possible. I get headaches from clenching my jaw, and when it's really bad, I can't even read because of the *noise* in my head. That's the best way I can describe it—noise. It's like my mind is spinning so out of control that I can't even make sense of it. It's just a jumble of chaotic thoughts clouding my brain.

That was the beauty of the Ativan. It stopped. Temporarily, sure, but it stopped.

Now I have only three more pills left. Three more days of comfort, and then I have to go back to feeling awful.

It's not fair.

And then, to add to my stress, I'm completely nervous about seeing Annie again tomorrow. I feel like someone has flipped a switch and made her into another person.

Annie tells me over and over that I'm still her best friend, but I don't know why she's pretending. I logged on to Facebook earlier and I'm still reeling from what I saw there. Annie's profile picture is now a shot of her and Courtney, obviously taken at a party I wasn't invited to. They're both making silly faces at the camera and laughing. They look so . . . happy.

She finally updated her relationship status to *In a relationship with Scott Hutchins,* which is basically like a knife stabbing me in the chest, and there's a new album titled *Annie Loves Scott* in her photos section that I tried hard not to open. I failed. Miserably. And now I've got a whole series of cutesy cuddling pictures burned into my brain. I feel like throwing up.

As if all that wasn't enough, there's a whole bunch of status updates that I don't understand. Cryptic things like *The red ones are better!* and *Hands off, Larissa!* that are followed by a string of *LOLs* and a bunch of confusing replies that make no sense to me. Evidence that she has a whole other life that I don't even know about.

Annie used to come over every day. We spent hours together in this room, doing homework, talking, and just hanging out together. I was more comfortable with her than with anyone else in my life. I was just myself, with no pretending or trying to be cooler than I am. It's like a slap in the face that it wasn't enough for her . . . that this other world is more compelling than the time we spent together. I know it's the holidays, but I've only seen her once over the break, and that was a rushed visit.

My stomach has been in knots all night, and I can't seem to calm down.

Three more pills.

Annie

Tell me again that there's nothing to worry about, I type in the chat window. I'm on the computer in the living room, flipping back and forth between my English paper and Facebook, having a fight/not-fight with Scott while my dad sits six feet away.

You're being dumb. She's nobody, he replies immediately.

I'm overreacting. I know that. Scott has been great ever since coming back from vacation. But he added Julia, the brunette from Florida, as a friend, and she's been tagging him in a bunch of pictures taken over the holidays. I'm a step away from booking a flight down south so I can slap her silly.

Ok. I won't bring it up again, I promise as a friend request notification pops up. I squint at the screen and read it again, convinced that I'm seeing things. *Sophie* sent it.

I look up and make eye contact with her across the room. *Huh.* I hover the mouse over the Accept button, considering.

Can I trust her?

She'll find out about Scott and about all the stupid stuff my friends and I post. She'll see pictures from parties and read all my status updates.

But then . . . I'll be able to see all that stuff on her profile too.

"Are you working over there?" my dad asks sharply. I click Accept and then minimize the window so my English paper appears onscreen.

"Yes, Father. I'm hard at work," I say, earning a snort from Sophie. My dad raises an eyebrow and Madge looks up from her book. God, I wish I could retreat to the privacy of my room and not have to endure Dad's version of "family time," where we all sit in the same room doing our own thing.

The computer pings as a chat message comes in. Sophie.

Wasn't sure you were going to accept there for a sec.

I smile at the screen. *This is a big step in our relationship.*

I figured we were ready to take it to the next level. :)

I sneak a peek at her and see that her eyes are crinkled up with a smile. It suddenly strikes me as hilarious that we're having a conversation right under our parents' noses. For all they know, we hate each other.

Warning, she writes, *I'm about to go through all your pictures.*

I've already started looking at yours!

Sophie laughs out loud.

"Homework funny?" Madge asks pointedly.

"Hilarious."

I find an album called *Troy* and open it. Holy shit.

Is Troy your boyfriend?

It takes her a moment to respond. I look over and see her chewing on her bottom lip.

We can trust each other, right? she types. *What happens on Facebook stays on Facebook?*

Absolutely! I could get into way more trouble than you for the things you'll find.

She raises her eyebrows at me from across the room, and I nod solemnly.

All right then, nosy. Yes, he's my boyfriend. What do you think?

What do I think? My God, he's the most gorgeous guy I've ever seen in my life. I mean, Scott is hot, but Troy is *hawt.*

Ummm . . . Wow!

I know, right? He's so amazing.

He does NOT go to our school.

Obvs. He's studying fine arts at university.

Whoa.

Yep. Remember—what happens on Facebook stays on Facebook.

Promise.

I click through the album, stunned at Sophie's rebellion. Here I was thinking she was Little Miss Perfect, and she has herself a secret older boyfriend. A secret older boyfriend who's also a sexy, tattooed artist.

I find another album with pictures of her with friends from school. Like me, Sophie never brings anyone home, and I realize as I browse through her pictures that I've never really thought about that side of her—the fun, relaxed side. There's this one picture in particular that gets to me. It's Sophie linking arms with a couple of friends. Her blond hair is glowing in the sunshine and her face is radiant. She's so *happy* that it makes me feel weirdly sad.

So . . . Scott Hutchins, right?

Oh boy. *Yep.*

He's the guy from the night I picked you up at that party. Is he your boyfriend?

Yes. That's the night we got together.

Cute! Lucky guy.

I blush. *Thx.*

I scroll through Sophie's wall posts, getting little clues about who she is as a person. It's crazy that you can live in the same house with someone and not know them at all. I've always thought of Sophie as stuck-up and spoiled, but from what I can see, she's friends with all kinds of people, and nice to all of them. There are no catty posts or snide comments on her wall.

You know, if you ever need to talk about anything, you can talk to me, she types.

I almost cry.

I gotta look out for my little sister, you know?

I blink back tears and then look up and give her a wobbly smile. Sophie winks at me and goes back to her computer.

She logs out of Facebook a few minutes later, but I keep the chat window open for the rest of the night.

Little sister.

Jessie

I was just about to log off Facebook and get back to my homework when Courtney posted a new status update: *Some people just don't know when they're not welcome.*

The bottom dropped out of my stomach. *I knew it.*

Ever since we got back from Christmas break, Courtney's been tormenting me in a million different ways that are apparently invisible to everyone but me.

It started with little snubs. Like the day I sat down across from her at the lunch table and she immediately got up and moved away, claiming that the sun was in her eyes. Or the time she went on a McDonald's run and remembered everyone's order but mine. Then came the "accidental" insults, like her rant about how ankle boots were *so last year* on the day I wore my new ones to school, and the time she insisted that my sweater looked exactly like one she'd donated to Goodwill two years ago.

Annie, of course, has been completely blind to all this. When I tried to explain what was happening, she told me I was being paranoid. "Don't be so sensitive, Jess. Court's treating you the same way she treats everyone else. She says the same stuff to me and Liss."

She doesn't, though. It's not the same.

So when I saw Courtney's Facebook status, I texted Annie straightaway. She couldn't ignore this, I figured. It was right there in writing.

Check Facebook, I texted.

I'm on . . . what's wrong?

Courtney's status.

??

My fingers shook as I dialed her number. I needed to know that she was on my side. That we'd still be friends even if Courtney kicked me out of the group. "It's about me, Annie!" My voice quavered and tears welled in my eyes.

"What are you talking about? It's probably about her family or something."

"No! She hates me!" I wailed. "This is totally about me."

I could hear Annie's sigh through the phone. "Jess, I love you, but you're being paranoid. Court's dealing with a ton of shit right now. Trust me when I tell you that she's not even *thinking* about you tonight."

I took deep breaths and tried to calm myself down. Maybe she was right. Why would Courtney be posting about *me* at 9:45 on a Monday night? I decided that I was overestimating my own importance.

I held on to that reassuring thought all night and into this morning. But by lunchtime there was no overlooking the fact that Courtney sighed audibly every time I spoke and rolled her eyes at everything from the lunch selections on my tray to the outfit I was wearing. I felt queasy, and inched my chair closer to Annie's. *You're not here for Courtney,* I reminded myself. *You don't care what she thinks.*

When Annie pushed her tray away and pulled out her science textbook, inspiration struck. I leaned in close, hoping no one would overhear. "Want to go study in the library with me?"

Annie looked up at me right as Courtney barked a cough that sounded suspiciously like *Lez* into her hand. The whole table erupted in laughter.

I watched as Annie shot an exasperated look at Courtney.

"What?" Courtney laughed. "I just have a tickle in my throat."

I gave Annie an *I told you so* look and waited for her to defend me. I was expecting her to be the girl I remembered from the locker room on the first day of school. Instead, she just shook her head at Courtney and went back to her homework.

What the . . .

"Oh, don't look so upset, Jessie," Courtney snapped. "I was just *kidding.*"

I shrugged my shoulders, struggling to keep my face blank. "I'm not upset," I lied, packing up my tray and getting up to leave.

"Jess . . ." Annie said. "Don't go! Courtney was just joking around."

"I know," I said, like it was no big deal. "I'm going to the library to study. Want to come?" My heart hammered in my chest.

Annie looked at Courtney and then back at me. "Just study here with us. We can quiz each other."

"No, thanks," I said, grabbing my tray and walking away.

I could hear Courtney laughing at me as I left, but it didn't hurt nearly as much as Annie's indifference. She *saw*, and she didn't even care.

Outside the cafeteria, I took a deep breath and blinked back tears before heading toward the library. I kept expecting Annie to fall into step beside me, but it didn't happen. Annie had made a choice, and she didn't choose me.

I sleepwalked through the rest of the day, feeling as if I'd taken a huge step backwards. I was alone again, but it hurt so much more than it ever did last year. All I could think about was where I'd sit at lunch tomorrow. I didn't want to go back to Courtney's table, but I wasn't sure where to go instead.

I could sit at the table Annie and I shared before Courtney came along, but that seemed far too pathetic. It would look like I was waiting for Annie to come back to me, and I could just imagine Courtney's comments. There was always the old table from last year, too. I could try to slip back into my old group and pray they'd take me back. Kevin would make a scene, but back in October, Charlie had practically begged me to join them. I thought about the day he'd found me in the library, right before my study session with Scott. He gave me that comic he drew and told me I should come meet the new girl at their table.

As soon as I got home from school, I turned my room upside down, hunting for Charlie's comic. I finally found it under a stack of textbooks and flopped onto my bed to read it. I figured I'd return it tomorrow at lunch as an excuse to join them.

He's talented, I thought as I took a good look at the cover. He'd drawn the outside of our school, with a crowd of students in front. I recognized Charlie and Kevin with the new girl, and I found Annie and me, our heads bent together as if we were sharing a secret. I felt a throb of sadness at the sight of us looking so happy together, and I fought the urge to text her a picture of the drawing. I knew she'd go wild for his artwork.

I held the book closer to my face and found Courtney and Larissa in the center of the crowd, surrounded by a group of goggle-eyed boys. *Typical.* Except . . . I squinted at the page. Courtney and Larissa were wearing superhero costumes. Ridiculously over-the-top superhero costumes, replete with sequins, capes, and boob-enhancing tops. Then I noticed the name on the side of the school: Sir John A. Macdonald School for Superheroes in Training.

The story started with Charlie and Kevin sitting in the cafeteria. Charlie had the power to turn invisible, and he was using it to check out his classmates without their noticing. Everywhere he looked, he saw people with incredible powers, like super speed, flying, and telekinesis. He slumped in his chair and moaned to Kevin about how lame his own superpower was in comparison. When he caught sight of me, though, his mood changed. My ability was empathy.

Hardly able to believe his eyes, Charlie found himself drawn to me. "You can see me," he marveled as he sat down at my table. "You're the only person who's ever been able to do that."

I didn't share his enthusiasm. "I don't belong here," I told him. "This is all a huge mistake."

As far as I was concerned, empathy was a useless superpower. If anything, it made me miserable. All around me, I could feel the suffering and insecurity and worries of others.

But, it turned out, empathy was something sorely lacking at Sir John A. Macdonald High School. Everyone was so competitive that they'd lost connection with one another. They'd all been so focused on being *the* hero that they'd lost sight of the fact that they were far more powerful as a team than they ever could be on their own.

I came to the end of the comic and felt surprisingly sad that it was over. I flipped the last page, hungry for more, and found a note Charlie had penned on the back cover:

> Jess,
>   Admit it . . . I was right: one good comic can change your mind.
>   I see the superhero in you, and I'd love to be your sidekick.
> Charlie

He'd written his number under his name, and I ran my fingers over the digits, amazed at how badly I suddenly wanted to call him. My brain was buzzing, and I had so many *questions*. I wanted to ask him how he did it. How he drew me in and made me *believe*. And with a comic book, no less. Not to mention the ending. How did he figure out such a perfect ending?

But . . . *I'd love to be your sidekick.*

I flashed back to the day in the hallway when Charlie interrupted my conversation with Annie to ask if I'd read this comic. What did I say? I remember lying and saying I'd read it. I think I called it *interesting*. And then I never talked to him again.

Oh God.

He thought I'd read it and dismissed it. He thought I wasn't interested.

My stomach churned. I couldn't call him now. He gave me this comic book in *October.* That was almost three months ago. What would I say to him?

Besides, I thought miserably, *he's with that new girl now.* I pictured them sitting in the cafeteria together and felt a wave of jealousy wash over me. How could I have missed this? He's a storyteller, like me. Or, at least, like I want to be.

I hugged the comic to my chest and wished I could go back and do everything differently. I wasted so much time trying to impress people who hated me that I never gave a second glance to someone who actually *liked* me.

Annie

I perch on the edge of Jessie's bed, fighting back tears. I want to ask her why she won't try harder. Why she's letting her insecurities about Courtney come between us. I want to ask her why she disappears every day at lunch and has stopped sitting with us entirely. I want to ask her why she messages me and calls me and begs me to come over, then sits there and pouts like I'm the worst friend in the world.

I open my mouth to say all those things, but what comes out instead is "You know, I've never been able to draw you."

"What?"

"I've been trying on and off almost since the day we met, but I can't do it."

Jess looks confused. "But you did draw me. I saw it. It was the first time you came over here." She gestures at her bookcase, to where we had sat that afternoon.

I shake my head, frustrated. "It wasn't right. I couldn't capture you." This feels important somehow. "It's like you have a shield up. Like I can't crack through to the real you."

"Or maybe you just never looked hard enough."

I let my head fall back. Here it comes. The guilt trip.

"I just don't get it, Annie," she says. "I don't understand why you don't miss me the way I miss you. And I really don't understand why you'd rather hang out with Courtney and Larissa than with me."

"Jessie, give me a break."

"What? I'm being serious. I just want to know!"

"I didn't choose them over you. You're choosing avoiding them over me!"

"That doesn't even make any sense."

"It does! You're the one who walked away. You're so stubborn about not forgiving them for something that happened in seventh grade that you would deny yourself all the fun just to make a point."

"They're horrible to me, Annie. I don't know how you can just forgive them for that. If someone had tormented you throughout middle school, I wouldn't betray *you* by going out and making friends with them."

"I'm not *betraying* you, Jess. You're so melodramatic! Court and Larissa *apologized* to you and are trying to make it up to you. You just refuse to listen."

"Yeah, right. You *heard* what Courtney said to me. You see how she treats me. And you think I should be okay with it just because she's *Courtney.* I'm sorry, Annie, but I don't see this fabulous person that you claim is underneath all her bitchiness. I just see a bitch."

I look at her, standing there with her hands on her hips, full of self-righteous anger. She suddenly feels so far away, and it makes me sad. "You want to know the truth, Jess?" I ask softly. "I *do* miss you. But not this you. I miss my friend from the beginning of school.

The one who knew how to let loose and have a good time. The one who was adventurous and smart and funny. We don't *laugh* together anymore. Doesn't that bother you?"

Her lips go white. "We don't do *anything* together anymore, Annie," she says. "*That's* what bothers me."

"How can you even say that? I'm here *right now,* Jessie. Right now! And all you want to do is talk about Courtney and make me feel guilty for having other friends. You make it so much *work* to spend time with you. I feel like I'm always walking on eggshells — like if I do or say the wrong thing, you'll get upset. And it's not fair that you're making me choose between spending time with you and being friends with Courtney and Larissa. If you weren't so stubborn, we could all be friends."

"They don't want to be friends with me, Annie! And I don't want to be friends with them. Why can't you see that? Why are you trying so hard to force me to play nice with people who have been awful to me? I don't *want* to forgive and forget. I just want to move on and make friends I can trust."

"What's that supposed to mean?"

"You see it, Annie. I know you do. You sit by and watch Courtney treat me like garbage and you do *nothing* about it. No, sorry — you make *me* feel guilty and like it's my fault. I don't like them, Annie, and I don't like who you're becoming when you're around them."

My whole body goes cold. "What I *see,* Jess, is a bunch of people who are bringing you into their group and treating you like anyone else. They're not handling you like you're fragile or damaged goods, which seems to be what you want in some kind of fucked-up way.

You need to stop playing the victim all the time and crying every time someone looks at you sideways." I'm so furious with her that my hands are shaking. "You're right, I don't rush to defend you or fight your battles for you. And do you want to know why? Because I see you as a strong and capable person, Jess, not as a pathetic loser who can't stand up for herself."

Her head snaps back as though I hit her. "I'm not *playing the victim*. I *am* the victim. And I can't believe you're blaming me for getting picked on. You're not the person I thought you were, Annie."

"You know what, Jess? Neither are you."

I want to throttle her for being this way. I storm to the door, bumping her shoulder on the way. "You're being a baby," I tell her. "I hope you know that."

"And you're ditching the best friend you'll ever have. You know, this pathetic place you want to escape from was here for you when you were lonely and sad about how things were going at home. I can't believe you'd just leave me and forget all the times I was there for you."

I go still, my hand on the doorknob. "I'm not forgetting those times at all. I wish you were still that same friend, but you're not. You've changed, Jessie. You're so busy keeping score of all the ways people are doing you wrong that you have no time left to be a friend to anyone."

I wrench open the door and walk out of her room without looking back. I'm done with feeling guilty.

Jessie

I was drifting in and out of sleep when the lights suddenly snapped on and my mother's voice filled the room.

"We need to talk."

I forced one eye open and groaned as the light assaulted my tired brain. "I'm napping."

"I can see that. It's four thirty in the afternoon and you've been in bed all day. Enough of this. What's going on?"

"It's nothing, Mom." *It's everything.*

Ever since my big fight with Annie, the days have been sliding past each other. It's like I'm floating above myself, watching some girl who looks like me screw up her life. Second semester is turning into an unholy mess, and yet I'm just drifting through the days without really caring.

"It's *not* nothing," my mom snapped, her arms crossed over her chest. "It's Annie, isn't it?"

I rolled over, hiding my face from her. "No."

"Jessie. You know, we're not blind here. Annie hasn't been over since she ran out of here weeks ago. What's going on?"

I considered my options. What answer would make her go away soonest?

"We're just having a fight. It's not a big deal, and I can handle it myself."

She sat down beside me on the bed. I felt almost repulsed by her and wondered what was wrong with me. "What did you fight about? Talk to me, Jess."

Yeah, right.

That was a minefield I didn't want to navigate. There were too many areas for her to find fault with. I wasn't ready to hear that I was wrong. Not even a little bit.

"It was stupid. We'll work it out."

"I don't think so. I've spoken with Dr. Morgan, and we feel you're showing signs of depression."

That woke me up fast. "What happened to you taking a step back and letting me manage myself? You have no right to talk about this stuff behind my back."

"I have *every* right, Jessica. When you stop taking care of yourself and start letting your health suffer, it's my job as a parent to step in. Now, you're either going to talk to me, or I'll book you an appointment with Dr. Richards, but I will *not* sit back and watch you let your health suffer."

"This is exactly the kind of thing that makes me not want to talk to you!"

"What kind of thing? Me *caring?* You talk all the time about how no one in Annie's family cares about her. You'd think you would be appreciative of having a family that *does* care."

"You go beyond caring, Mom."

"What's that supposed to mean?"

"You interfere. You've interfered since day one. I just want to handle this on my own."

"You're doing a fabulous job," she said. "You've stopped eating, studying, and interacting with other people. Clearly I'm not needed here."

"You have no magic cure, Mom. What are you going to do, call up Annie's parents and tell them to make her play with me? It's complicated, Mom. It's high school."

"I'm aware of high school, Jess. I went there myself, you know."

"Yeah, like five hundred years ago. *And* you were pretty and popular. *And* you had a boyfriend. Your life was easier than mine."

The fight went out of her a bit. "I'm not saying your life isn't hard, Jess. I *know* it is. That's why I want to help."

I stared hard at her, seething.

"It's incredibly painful when friendships fall apart. But I know one thing: you and Annie fit together so well. You really care about each other. Things will work out."

"How? How will they work out?"

"I think it might be time for you to tell Annie about your anxiety."

"What? God, no!"

"I don't know what you girls fought about, but I'm sure there are many things about you that are puzzling for Annie. She's expecting you to react like anyone else, without understanding your situation or limitations."

"My *limitations?*" My fury was white-hot. "I'm not a *freak*, Mom. And there's no reason Annie needs to know anything about my anxiety. It has nothing to do with why we fought. Telling her about that stuff wouldn't fix anything. It would just complicate things."

"Just hear me out. You and Annie are like puzzle pieces. From the first time I met her, I saw how well the two of you fit together. You snapped into place and complemented each other perfectly. High school is a messy time, and your puzzle has gotten all jumbled up. But I have every faith that with a little effort, the pieces will fall back into place. For you, that effort might mean being brave enough to show Annie the real you. Annie loves you. I know that. Telling her about your anxiety will show her that you trust her, and it'll give her the chance to understand you better."

Things are so simple in my mom's world. "I'll think about it," I lied. I didn't bother to tell her that the real reason our pieces don't fit together anymore is that pieces from other puzzles have snuck their way into our box. Courtney, Larissa, Scott . . . they don't belong in our puzzle, and it's become impossible to sort it all out and see what belongs and what doesn't. Annie is stubbornly holding on to all these misfit pieces, trying to force them to fit. She won't listen to me when I tell her it's not right.

Annie

My heart plummets as Mrs. Avery swings her car into my driveway. I really, really, *really* don't want to do this.

I take deep breaths as I walk down the front steps and climb into her car. This is going to be a disaster. I'm sure Jess has told her about all the things I said during our fight, and I'm so ashamed that I can't even look Mrs. Avery in the eyes.

"Thank you for agreeing to meet with me," she says. "I thought we'd go back to the same coffee shop we went to in the fall. Does that sound okay?"

I nod and squirm in my seat. She doesn't *seem* angry with me. I sneak a peek at her as she drives and silently curse Jess for crying to her mom about our fight. How am I going to explain myself to Mrs. Avery?

By the time we sit down with our drinks, my heart is beating so fast that I'm afraid I might faint.

Mrs. Avery frowns at me over the top of her coffee cup, and I'm convinced that she hates me. "I don't know if I'm doing the right thing talking to you, Annie," she begins, "but I feel like there are some things about Jessie that you should know."

I blink in confusion. "Is she okay?"

"She's taking the fight you two had very hard, but that's not the reason I brought you here to talk. I'd like to explain some things about Jessie that might make you understand her a little better."

"So . . . so you're not mad at me?"

"Mad at you? Of course not. Did you think I brought you here to lecture you about the fight?"

I shrug and try to swallow the lump in my throat. "I thought you might be disappointed in me."

"I was sorry to hear that you and Jessie fought, but I'm not disappointed in you at all. In fact, I think I probably understand where some of the tension between the two of you is coming from."

She tells me about how Jessie had a kind of breakdown in seventh grade after everything fell apart with Courtney and Larissa. Jess started having panic attacks and refused to go to school. Things got so bad that her parents had to take her to a doctor, and that's how they found out that she was depressed and that she has an anxiety disorder.

"Jessie's social anxiety makes her see judgments from other people even when there are none," Mrs. Avery explains. "She gets fixated on all the negative things people might think about her, and then she has trouble sorting out whether her fears are realistic or not."

"So that's why she's always so worried about what Courtney and Larissa think." I breathe a sigh of relief. "I thought she was just being paranoid. They apologized, and we were all trying to convince her to move on, but she just couldn't let go of the idea that they hate her."

It all makes so much sense now: Jess feeling like every status update and comment is about her, how she doesn't like to go to parties or hang out at the mall, and how she hides away in her room all the time. "I feel terrible," I tell Mrs. Avery. "I wouldn't have been so hard on her if I'd known."

"It's not your fault, Annie," she says, pulling a collection of books and pamphlets out of her bag and placing them on the table between us. "I can imagine it must be confusing for you sometimes, trying to wrap your head around her reactions to things. I was hoping that if you took a look at some information about anxiety, it might help you understand her better. I know how close you and Jessie are, and it pains me to think that her anxiety might come between you."

"Of course," I tell her, sliding the books over closer to me. "I just . . . why didn't she tell me? We're supposed to be friends."

"Oh, Annie, you *are* friends. And your opinion means more to Jessie than you could possibly understand. I think she was worried that you might see her differently. She was afraid of complicating things between you."

That makes sense, I guess, but I'm still disappointed. "I'm glad you told me."

"Me too . . . I think. I've taken a risk, trusting you with this, but I think you're a very trustworthy person. Jessie wouldn't be happy if she knew I'd interfered, and she'd be devastated if this got out. I'd really appreciate it if you didn't tell her—or anyone else—about this conversation."

"I won't," I promise.

On the drive back to my house, my mind is in overdrive trying to work through everything Mrs. Avery told me. I can't stop thinking about our fight and how I got so mad at Jess just for being who she is. I was such a hypocrite, expecting her to make allowances for Courtney's personality when I wasn't doing the same for her. An idea starts to take shape in my mind. I can't change the way Jessie sees things, but maybe I can change the things she sees.

When Mrs. Avery drops me off at home, I slip inside the front door and stash the books she gave me in the closet. I peer out the window and wait for her to drive away before sneaking back out and rushing down the street to Courtney's house.

I'm on Court's front porch before I realize I need to slow down and figure out what the hell I'm going to say. Obviously, I can't tell her about Jessie's anxiety, so how am I going to convince her to cut Jess some slack?

I'm pacing the porch and muttering ideas to myself when Courtney whips open the door and scares the shit out of me.

"Are you having some kind of psychotic episode out here?" she snaps.

"Oh my God, you scared me," I yelp, nearly jumping out of my skin.

"I scared *you?* I was about to call 911 before I recognized you."
She grabs my sleeve and yanks me inside. "What's with the talking
to yourself?"

I shrug and follow her into her room. "I was just trying to figure
out how to talk to you about something."

"No, I will not go out with you," she deadpans, flopping down
on her bed. "Does that answer your question?"

"Funny. No."

"Well, spit it out, then."

"So . . . you know how Jessie hasn't been eating with us anymore—"

"Oh, Jesus Christ, Annie," she groans. "We're not really going to
have *another* Jessie talk, are we?"

I run my hands through my hair. "No. Well, yes. But this is different."

"I doubt that," she mutters, picking up the remote and turning
on her TV.

Clearly I should have rehearsed more.

I step between Court and the television. "Listen," I say in my
best don't-fuck-with-me voice. "I found out some stuff today, and
things have got to change."

Courtney smirks, and I see red. "I'm serious, Court." I grab the
remote out of her hand and flick off the television before hurling
the remote onto her bed for effect. I must whip it harder than I
thought, because it bounces off and sails right through her open
window.

Our eyes meet in shocked silence, and then we both race to look outside. The remote is just out of reach, stuck in a patch of snow on the roof below.

"Well, that's just fucking great," Court says. "Any other weird shit you want to pull today?"

I take one look at her pissed-off expression, and I can't help it — I burst out laughing.

Courtney tries to keep a straight face, but a smile tugs at the corners of her mouth, making me laugh even harder.

"You're crazy," she mutters, and a little snort escapes as she pulls her head back inside. I fall to the floor, clutching my sides and trying to catch my breath.

"I can't believe you threw my remote out the window," she says, giving in to the laughter.

"It bounced!" I squeal. "Who leaves their window open in the middle of winter, anyway? And where the hell is the screen?"

"It . . . was . . . hot in here," she manages. "And I took the screen off because that's how I sneak out at night."

"Well, next time you sneak out, just grab the remote on your way."

She grabs a pillow and thwacks me on the head with it, and we both lose it completely.

It takes forever for the laughter to subside enough that our breathing returns to normal and we can talk again.

"So tell me about the Jess thing." She groans softly. "I'm all ears."

"And open-minded?" I prompt.

"Don't push your luck, Miller."

"Right." I sit cross-legged on the floor and consider my options.

I know I promised Mrs. Avery that I wouldn't say anything about Jessie's anxiety, but here's the thing: Courtney's not the bitch everyone thinks she is. I've seen the real her underneath all that.

"What if I told you there was a good reason why Jess does all that stuff that annoys you—" I begin.

"This should be good," she quips. "Like, she was abducted by aliens and is suffering the effects of mind control?"

"Good one. But no. Remember when you told me that the thing that bugs you the most is how sensitive Jess is, and how much you hate it when she overreacts?"

"Mmhmm."

I take a deep breath and push back my feelings of guilt before telling Courtney about Jess's anxiety.

Courtney listens to it all, then lies back on her bed and stares up at the ceiling. "Why did you tell me all that?" she asks.

"Because I trust you. I knew that if I told you the truth, you'd help me help Jessie."

She bites her lip, thinking hard. "Okay," she says finally. "I'll try."

Jessie

I've fantasized about Annie and me making up a million different ways, but I can safely say that none of those scenarios took place in a high school bathroom.

So imagine my surprise when after almost three weeks of not talking, Annie waltzed into the washroom while I was fixing my hair today, smiled at me, and said, "Hi, Jess, I've been looking everywhere for you."

I thought I was dreaming.

And after all that time spent thinking about what I'd say in the event that she spoke to me again, the best I could come up with was "What?"

She took a deep breath and squared her shoulders. "I owe you an apology."

I had to brace myself against the sink. It was so bizarre. Annie was standing there like she was making a presentation in class, and her words were all wrong. It didn't even sound like her. My Annie would have said, "I'm sorry," or "Can you forgive me for being such a bitch?"

"I owe you one too," I said, cringing at the distance between us.

"Thanks. I guess we both kind of freaked out, right?"

"Right." It came out in a whoosh of feeling, and Annie seemed to relax a bit.

"I've missed you," she said, running up and giving me a tight hug. "Friends again?"

I forced a smile onto my face and allowed myself to believe this was really happening. "Friends. My mom will be so relieved to see you after school. I think this fight has been even harder on her than on me."

Annie laughed. "I miss her too, but I'm going over to Scott's today. I want us to hang out soon, though. What day is good for you?"

Any day. Every day. "How about Friday?"

"Hmmm . . . Friday I'm going to the movies with Scott, Larissa, and Jonathan. Do you want to come?" Her voice trailed off, making the invitation sound as insincere as it was.

I wanted to joke with her about me being the loser with no boyfriend, but instead I said, "Nah. I have . . . I mean, I was going to invite you back to Avery Family Games Night." My heart constricted at how pathetic my Friday night sounded.

"Holy shit! I forgot about tacos and games! We should so do that again sometime."

It happens every Friday night, I thought to myself. "What day is good for you?"

"What about Sunday afternoon?"

"Sure! My house?"

"Absolutely! I miss hanging out at your place." She paused to check her reflection and smooth her hair. "Listen, I had a long talk with Courtney about the way she was treating you, and things are going to be different from now on, I promise. Please say you'll sit with us at lunch today, okay?"

She didn't even wait for a response. She just flashed me a quick smile and walked out, leaving me standing there with my mouth hanging open.

I was relieved we made up, but it seemed so anticlimactic. After weeks of worries and tears and gnawing sadness . . . after all the panic and self-doubt and desperation . . . to have Annie just toss an "I'm sorry" at me and then go about her day as if nothing had ever happened . . . it was so unsatisfying. I felt like all that time was a complete waste, because I was right back to where I started before our big fight. Maybe even a step or two back.

I spent the rest of the morning stressing about what to do at lunch. I didn't want to eat with Courtney and the others, but I *did* want to spend time with Annie.

I had absolutely no idea what made her apologize. It felt so tenuous. I was afraid that if I ditched her at lunch, she'd get mad again. So I swallowed my fears (and more than a little of my dignity) and went back to Courtney's table in the cafeteria.

"Well, well, well," Courtney singsonged when she saw me. "Look who's back."

"Isn't it great?" Annie's smile was wide.

Courtney nodded her head and crinkled her eyes. "It's good to have you back," she told me. I braced myself for the punch line, but she just smiled and went back to her lunch.

What the . . .

"So now that we have you back with us," Larissa said, "I can't wait to hear your ideas for Annie's birthday party. I'm sure she's told you all about it, right?"

My heart plummeted.

"Not yet," I said, with what I hoped sounded like confidence, "but I'm sure she'll fill me in."

Annie gave me a look that I couldn't read. "Will you come?"

I took a deep breath and looked around the table. "Of course I'll come. And I'd love to help you guys plan."

Annie squeezed my hand and beamed a smile at me. "Thanks, Jess."

"So . . ." I said, hoping to smooth things over further. "What are we doing? A sleepover? Should I get movies or snacks?"

Larissa burst out laughing, and Courtney ducked her head to hide her smirk.

"You are so *cute*," Larissa said, shaking her head. "We're having a proper party. At my house, of course. And if you want to bring something, you can bring booze. Otherwise, just bring yourself."

I tried to catch Annie's eye. *Booze?*

"There's no way I can bring anything," Annie apologized. "Madge keeps the liquor cabinet locked."

"What about Sophie?" Larissa asked. "Can you get her to buy us something?"

"Hmmm . . . let me ask her. I can't make any promises, though. It totally depends on her mood." Annie rolled her eyes, and they all laughed. The weeks I'd been out of the loop suddenly felt like years.

"What about you, Jess?" Larissa asked, shooting a look at Courtney. "Any older friends who can hook us up?"

I don't know anyone, of course, but I didn't want to admit that. "Let me look into it."

Courtney bit her bottom lip and exchanged a look with Annie. "Don't worry about it, Jess," she said gently. "We've got it covered."

Whatever conversation Annie had with Courtney, clearly it had an impact.

I should have felt relieved, and even grateful. But instead I was more than a little insulted. I felt like everyone was being fake and treating me like a kid. I resolved to track down alcohol for Annie's party if it was the last thing I did. I wanted to earn Courtney's respect, not have her feel sorry for me.

Annie

I rush into my bathroom, tripping over the clothes spilling out of my hamper and banging my knee against the vanity. *Shit!* I'm running stupidly late this morning.

I snatch up my toothbrush and scrub my teeth as quickly as possible, calculating how late I'll be for first period. Detention late? Or just lecture late?

One look in the mirror confirms that it will definitely be detention late. I look like death. It took me forever to fall asleep last night, and it shows on my face. My cheeks are sickly pale, and there are dark circles under my eyes.

Concealer. Need concealer.

I shuffle through the bottles and tubes littering the countertop but come up empty-handed. *What the hell?*

I wrench open the drawer, nearly yanking it right out of the vanity. It's got to be here somewhere. I empty the contents of the drawer onto the countertop—brushes, mascara, Band-Aids, tampons . . . I've got everything in here except concealer.

That's when I remember—the makeup kit Madge gave me for Christmas. It's still sitting, untouched, on my dresser. I skid into my room and pop it open, and there it is—concealer! Thank God.

Back in my bathroom, I'm dabbing it under my eyes when a horrible feeling creeps up my spine. I look at the countertop where I tossed the tampons out of my drawer. When was the last time . . .

The room goes hazy.

Think.

Were Jess and I speaking then? Did I have it on spring break? Was it before or after the history assignment was due?

I have absolutely no idea. It could have been last month or three months ago for all I can remember.

As stupid as this sounds, I've never kept track of when my period comes. I can always tell when it's on its way, since I start getting cramps and feeling gross, so I just wait for the signs and make sure I'm prepared. I stumble over to the bathtub and sit on the edge, taking deep breaths and trying to sense some sign that my period is coming, but there's nothing. Not even a twinge.

Fucking hell. I can't be — can I?

I get up, smooth out the concealer under my eyes, and head into my room for my bag. My first class is a write-off. I check the clock on my nightstand and make a decision. I'm headed to the pharmacy and then to find Jess.

She's the only person I trust with this. The only person who understands having a secret you can't tell anyone else.

Jessie

Do you ever have days when you swear you're dreaming? When reality is so ephemeral . . . so slippery . . . that your mind skates along the edge of disbelief?

That was my day today.

Annie herself is like a dream. One minute I think I have her figured out, and the next she morphs into someone new.

Every time I get comfortable—every time I relax into our friendship—it takes a dizzying new turn. Today was the most dizzying turn of all.

Annie texted me before school this morning to say she was running late and that I should go on without her. I walked to school alone, worrying over her having ditched me so close to us making up from our fight.

By the time first period was over, I'd convinced myself that she had reconsidered our friendship. So when I spotted her scanning the crowd in the hallway, it didn't even register that she might be looking for me.

As soon as she saw me, though, relief spread across her face. She made a beeline through the foyer, cutting off kids as if she didn't even see them.

She grabbed me by the arm and leaned into me. "Thank God you're here. I've been dying to talk to you all morning." She looked panic-stricken, and my mind got tangled up between relief that she was happy to see me and fear over the look in her eyes.

"What's wrong?"

"In here," she hissed, dragging me into the bathroom by the arm. "I need your help." She held up a finger for silence while the bathroom emptied of the between-classes crowd.

I felt lighter. Annie chose *me.* She had a problem and she was turning to *me.*

"Promise you won't tell anyone?" She sounded excited. Her words were vibrating with an unnerving mixture of hope and dread. She pulled a plastic bag out of her backpack and clutched it to her chest. With her eyes wide and cheeks pink she looked like my Annie again. She looked like the first day of school.

"Of course not!"

"Okay . . ." She dragged out the word like she was about to reveal something wondrous, and my eyes widened with expectation.

But what she pulled out of the bag was a red and white box that took my breath away. The room swam around me as though we'd suddenly been plunged underwater.

"I know!" she practically shouted, and I looked reflexively toward the door, afraid we'd get caught. "I know it's terrible and awful, and I should be crying and freaking out . . . and I'm not exactly *happy* about it or anything. God, I don't even really believe it could be true . . . but I'm late, Jess. I'm late and I'm freaking, and I just have to *know,* you know?"

She finally stopped talking and looked at me, waiting for me to say something. Waiting for me to reassure her. To put my arm around her and tell her everything would be okay. I could see the scene unfolding the way she wanted it to, but I just couldn't make myself cooperate.

Instead, I blurted, "You had *sex!*" I'd meant it to be a question, but it came out an accusation.

"Duh."

"What were you *thinking?*" I had suddenly become my mother. I knew I was handling it all wrong. I didn't really care so much that she'd had sex, beyond being insanely jealous and enormously curious. What really bothered me . . . what still cuts me so deep that I can barely breathe, is that she did it without talking to me. She thought about it, debated it, made her decision, and did it without ever, not even once, mentioning it to me.

"Jesus, Jess! I need *help,* not a lecture."

I took a deep breath and tried to focus my thoughts. "Okay. Let's think about this logically. You still have a week before your period is due."

"What?"

"Your period. It's due next week."

"I don't even want to know how you know that, but I'm late from the one *before.*"

"You're three weeks late and just noticing *now?*"

"I don't keep track of these things!"

I eyed the box. "You haven't taken the test yet, right?"

She shook her head.

"Let's do it, then," I said, slinging my backpack into the corner. "It's not like either of us will be able to focus in class until we know."

Annie disappeared into a stall, and I heard the package rip open. A moment later, a little folded booklet came skidding out from under the stall. "Read that! I'm too nervous."

I scanned the pamphlet, my hands shaking. "Sounds pretty easy. Take the cap off, pee on the 'absorbent tip,' and then put the cap back on. We should know in three minutes."

We shared a giggle at the term *absorbent tip* before the bathroom fell silent. When I heard Annie peeing, I got so scared I thought I might throw up. What the hell were we going to do?

She came out of the stall holding the stick in front of her as if it were a weapon. She set it on the edge of the sink, and we stared at my watch as the seconds ticked by. Neither of us peeked at the test.

At two minutes and seventeen seconds, we heard the bathroom door pull open. We both moved to block the test from view. A nervous-looking girl peered at us, obviously curious about why we'd formed a human wall in front of one of the sinks, but she thought better of asking. We stayed motionless, not even talking, until she finished, washed her hands, and left.

"Three minutes have definitely passed." Now that it was time to look, I wanted to run away.

Annie looked at me for a long moment. "Thanks for this, Jess," she breathed.

I nodded at her, and we both turned around at the same time. In front of us was the white plastic stick. There were two pink lines in the little window.

"I don't suppose two lines means negative?" she asked.

I didn't answer. I just passed her the booklet that contained the bad news. Two lines meant pregnant. Two lines meant a *baby.*

Annie picked up the pregnancy test and tossed it into the garbage. "Well, fuck . . ." she said awkwardly, not meeting my eyes.

"I won't tell anyone," I reassured her. "And we'll fix this, I promise. We just need information. We can go to a guidance counselor if you want . . . or maybe your family doctor? I'll go with you. We can find out where to get it done there."

She was nodding her head along with what I was saying, until I got to my last sentence. Then she stopped and looked at me, confused. "Get what done?"

"You know, the . . . *procedure.*"

She was still looking at me blankly.

"The thing . . . the *abortion.*" I whispered the last word, feeling the crushing weight of it in my chest.

"Jess!" Her eyes widened in shock, and she backed away from me as though I were something monstrous. "Who said anything about an *abortion?*" Like me, she couldn't say the word without whispering.

"Well, it's not like you can *keep* it!"

"This is all so . . . I *just* found out. You can't expect me to know what I want to do right this instant!"

"What do you mean — know what you want to do? What options do you have? You can't seriously be thinking about having this baby. You're *fifteen,* for God's sake. Are you really going to walk through these halls with a giant pregnant belly for everyone to see?"

"Oh my God," she whispered, tears filling her eyes. "I didn't . . . I mean . . . I haven't thought about it. I just . . ."

"Look, Annie. Let's call your doctor and make an appointment. We can ask him about . . . abortions . . . and get information. You don't have to do it if you don't want to, but I'm assuming that there's some kind of time limit on this sort of thing. Let's get information first and then decide what to do."

She gave her head a quick shake, as though she were waking from a dream. "I got it, Jess. Thanks, though."

"You got what?"

"I'll go to the doctor and everything. I don't need you to come."

"But I *want* to. I want to help you."

She looked at me strangely. "I know you want to help, but the only two people who get a say in what we do are me and Scott."

"Right. Of course. I just thought . . . I mean, you said you needed my *help*. Why did you drag me in here if you didn't want me to help?"

"I wanted you here for moral support. Not to schedule an abortion for me. I need to *think* about things and talk to Scott. This is serious, Jess! It's a *life*."

Her words shamed me. I *know* it's a life . . . and yet I can't help feeling like it's not, too. This was Annie's life we were talking about, and I couldn't believe she wasn't putting herself first. She made a *mistake*, for God's sake! I couldn't wrap my head around the idea that she might consider throwing her entire life away at fifteen because of a *mistake*.

I nodded at her, embarrassed. "I just want to help," I said as she fumbled with her bag. "Any way I can, Annie. Seriously. I'm here for you."

"I know you are," Annie said, and she gave me a little hug before rushing past me. "I just need some time to think."

I stayed in the bathroom and watched her go, feeling as if the world were spiraling away from me. How could something so momentous happen in this dingy little room? I gathered my stuff and headed for the door, passing the trash can on the way out. I didn't want to look inside but couldn't help myself. The plastic stick was sitting there, right on top of the wastebasket for anyone to see. It looked almost obscene, and I couldn't believe she hadn't hidden it at the bottom of the trash or wrapped it in the plastic bag before throwing it away. I stopped, debating, and then grabbed some paper towels and threw them on top, pushing the test down and hiding it from view.

Annie

Before now, I'd always thought that people who couldn't make up their mind about something were full of shit. I figured they knew what they wanted but didn't have the balls to admit it and so pretended to be torn. I'd never been torn before.

I am now.

Some days I fall asleep willing myself to miscarry in the night. I don't want to deal with this shit. I think of my dad finding out, or Madge's face when she hears . . . even of Scott's reaction, and I want to be sick, I'm so scared. On those days, I know I need to figure out how to have an abortion. I lie in bed imagining I'm starting to feel cramping coming. I close my eyes so tight I can see flashes of light on my eyelids, and I put all my energy into ending this pregnancy. I send every negative thought I can muster down into my belly and try to push the little baby out of me along with all my frustration and fear and anger.

And then there are days like today. Today, I swear there is a little ball of light inside me. It's like . . . like I have a treasure no one knows about but me. And it's something so precious that I have to protect it no matter what. On days like this, I start to think about other ways this story could end. I imagine myself having the baby and giving it up to some fabulous couple who are dying to have a child. They're smart and rich and young, and they give my little girl or boy the best of everything, and I get to go through the rest of my life knowing I did something selfless and beautiful.

Or I could keep the baby. I imagine myself holding my little one for the first time. In that fantasy, it's always a girl. I look into her little eyes and fall in love and know that no matter what happens, we'll have each other. I keep the memory of my own mother alive by being exactly that type of mom to my baby. It's us against everyone else — everyone who doubted or abandoned me when I got pregnant — and she grows up never having to know anyone like Madge.

And this is what I mean by being torn. Because on the days I don't want to be pregnant, the feeling is just as strong and as real as on the days when I want to have this baby.

So here I am, less than a week before my sixteenth birthday, holding on to a secret that could completely change my life.

Jessie

Oh my God. Oh my God. Oh my God.

I can't get last night out of my brain. I feel like puking every time I think about it, but no matter what I do, the horrifying scenes keep playing over and over again in my mind. It doesn't help that my mother has been screaming at me about it all day. And she doesn't even know a fraction of what happened.

Annie betrayed me.

The night started out so promising, which is what really kills me. I remember how confident I felt on the way to the party. I'd cashed in on my mother's relief that I was actually attending a real high school party, and we'd spent the entire day preparing. She bought me an outrageously expensive new outfit, took me to the salon to have my hair smoothed into shiny waves, and to Sephora to have my makeup professionally done. I felt pretty and hopeful and excited. I was so, so stupid. What made me think that dressing up would make me into someone new?

Things started into a downward spiral pretty much from the time I walked into Larissa's house. My finger had barely touched the doorbell when a frazzled-looking Larissa whipped open the door and yanked me into the house by my jacket. "Hi, Jess," she said absently, spotting some boys sneaking through a door behind her. "Back downstairs!" she yelled, her hands shaking as she pointed them back to the basement. "Can you help?" She begged me. "My parents aren't home and things are getting out of control. This is the first time they've trusted me with an unsupervised party, and way too many people are here. I think Courtney invited the whole world."

She didn't even notice my new hairstyle or my two-hundred-dollar jeans. And when I pulled the bottles of vodka I'd stolen from my parents' liquor cabinet out of my pockets with a flourish, she jumped between me and the basement door and hissed, "Put those away!

"There's way too much booze down there already. I want everyone to stop drinking," she explained, wringing her hands. "Someone's gonna puke on the carpet, I just know it."

I stuffed the bottles back in my jacket and left it on the couch in the living room. This was not starting out the way I had hoped.

"Should . . . should we go downstairs?" I prompted.

"In a sec. I'm giving everyone till nine thirty to arrive, and then the doors stay closed. I just want to make sure no one is hanging around the front of the house before then. My neighbors will notice if tons of people show up at once."

I sighed and leaned against the wall, reassuring myself that my entrance would be grander if I was the last to come downstairs.

"Grab a Coke or something," Larissa said, waving her hand in the direction of the kitchen. I bit my lip and considered. It was a shame to have gone to the trouble of stealing all that vodka for nothing. And maybe a little liquid courage was just what I needed.

I grabbed one of the bottles on my way past the couch and scurried into the kitchen. I found a stack of red plastic cups on the counter and fumbled with the cap on the vodka bottle before sloshing some into the bottom of a cup. How much was I supposed to add? I eyed the inch of clear liquid at the bottom of the cup and decided to fill it halfway. I wanted enough to take the edge off, and I probably wouldn't get the chance to mix another drink, with Larissa watching everyone like a hawk.

I topped up the cup with Coke and then stashed the vodka bottle under the sink. I was expecting the worst when I took a sip, but it wasn't bad at all. I took a huge gulp for courage and then joined Larissa by the front door.

At nine thirty she turned out the lights. "Thanks for the help. Let's go have fun." Her voice was strained, though, and I realized she wouldn't be enjoying the party very much.

"Larissa!" Emily Watson called happily as we came down the stairs. "We're almos' out of drinks!"

Larissa grabbed a can of Coke off the nearest table. "Drink this."

"But there's nothing left to put in it," Emily whined, sticking out her lower lip.

Larissa shrugged and wandered off. Emily regarded me coolly. "I don't suppose *you* brought any alcohol."

"Nope!" Larissa shouted from a few feet away, shooting me a warning glance.

I sighed and shook my head, then took another gulp of my drink and turned to survey the room. So much for unveiling my new look. No one really seemed to care who else was here. They were huddled in couples or small groups, talking and laughing. I'd imagined my first high school party looking different than this. This just looked like people hanging out after school.

Annie caught my eye from across the room and gave a happy wave. Then Scott pulled her over to a snack table and I lost sight of her in a group of people.

"Where's Courtney?" I asked Larissa, working hard to appear casual.

"Oh shit! I almost forgot. She went on a booze run like an hour ago. Her fake ID is totally sketchy, though. She'll never score anything."

I ventured over to the snack table and grabbed a handful of chips . . . and then I started to panic. Even though no one had even noticed me, I suddenly felt like there was a spotlight on my isolation. I searched the crowd for Annie and found her sitting on a couch in the back corner with Scott. Clearly, they wanted to be alone. I feared looking like a loser far more than I feared intruding on a private moment, though, so I took another sip of my drink and made my way over there.

"Happy birthday, Annie!" I shouted over the music.

She smiled up at me and rolled her eyes. "You're the first person to say that to me." Scott nudged her, and she laughed. "Okay . . . the *second* person." She patted the couch beside her, and I sat down. "Larissa and Courtney were just looking for an excuse to party. They say it's for my birthday, but you'll notice they're not overly interested in what I'm doing."

Scott put his arm around her consolingly. "Poor you," he joked. "Stuck here with me and Jess." He leaned over and winked at me, turning my insides to liquid fire.

"I guess I'll just have to cope," Annie said, laughing.

I pulled an envelope out of my bag and presented it to her with a flourish. "Happy sixteenth!"

Annie's eyes went wide as she opened the card and found the gift certificate to Morton's Art Supply inside. "Jess!" she said, blinking back tears. "This is my favorite place in the world." She gave me a long hug. "Thank you."

I pulled back and searched her eyes. She's been in denial about the whole pregnancy thing. She won't even talk about it.

Annie winked at me and clutched the card to her chest before leaning forward and resting her forehead against mine.

"You okay?" I whispered.

She nodded. "This helps."

I took another sip of my drink and settled back into the couch, feeling warm and . . . happy. The alcohol was starting to do its job, and I felt so wondrously relaxed and content. Prozac alone has never done this for me. Prozac mixed with alcohol was amazing.

And that's where my memory gets choppy. The parts of the night

I do remember are vivid, but no matter how hard I try, I can't piece together what happened in between those memories. It makes me sick to think of what I may have forgotten.

After being on the couch with Annie and Scott, I suddenly found myself in a group of girls who had their claws out, gossiping mercilessly about our classmates. Emily was there, and Larissa, which is tragic, because I remember clearly how I bashed Courtney and called her a bitch. I felt like I was flying at the time, though, and I suddenly understood why Courtney is so mean. I felt powerful and beautiful and free. Being on the inside was like a drug, and when the other girls laughed at my impersonation of Courtney, the pure joy of it flooded my veins.

A heartbeat later and I was back on the couch with Scott. I don't know where Annie was. I was sleepy, and I leaned my head on his shoulder. He was asking me something, but I couldn't make out the words. I knew I should lift my head and look at him, but it felt so good to lean into his strong arm and pretend that he was my boyfriend for a few minutes.

"Are you okay?" he asked, moving away from me so that my head bobbed.

He caught hold of my chin and searched my face with those puppy dog eyes of his. "Mmmhmmm," I said, smiling. "So happy tonight."

His face melted into a smile that showed off his dimples. "Jessica Avery," he scolded playfully, "you've been drinking."

"Shhhh!" I said, flirting with him. "Don't tell my mom."

His laugh was deep, and I felt it vibrating in my chest. He was so perfect. *I love you,* I thought to myself.

But when his eyes widened and he jumped up off the couch, it dawned on me that perhaps I'd said the words out loud.

"I think maybe it's time we got you home," he said, backing away like I might leap on top of him. *I definitely said them out loud.*

Then I was dancing in a crowd by the speakers and the room was swirling around me in the most intoxicating way. I felt like I was one beat ahead of the music all the time, dancing the way I'd always wished I could. *This must be the key to dancing,* I thought. *Letting go.*

Then Courtney was beside me. "I see we've conquered our anxiety for the evening," she shouted over the music. The words slithered out of her mouth and wrapped themselves around my chest, squeezing with that familiar pressure. I wanted to punch her for ruining my moment of freedom. I was suddenly hyperaware of my body, and I went from dancing with abandon to stumbling over my own feet.

I pushed my sweaty hair back and met Courtney's gaze. "What did you say?"

"You know, your crippling anxiety that prevents you from being normal — it doesn't seem to be a problem tonight. You seem super comfortable hanging out with all my friends and calling me a bitch."

The room swayed while I tried to make sense of what she was saying. Now that I was standing still, the room should really have stopped moving. I opened my mouth to toss a witty comeback her way . . .

And instead I puked. All over Courtney.

Larissa screeched, the music stopped, and all of a sudden all eyes were on me. I swayed for a moment, and Annie was there to prop me up. *Annie. Courtney.* A horrible truth was revealing itself in my mind.

"Have you been drinking?" Annie asked, her face contorted with disbelief. I stared at her, letting Courtney's words play back in my head. *Crippling anxiety.*

"Jessie," Annie said slowly, looking worried, "is it okay to mix alcohol with your medication?"

My medication? I yanked my arm away from her and swayed dangerously, afraid I might throw up again. "What are you talking about—medication?"

Annie fidgeted, looking around for support.

"Oh for *fuck's sake*," Courtney yelled, pulling her soaking shirt away from her body. "Your *crazy girl* meds. The ones that keep you from being a complete and utter psycho like you are right now."

The last thing I saw before the room went black was Annie's guilt-ridden face.

The next thing I knew, I was being loaded into my mom's car, and she was on the phone with someone asking about drug interactions. Annie was crying and apologizing over and over again. And that's when I put it together. I heard my mother's voice in my mind—*I think it might be time for you to tell Annie about your anxi-*

ety. I leaned forward, puked all over her car, and then surrendered to the darkness again.

That's all I remember before waking up this morning with a headache so intense I thought someone was cracking my skull open.

Mom has been in and out of here all day, presumably checking to see that I'm still breathing before screaming at me over and over again about responsibility and taking care of my health and how I could have killed myself. I let her words bounce off me and roll around on the floor. She told Annie. She took my deepest secret and just handed it over like it was nothing. And then Annie told Courtney, who told the world. I will never, ever trust any of them again. They have ruined my life.

My phone has been buzzing all day with messages and voice mails from Annie. I open the texts and delete them immediately. I want Annie to see on her phone that I got her messages but didn't reply. I want her to suffer.

I thought she was different. I thought *we* were different. But she betrayed me just like Courtney and Larissa.

When I think about last night, I may as well be back in seventh grade, alone on the playground, because I feel exactly the same way I did back then — small and worthless and ashamed.

Annie

Jess is a total bitch.

I've talked to her mom twice now, so I know she's awake and that she's okay, but she refuses to pick up the phone when I call. I've sent her a million texts that she won't reply to, and I just tried messaging her on Facebook to find that she unfriended me.

Happy Birthday to me, right?

I know she's mad I told Courtney, but she won't even let me *explain*. I did what I did to help her. I was being a *friend*.

If she were truly *my* friend, she would hear me out. She'd let me explain, at least. And then we'd talk about it. But no. Like always, Jessie is convinced that she's right and that everyone is against her. She's probably pouting in her room, thinking about how awful I am. Like I'm the one who got wasted and started hanging all over *her* boyfriend.

I read the books Mrs. Avery gave me, and I feel like I understand about her anxiety and depression. But here's the thing: I don't think those are excuses for being a shitty friend. I don't see why I always have to be the one to overlook stuff and be *understanding* and she gets to be as immature and demanding as she wants.

Not to mention that you'd think she'd be cutting me some slack right now. She's so fucking self-involved. She is the only person on *earth* who knows that I'm pregnant. Shouldn't she be worrying about *my* feelings for five minutes? Shouldn't she make some allowances for me?

I leave her one last voice mail. I tell her I'm sorry and that it was a misunderstanding. I tell her I want the chance to talk to her about it and show her my side of things. I'm not going to chase after her forever. If she values our friendship, she'll give me a chance and call me back. If I don't hear from her, then I'll know her answer.

Ugh.

I so don't need this right now, on top of everything else.

Like I wasn't feeling shitty enough.

All last night at the party I felt like such a fraud. It's eating me up inside, keeping this secret from Scott. I *know* I should tell him I'm pregnant. This affects him, too, and he should know. But I just can't bring myself to do it.

It'll change everything. The easy, fun connection we have will get strained and awkward. We'll have real, grown-up decisions to make. I'm not ready for that. I want to be happy and carefree and *young* for a while longer. I've been sixteen for only twenty-four hours, for Christ's sake.

Plus, I have absolutely no idea how he'll react to this news. I don't even know how I *want* him to react. Even the thought of having this conversation with him short-circuits my brain. This cannot be real. It cannot be happening to me.

What if he breaks up with me? What if he decides this is all too much for him and he just leaves? What will I do then?

If I get an abortion, I might not even need to talk to him. Maybe I can just pretend that none of this ever happened. I can stay with Scott and keep all my friends and still be *me*.

I can't tell him yet. I need to decide what I want to do first. I don't want to ruin everything for no reason.

Jessie

She's *done?* What the hell was that supposed to mean?

I stabbed at the screen of my phone, replaying Annie's last voice mail.

How *dare* she?

Even the tone of her voice made me livid. She was so *smug:* "I've called and texted you all day, but you refuse to talk to me. You even blocked me on Facebook. That's not how friends treat each other, Jessie. And the day after my birthday, too. If you're really my friend, you'll call me and we'll talk this through. You don't know my side of the story at all. I have so many things to tell you, but I'm done chasing you. If you don't want to talk to me, then fine. Walk away. But if you *do* value our friendship, please call me back and we'll talk."

I could almost see her shrugging her shoulders and giving up, and it pissed me off. She expended what? . . . Like five hours of effort into making it up to me? A bunch of worthless texts and phone calls? If it had been me, I would have gone to her house, sent her apology flowers — anything to show that I was sorry and that I cared about her.

I threw my phone down and pulled my laptop toward me. I'd been trolling Facebook all day, looking for references to the party. I hit Refresh and held my breath as it reloaded. Still nothing. I wasn't sure if I should be relieved or upset.

I pulled up my friends list and scanned through it, feeling sick. All those people, and none of them real friends. Annie wasn't on the list, of course. I unfriended her the minute I woke up today.

I picked up my phone again, suddenly desperate to erase every bit of evidence of our friendship. I deleted all her messages and texts and then pulled up her number and blocked her from my contacts, but it still felt unsatisfying. It still felt as if she'd had the last word.

I looked back at my laptop screen. Scott was on Facebook. I could see the little green light beside his name on my chat sidebar.

Why should I keep her secrets when she didn't keep mine?

All it would take was one little click and a carefully worded message.

Hi, Scott. I'm so sorry about last night. I was really drunk and stupid and I don't even remember half of what happened. But I do remember wanting to tell you something. Annie has been keeping a huge secret from you. You really need to ask her about it.

Annie

I can feel Jessie's eyes on me, but I refuse to turn around. She flounced past me on her way into class earlier, her nose in the air, sighing loudly as she passed my desk. Her whole *woe is me* routine is bugging the shit out of me. She's been skulking around all morning, looking *wounded* and waiting for me to make things right.

I apologized already. It's her turn to apologize to *me*. And not just for ignoring me and being a bitch—she owes me an apology for slobbering all over Scott at the party. I mean, *come on.* It takes a shitload of nerve to play the victim when you're a backstabber who'd make a move on your best friend's boyfriend.

Scott. The back of my neck goes hot with sudden realization. I haven't heard from Scott all morning. Weird.

I reach down and ease my phone out of my bag, careful not to let Miss Fletcher see it. I must have missed his text this morning. I rest the phone inside my desk and open my messages. Not a single text from Scott. He *always* messages me first thing in the morning.

I chew on my lip, my mind turning over the possibilities. Is he home sick? Did he lose his phone again? I wait for Miss Fletcher to write something on the board before firing off a quick text: *Haven't heard from you all day! Everything ok?*

It takes about three seconds for the reply to come in. *We need to talk.*

Why? What's wrong?

Let's talk at lunch.

You're freaking me out. Is everything ok?

We'll talk at the diner.

The diner? We're not supposed to leave school property at lunch, though no one really makes a huge deal about it. Almost everyone eats in the cafeteria. Joel's Diner is a twenty-minute walk from school, and it's hard to get there and back in time for class.

Ok . . . meet at my locker?

Meet you at Joel's.

What the hell? Butterflies swoop in my stomach. Something's wrong. Scott sounds so *mad.* I rack my brain trying to think of a reason why. Did we have plans I forgot about? Was I supposed to message him last night? We chatted over Facebook in the afternoon, and he wasn't mad at all . . .

I'm shaking by the time I walk into Joel's at lunch. I practically ran the whole way, so I'm surprised to see Scott already here. He's in a booth at the back, already ordering from a waitress. Nice that he waited for me.

I give myself a mental shake. *Stop freaking out like a pathetic girl. You haven't done anything wrong.*

I walk up with a confidence I don't feel. "Hi," I say, trying hard to sound bright and cheerful.

Scott doesn't even look up at me. "Order fast so we're not late for class."

The waitress raises her eyebrows at his tone. "I'll have a burger and fries," I mumble, sliding into the booth. "And a ginger ale, if you have it."

She scribbles down my order and rushes off. I'm gripped with the sudden urge to call her back and ask her to sit down so I won't have to face this alone.

I look up and meet Scott's eyes. He's staring at me.

"Are you going to tell me what's wrong?" I ask.

"Are you keeping secrets from me?"

My blood runs cold. He can't possibly know. "Secrets? No . . . what makes you think I'm keeping secrets?"

He closes his eyes for a moment, and when he opens them again, they're so sad that it breaks me. "If there's anything you need to tell me, Annie, just say it. Please don't lie to me."

This isn't the time or the place. I'm not ready to have this conversation yet. But the hurt in those eyes that I love so much . . .

"I'm pregnant." *Holyfuckingshit.* I want to reach out and grab the words and push them back into my mouth.

Whatever Scott thought I was going to say, that sure wasn't it. His face goes completely white. "What? When did this happen?"

"I missed my period last month and I took a test and—"

"Last *month?* You've known this for a month and you're just telling me now?"

"No. Almost. Wait . . ." My head is spinning.

"Why would you wait?"

"Hold on a second. You've got it all wrong. I missed my . . . you know . . . and then it took me a while to realize I was so late. Then I took a test. So really, I think I've known for all of two weeks or so. But why is that important?"

"What do you mean, *why is that important?* How long do we have left to take care of it?"

"What are you talking about?"

He leans in close, his eyes dark. "I mean, what were you waiting for? Till it was too late?"

"Too late for what?"

"An *abortion.*" He hisses out the word, looking around nervously.

"What? No! Of course not. There's still lots of time for those decisions. I was . . . just . . . I wanted to tell you at the right time."

Scott's fury is white-hot. "The right *time?* Are you fucking serious? What right time would there possibly be for you to tell me you're ruining my life and that you've been hiding something major from me for a month!"

"Two weeks . . ."

"Whatever!" He's obviously not worried about being overheard anymore. The waitress fidgets by the counter.

"Calm down. I'm not keeping secrets. This was hard for me, too. I totally freaked out and got scared. This isn't exactly the kind of information you can just toss out there, you know?" I reach for his hand, but he pulls it away. "Come on, Scott. Of course I was going to tell you. Of course you need to know. Because this is your child and we need to make these decisions together."

The panic in his eyes takes my breath away. "My *child?* Annie! What's wrong with you? We're sixteen years old. We can't have a child! What are we going to do, drop out of school and get jobs at the Dollar Store to support it? You're insane."

"I never said we were going to keep it, I just said we had to talk about it. And talking usually involves conversation, not someone yelling at the other person." The tears are out in full force now, and I swipe at them angrily. I don't want to cry in front of him.

"How did this happen, anyway?" His eyes are accusing.

"What's that supposed to mean? Are you telling me you don't remember us having *sex?*"

"Of course I remember that. But you were supposed to be on the Pill."

"What the fuck are you talking about?" I'm the angry one now. "Who said anything about the Pill? What did you think, that I'd go up to my dad and ask him to fill my birth control prescriptions? Where the fuck would I get the Pill?"

"When I asked you if we could stop using condoms, you said it was okay."

"*Excuse* me?"

"When. I. Asked . . ."

"I heard you. But first of all, you didn't *ask if it was okay.* You announced that you hated condoms and said you couldn't feel anything, so you wanted to stop wearing them. There was no question in there. And we *never* talked about the Pill. I said it was okay because I wanted you to enjoy it, not because I was on birth control."

"Then you never should have said yes."

"Why is it all *my* responsibility to take care of the birth control? You never even *asked*. And why would I have insisted on condoms from the beginning if I was on the Pill?"

"I just figured you were worried about AIDS."

"Bullshit. You didn't think I was on the Pill. You just don't want to admit this is as much your fault as it is mine."

"No, Annie. I *did* think you were on the Pill, because I thought you were a smart girl. I assumed you wouldn't risk ruining both of our lives like this."

"Well, if you were so concerned, you should have talked to me about it."

"My mother was right." He mumbles the words as he sits back, staring off into space, but I feel like he shouted them.

"Right about what?"

"Right about you."

"And what exactly did your mother say?"

"That you were out to trap me. That girls like you are looking for some guy to drag down and force them to take care of you."

"Girls like *me?* What kind of girl am I?"

"You know, from a broken home. Unhappy. She said you'd try to trap me into a relationship because you don't have enough love in your life, and I didn't believe her."

"But you do now."

"What am I supposed to think, Annie? People don't do things like this. Girls don't sleep around like this without taking birth control. You weren't even on the Pill, for Christ's sake. That makes no sense to me. I mean, who would do that?"

Girls like me.

I stand up and walk right out of the restaurant. With every step, I expect him to chase after me. I expect him to grab me by the arm and apologize and say he's just overwhelmed and scared. I expect him to tell me he loves me. But he doesn't.

I walk all the way home in a complete daze. I'm actually surprised when I see my house in front of me. I'd meant to go back to school, but I'm relieved to be here instead. I stumble into my room and bury myself under the covers before gathering the courage to check my phone.

Not a single call or text.

He let me walk away and didn't even check to see if I was okay.

Jessie

My stomach hurt and my head was pounding. I felt like something terrible was happening and there was nothing I could do to stop it. My heart kept fluttering and my brain was buzzing and I didn't think it was normal—even for a panic attack. What if I had some kind of heart condition and I was just ignoring it because I thought it was anxiety? What if I died sitting there waiting for my Ativan to kick in?

I'd faked a stomachache so I could stay home while my parents went out to dinner. As soon as their car pulled out of the driveway, I turned their room upside down looking for the key to the medicine cabinet. I finally found it under my mother's table lamp.

I was practically hyperventilating, worried that Mom might have thrown out the old prescription when I got my new one. It was right there on the shelf, though. Twelve pretty little white pills. I took five of them and put the rest back. I could make five last.

I'm not proud of myself. This isn't the person I want to be. I want to be honest and trustworthy. Not the kind of girl who steals drugs and breaks the trust of her only friend.

Annie.

I was so scared to go to school this morning. In my rage last night, I felt totally justified telling Scott about Annie. When I woke up this morning, though, I wasn't so sure.

I had a feeling things were going to get ugly today. What if they fought in the cafeteria? What if Annie came to me crying? What if she found out that I stabbed her in the back and she confronted me?

Not to mention my panic about the whole anxiety thing getting out. I was sure everyone would be talking about how I barfed all over Courtney after mixing alcohol with my *crazy girl* medication. Who could resist repeating a story like that?

I spent all night on Facebook and Twitter, searching compulsively for any references to me. Were people laughing at me? Were they saying I'm crazy?

I couldn't find anything, though. It was as if Saturday night never happened. Which was even freakier, somehow. At least if I'd found evidence, I'd know what to expect.

By the time I got to school, I was a jumpy mess. I tried to put my head down and ignore everyone, but all my senses were heightened. I was aware of every whisper, every averted gaze, and every bout of laughter in the halls. My therapist would say that I was interpreting people's actions through the lens of my anxiety and that I should use my strategies to remind myself that their behaviors likely had nothing to do with me at all. But my therapist is pretty much full of crap, because she's never had to walk a high school hallway after being exposed as a freakshow mental case.

The only thing worse than the stares of my fellow students was my worry about the Annie situation. I expected her to be depressed or hysterical or angry. I expected drama. But when I caught sight of her in the hallway, she was walking along with Courtney, laughing.

My first thought was, *She hasn't talked to Scott yet.*

My second thought was, *What a bitch.* Because she should be mad at Courtney for what happened to me at the party. Courtney shamed me and betrayed Annie's confidence. Why were they walking along like nothing had happened?

So much for Annie's whining messages about how much I mean to her.

The anger calmed my nerves, and some of my guilt evaporated.

By second period I was slumped in my seat in history, staring at the back of Annie's head and hating her. She'd been ignoring me the whole class. For someone who claimed to be sorry, she sure wasn't showing it.

My anger bottomed out and was replaced by cold fear when she suddenly went rigid in her chair and started texting frantically. When the bell rang, she gathered up her stuff and made a beeline for the door.

I swung out of my desk and followed her into the hallway, where a familiar-looking girl stepped into my path, making me trip and drop my books everywhere.

"I'm so sorry, Jessie," she said, bending down to help me gather my stuff.

"It's okay," I muttered, searching up and down the hallway for Annie. I had no idea which way she'd gone.

I took the last of my books from the girl and started toward the cafeteria, hoping to find Annie there, but the girl stepped back in front of me. "Jessie?"

Oh, great, I thought as I recognized her. It was the new girl— Charlie's girlfriend. "Yeah?"

"Um . . . my name's Jody. Charlie said he told you about me? I was just wondering if you wanted to sit with us at lunch today."

"What?" I needed to find Annie, and this Jody girl was seriously starting to annoy me.

"I know you normally eat with Courtney, but I thought you might need someone to sit with today."

I felt my chest constrict. "Why would you think that?"

She shrugged. "I heard about what happened over the weekend, and I thought you might need a friend today."

"Thanks anyway," I said, skirting around her. "I'm good."

I raced to the cafeteria but couldn't find Annie anywhere. She wasn't in line or at Courtney's table. I scanned the other tables, wondering if she and Scott were sitting alone together, but there was no sign of either of them. Where could they be?

I checked every stairwell, peeked into the bathrooms, and scoped out the field. I was frantic all afternoon. Annie didn't go to any classes after lunch. I waited outside each of her classrooms until the bell rang, hoping to catch a glimpse of her.

I checked her Twitter account on my phone, but she hadn't tweeted since the weekend. I even trolled Courtney's Facebook for any gossip, but there was nothing.

Not even the whispers of *freak* and *psycho* I heard in the halls could distract me from my thoughts about Annie. I needed to know what was happening, but I was locked out of her life.

After the final bell rang, I came home and lied about having a big assignment so I could monitor her online activity. But Annie is completely silent. I even tried re-adding her as a friend on Facebook, but she hasn't responded. No one is saying *anything* online.

I've never been more aware of how isolated I am than tonight. It's as if I have absolutely no connection to the world outside my head. There are life-changing things happening, but I'm so far adrift that the ripples don't even reach me.

Annie

You're being paranoid, I tell myself, hunching my shoulders and scanning the hallway for Scott. I have that ticklish feeling I get on the back of my neck whenever people are staring at me.

I wasn't ready when I talked to Scott yesterday. Everything came out all wrong. I need to find him this morning and make things right.

I head toward his locker, trying to shake off the sensation that people are whispering about me. *No one else knows,* I remind myself. *Stop freaking out.*

I yelp as a hand reaches out of the crowd and grabs me. "Holy shit, Larissa," I squeak out. "You scared me."

She searches my eyes and I feel my stomach hit the floor.

"What?" I ask her.

"Is it true?" she whispers dramatically.

"Is what true?"

"Are you *pregnant?*"

"What? Where did you hear that?"

"It's all over school! Didn't you check Facebook this morning?"

Larissa pulls me into the nearest stairwell. "Late last night, Scott changed his Facebook status to single." She pauses, searching my face for a reaction. "So everyone started commenting and asking what happened. He put up a status that said 'Don't believe anything Annie says.' So I had Jonathan call and get the scoop. He told Jon that you got pregnant on purpose to try to trick him, and that you're some kind of psycho girl who wants to drop out and get married."

"He's lying," I whisper. "I don't want to get married, and I wasn't trying to trick him."

"So you *are* pregnant?" She has an expression on her face that I can't read. But I'm so confused. So alone. I need someone to know my side.

"Yes."

"Oh. My. God. Annie! How?"

I just stare at her.

"Okay. I get the how. But didn't you guys use stuff?"

"He used a condom forever, but then he said he wanted to stop. I agreed, and he says it's my fault because he figured I would only agree if I was on the Pill." I want her to rant and rave over the injustice of it. I want her to take my side.

"Didn't you guys ever *talk* about it?"

"Not enough, apparently."

"What are you going to do?"

"I don't know!" I wail. "Larissa, what can I do? How do I fix this? I'm scared, and I don't have anyone to help me."

Larissa takes a step back, shocked by my sudden outburst. "You'll figure something out, Annie, I know you will." She gives me a quick hug and heads for the hallway. "Maybe talk to your guidance counselor?" And then she's gone.

I sink to the floor and sit under the stairs, still wearing my coat.

Everyone knows. Scott opened his big fucking mouth and told everyone.

He's such a coward, I think as tears of frustration well in my eyes. I know *exactly* why he did this, and I could claw his lying eyes out of his face over it. He was scared I'd tell everyone how he abandoned me when he found out I was pregnant. He was scared of being the "bad guy," and he didn't want anyone thinking that he'd been part of this willingly. So he lied and said I got pregnant on purpose.

Feelings rush through me in waves. I'm angry and sad and ashamed and afraid. I pull my jacket up around my ears and wish I could make myself invisible forever.

It seems like only minutes have passed, so I'm startled when feet start pounding on the stairs above me. I check my phone to find that first period evaporated while I was hiding here. I wait for the halls to clear and then stand up on stiff legs. I'm suddenly sweltering in my jacket, so I slip it off, a loose plan forming in my mind. I head for my locker to drop off my jacket. Then I'll go and make an appointment in the counseling office.

When I reach my locker, though, I'm gripped by nausea. Someone has taken a bright red lipstick and written the word *SLUT* all over my locker door. I reach out and touch the oily surface of the letters and then turn around and run.

Jessie

The drama on Facebook was out of control tonight. Actually, drama sounds too benign. It was a train wreck. It was a massacre.

It started right after school, when Courtney posted the status *I wish a certain slutty ex-friend would quit messaging me. I hate LIARS.* A flurry of responses ensued, mostly from wannabes hoping to endear themselves to Courtney.

Hugs Courtney.

Who's the ex-friend? I hate liars too!

Oooh! Sounds like a good story!

Then Larissa weighed in, unable to contain the fact that she knew who Courtney was talking about: *Don't tell me you haven't heard about Annie yet??*

That's when the rumors got out of control. First, people swore they'd seen her sneaking around with other guys, cheating on Scott. Then someone claimed that they'd walked in on her having sex with a senior in the boys' bathroom. And then the big bombshell came. *Annie is pregnant! I bet she doesn't even know who the father is.*

I couldn't stop reading. It was like some gruesome accident that you know you don't want to see but can't resist peeking at. I kept refreshing the feed, even while it made me feel sick.

I never understood what Scott saw in her. She's so UGLY.

She puts out, obvs! Why else would he waste his time with her?

How can you even tell she's pregnant? She's FAT already!

I imagined Annie sitting in front of her computer, unable to tear her eyes away from the comments. I felt sorry for her and angry with her all at once. If she'd just listened to me about Courtney, she wouldn't be in this situation. Courtney is evil. She's always just one step away from turning on people. Why didn't Annie *listen* when I told her not to trust Courtney?

Annie

I don't know what to do. I don't know what to do. *What the fuck am I supposed to do?*

This is all so fucked up. I can't even believe it's happening. I knew—I *knew*—it would be bad if people found out I was pregnant. But I never expected *this.*

I've avoided the Internet for days. After what happened at school on Tuesday, I knew that Facebook would be exploding with the news. I made a promise to myself that I would ignore, ignore, ignore. I told myself it would all blow over in a few days. *Don't read it—it will just upset you.* But here I am, glued to the computer screen, hitting Refresh over and over again.

I shift in my seat as the page reloads. It's after midnight, and I've been in front of this computer for hours. *Just one more refresh,* I promise myself. *Then I'll go to bed.* There are more than a hundred responses to Courtney's original status now. Imagine that. Over a hundred comments about how ugly and slutty and fat I am.

I break my promise and refresh the screen for another half hour before finally turning off the computer and crawling into bed.

I burrow under the covers and try to wrap my mind around what just happened. It's bad enough that people I thought were my friends are saying horrible things about me, but almost worse that people I don't even know have mean things to say. Why would someone who has never even talked to me take time out of their day to rip me apart online?

More than one hundred comments, and not one person defended me.

Just as I'm finally drifting off to sleep, my cell phone dings. I almost ignore it, desperate for the nothingness of sleep. Curiosity gets the better of me, though, and I lean over to find a text from a number I don't recognize. I slide my thumb across the screen to unlock the phone, and there it is. *Fucking bitch.* My eyes snap open and I stare at the screen, wondering who sent it and how they got my number. I'm about to respond when another text comes in from another unknown number: *Ugly slut! Everyone hates you.*

Text after text arrives. I stop reading them. I just let the number of messages climb higher and higher. Tears stream down my cheeks as the phone vibrates in my hand over and over. My mind is screaming at me to shut it off and put it away, but I can't. I lie there noting each message that comes in. Counting them without really counting. Accepting them like blows.

When the texts finally stop, I sit staring at my phone for a few minutes, and then I do something that I'm quite sure proves there's something seriously wrong with me. I read them. Each and every one. Even though I know I should just delete them unread, some sick and demented part of me wants to know. So I read every hateful message.

When I'm done, I lie awake while the words float around in my brain. Three o'clock melts into four, and four o'clock turns to five, and I still haven't slept at all. Every time I close my eyes, I see the words. *Slut. Bitch. Loser. Fat. Stupid. Worthless.* I hear angry, hate-filled voices hissing at me in the dark. Voices of people who used to be my friends.

Why?

I'm still the same girl who sat with them all at lunch last week. I'm still the girl Scott said he loved. How can I walk through one day and into the next and suddenly be so hated, when I haven't changed at all? How can someone be considered pretty and popular one day and be a stupid, fat slut the next? Was there something in me that they've only just noticed?

I think of Madge and the way she looks at me—like something stuck to the bottom of her shoe. Has everyone seen that part of me now? Are they mad because I had them all fooled and now they've seen the truth? Do I *deserve* this?

I've spent hours thinking about myself and what I've done. It's true that I wasn't as careful as I should have been about sex. I didn't make Scott wear a condom, and I wasn't on birth control. Is that totally fucked up? Is that why everyone thinks I'm a freak? It's a lie what Scott said—I wasn't trying to trap him into anything, and I didn't set out to get pregnant. I never thought of him as needing to be trapped.

Why is everyone so mad that I had sex with Scott? I can't figure out why that makes me this horrid slut when all my friends are having sex too. Larissa can bat her eyelashes and play the innocent all she wants, but everyone *knows* she's been sleeping with Jon since practically the day they started going out. Why aren't people writing on *her* locker and sending her ugly texts? Where did I go wrong?

The sun is starting to come up. I don't want to go to school today. I won't go. Tomorrow I'll hold my head high and pretend I'm okay. But not today.

Jessie

It's been a whole week, and Annie still hasn't come back to school.

This is *not* my fault. So why does my stomach churn every time I think about my message to Scott? I keep going back and rereading it until the pressure in my chest is unbearable.

I only meant to nudge him. He was going to find out at some point anyway. Annie said herself that she was going to tell him and that they'd make decisions about what to do together.

And it's not my fault that everyone at school found out. That was one hundred percent Scott, the disgusting jerk. I can't believe he turned out to be this person. I'd never have said anything if I'd known. He was supposed to be the quintessential hero, not a villain in disguise. What kind of guy drags a girl's name through the dirt and then walks around school like *he's* the victim?

Annie hasn't responded to any of my messages, and her phone has been off all week. I keep hoping and praying that she'll come back to school and everything will be okay. She'll be tough and angry and sarcastic and funny, and she'll bounce right back because she's *Annie* and because Scott and Courtney and everyone else pale in comparison to her.

But day after day I wait by her locker to find no sign of her, and her desk sits empty in history class.

I can't believe she's still hiding out at home. She's not allowed to be this fragile. She's *Annie.*

Annie

Please God, tell me I'm imagining things.

I swear Madge is checking out my stomach. Like every two minutes.

I keep *almost* catching her, but every time I look over, she does that thing people do when they suddenly look away and pretend they're not watching you.

"Broccoli, Anne?" she asks, passing it to me. I shake my head and put the bowl down without taking any, and Madge's eyebrows shoot up so high I swear they're going to take flight. I bite my lip and consider. Is this the face of an overly controlling stepmother or a woman concerned with the nutrition of my unborn child?

I swallow a crazed giggle. The paranoia is making me downright manic.

On a whim, I jump up from the table and grab a Coke from the fridge. My stomach flops over as I head back into the dining room and pop open the can. Madge jumps like it's the sound of gunfire, and her lips go white as she presses them into a straight line.

Shit. Shit. Shit. Shit. Shit.

She can't know. I'm being paranoid.

"Delicious as ever, Madeleine," my dad says, getting up and planting a kiss on Madge's forehead. She smiles up at him, but it's a sad smile that doesn't reach her eyes. She looks over at me as my dad leaves the room. "Would you help me clean up please, Anne?"

Sophie starts reaching for dishes, but Madge puts her hand on her arm. "I need a few minutes with Anne, please."

Fuck.

I slump in my chair as Sophie scurries out of the room. *My life is over.*

The second Sophie clears the doorway, Madge is on me. "I cannot believe you've gotten yourself into this situation." Her words are heavy and dark, and they press down on me, pinning me to my chair.

I blink at her while the enormity of what she's said sinks in, and then my mind goes wild. I'm cursed. First Scott, then school and Courtney and Facebook, and now Madge. Why can't I get two freaking seconds of peace to figure things out? I want to run away and hide in my room, but Madge *knows* and she's going to tell my dad and I'm not ready for any of this. I put my head in my hands to try to hold my brain together.

"So it's true, then," she says, heaving a sigh and slumping in her chair. "I'd hoped it was just an online rumor."

"Online . . . " A terrible thought worms its way into my head. "Sophie."

I flash back to the day she added me on Facebook. Of course. She saw the whole thing play out online. Something cracks open inside me. Sophie watched me being attacked and never once came to my defense or tried to talk to me about it. She just ratted me out to her mother instead. *What happens on Facebook stays on Facebook.*

"She saw something on the computer and let me know. You should be thanking her. You're in way over your head." Her message is clear: I'm a stupid *kid* who played at grown-up things.

I let my head fall forward so it's resting on the table. I just want to give up. My life is a nightmare I can't wake up from.

"How could you let this happen, Anne? You're supposed to be smarter than this. Your father is always going on and on about what a smart girl you are and what a good head you've got on your shoulders." Madge stands up and starts pacing the room, throwing words at me like daggers. She's *enjoying* this, I realize. I've let her win. I've finally proved that I'm the screwed-up kid she always believed I was.

She pauses and turns triumphantly toward me. "What do you think would happen if I told your father about this?"

I shrug, refusing to show her the fear she's hungry for.

"Shall we tell him, then?"

I nod with as much dignity as I can muster and move to get up, but she puts her arm out to stop me and searches my face. "You're really prepared to do that?"

What the fuck? "Yes. I mean . . . No. Do I have a choice?"

"There are always choices." She sits down beside me, pinning me with her gaze. "Your father would be heartbroken, you know. And men are unpredictable. If he's brought into this, it might limit your choices."

"What choices?"

"Men don't always understand the challenges we women face. I'm presuming you recognize that you are in no position at sixteen to be raising a baby. Correct?"

I duck my head in response.

"Good. Which then leaves you with two choices . . . having the baby and putting it up for adoption, or having an abortion. If your father gets a say, I'm not sure abortion will still be on the table."

My mouth falls open in horror.

"Oh, don't look so shocked, Anne. Surely you've thought of that possibility." She takes a deep breath. "Listen, being a mother is not an easy road, even for those of us who do things in the right order and at the correct age. You are in no position to care for a baby. You can't even manage to take care of yourself."

Why isn't she marching me into my dad's office and exposing me as a total fuckup? Madge doesn't give a shit about me, I know that.

"Why would you help me?"

She sighs and crosses her arms over her chest. "I've worked very hard to build a life with your father, Anne. A baby in this house would be a disaster, and I couldn't bear to see what it would do to your dad."

I watch her face, looking for signs that she's lying. That she's trying to trap me.

"What about adoption?" I don't want to admit it, but I've been thinking more and more about having an abortion. The whole problem could just go away. I could go back to being Annie again. I could even pretend that I was never pregnant and that this was all a big misunderstanding.

Madge cocks her head to one side, as though she's talking to a young child. "A noble alternative, sure, but it hardly solves your problems, does it?"

"What's that supposed to mean?"

"You'd still have to deal with being pregnant. You'd have to admit it to your father. And it's hardly gone well with your friends so far, has it? Do you want all your teachers to know too?"

"No. But . . . I don't know. I need more time to think."

Madge eyes my belly. "You probably still have a bit of time, but if you want to put an end to the rumors, I'd get it done soon." She twists her face into an expression I'm sure she means to be comforting. "I'll tell you what, Anne. I'll do the research and figure out where we need to go. I can make you an appointment, and we'll take care of this problem."

I know she's being selfish, but it's pretty damn tempting to let her take over. If Madge gets her hands dirty helping me arrange an abortion, she'll hardly be able to rat me out later. I smile encouragingly at her and nod.

A slow smile stretches across her face. "Good. I knew you'd listen to reason." And then her eyes harden. "I don't think I need to tell you that this would be best kept between us. We don't need everyone getting all worked up over a little accident, right?"

"Right," I say, eager to escape the conversation.

"Go on, then. I'll make the appointment and we'll put this be-hind us." She waves her hand dismissively, and I scuttle around her and fly through the dining room door to find Sophie pacing in the hallway outside.

"I'm so sorry—"

"Fuck you, Sophie," I hiss, pushing past her roughly. "Never talk to me again."

"Annie!" she calls after me, but I don't turn around. I race to my room and lock the door behind me, then collapse in relief with my back against the door.

Jessie

I hunched over my history textbook, my elbows on the table and my hands resting like blinders against the sides of my head. Studying in the cafeteria was about the dumbest idea I'd ever had. I'd hoped the chaos would drown out the noise in my head, but I couldn't focus any better than in the library or at home.

I let my head fall forward onto my textbook. I was going to bomb the test. It was inevitable.

"Still too busy to eat lunch with us?"

I squeezed my eyes shut and hoped I was imagining things.

"Jessie? I know you're under there."

I turned my head to the side and peeked out from under my hair.

Jody.

"Hi," I mumbled, sitting up. "I was just . . ."

"Hoping the information would jump out of the textbook and into your brain?" Jody dropped into a chair across from me and pried open a bag of chips. "Want one?"

I shook my head, squinting at her.

"So, how come you're sitting over here all alone?" She leaned forward and winked at me conspiratorially. "What's taking you so long to come join us?"

"Oh! I just . . . I figured . . . I mean, I have to study."

"Mmhmm. Okay, I'm going to be totally honest with you. I'm here on a mission, and I'm not leaving until you agree to come talk to Charlie. I can't take one more day of watching him pine over you."

"Charlie?" I sputtered. "But . . . I thought you two were . . ."

Jody laughed and shook her head at me. "You're kidding, right? That boy is completely obsessed with you."

I blushed. "*Was* obsessed, maybe. I'm pretty sure I screwed things up bigtime."

"Ah. I presume we're talking about the infamous comic book?"

I groaned and let my head fall back onto the table.

"So you did read it?"

"I'm a loser," I moaned.

"Not according to him, you're not."

I raised my head and met her eyes. "I told him I'd read it, but I really hadn't, and then I picked it up months later. I felt like too much of an idiot to say anything, so I've been ignoring it ever since."

The right side of Jody's mouth twitched as she tried not to smile. "You two are perfect for each other. You're both a comedy of errors."

I hid my face in my hands.

"I'm serious," she said. "This is the kind of story you'll tell your grandkids one day."

"That's assuming he'd ever want to talk to me again."

"Trust me," she said, crossing her arms over her chest. "He's been mooning over you since the day I met him. Let's go."

"What?" I asked, my eyes bugging out of my head. "You mean right now?"

"Right now."

"But what will I say to him? What if he hates me?"

"Just tell him what you told me. He'll be relieved."

"You think?"

"Come on!"

I followed her over to my old table, my heart pounding with every step.

"Hey, boys," Jody called out as we approached. "Look who I found."

Charlie looked up and met my eyes, and for a split second I saw a flicker of something that looked like hope. Then his eyes dulled, and he nodded at me casually. "Hey, Jessie."

"Jess and I were just talking about comic books," Jody sang, pulling out the chair beside Charlie and shoving me into it.

"Yeah?" he asked cautiously as I stumbled into the seat.

"Yeah. I . . . I finally got a chance to read the one you gave me."

His brow furrowed. "But you said . . ."

"I know. I hadn't looked at it yet."

"Then why . . . "

"I was—" I groped for words, looking to Jody for support. She nodded at me encouragingly. "Trying to impress you?"

He barked out a laugh that warmed my insides. "Impress me, huh? Interesting strategy."

I blushed and looked down at the table. It *seemed* to be going okay. At least he hadn't gotten up and stormed off.

"So," he said slowly. "What did you think?" The hopeful look was back, and my heart started to beat alarmingly fast.

"That you were right," I said shyly. "One good comic can change everything."

Charlie ducked his head and then flashed me a smile that made my heart leap.

"This is some painfully awkward shit," Kevin broke in, earning a smack from Jody.

"Shut up, Kev," she said affectionately. "This is romantic."

Annie

I blink in surprise as Madge shifts her car into park and yanks the key from the ignition. We can't possibly be here already.

I look out the window at the squat gray building that looks absolutely nothing like I thought it would, and then let my head fall back against the seat.

Madge sighs, and I can feel her eyes burning their disapproval into me. I don't want to get out of the car, but I don't want to stay in here, either. The seat belt is too tight and Madge is sitting too close and I feel like this giant SUV is crumpling in on itself, trapping me inside. I suddenly realize that I've never sat in the front seat of Madge's car before. We've never done anything together that's just the two of us. Our first stepmother-stepdaughter bonding day, and it's a trip to the abortion clinic.

Why isn't she getting out of the car? I shift in my seat and reach for the door handle, desperate to escape.

"Wait a minute, Anne," Madge says. I freeze, my fingers hovering inches from the handle. There's a little flutter of something in my chest. Is she having second thoughts?

My eyes flick to her face, and I watch as her gaze travels past me to the building outside. She looks as conflicted and unhappy as I am. I feel a smile creeping up from somewhere in my body, but before it makes it to my lips, she says, "I hope today is a lesson to you. I don't want to ever have to bring you back here again." Then she climbs out of the car and marches to the sidewalk, where she waits for me with arms crossed.

I want to refuse to get out of the car. I want to hole myself up in the back and scream that I won't go through with this. I want to take out my cell phone and call my dad and confess everything and beg him to make Madge stop. But I don't. I see the look on her face and I imagine the way Dad would look at me. I think about the kids at school who used to be my friends and how they see me as a dirty slut because I had sex with Scott. And I imagine nine months of walking the halls with a growing belly.

And the weak part of me wins. That sniveling, pathetic, scared part of me that always wins. *I'm not cut out to be a mother,* I think as I follow Madge into the building. *A mother wouldn't be this cowardly.*

I hang back while Madge checks in with the receptionist. She can do all the talking, I decide. Let her bear the weight of this decision. I'll get through this by just following along and doing as I'm told.

But then there's a social worker leading me to an office and telling Madge to sit outside in the waiting room, and all my plans go up in smoke.

"I'm Janet," she tells me, gesturing at a chair. "Please, have a seat."

She perches a pair of half-moon glasses on her nose before flipping through a clipboard full of notes. "Your mother faxed over your background health information for us, but I'd like you to take a look at the forms and verify that everything is correct."

I want to tell her that Madge isn't my mother, but I can't seem to find my voice. I hold out a shaking hand for the clipboard and pretend to read the forms while Janet watches.

"Part of my job today is to make sure you understand all the options available to you, and that you're confident in your choice to have an abortion."

The word just rolls off her tongue, and I look up in surprise. I've heard *abortion* so many times lately, but it's always been whispered or hissed or shouted. I've never heard it said like a regular word before.

I pass her back the clipboard and nod, suddenly grateful that Madge isn't here. Janet's eyes crinkle when she smiles at me, and the lines around them look like kindness. I flex my fingers and imagine drawing her face.

I have to fight to focus on the words she's saying. She talks about adoption and giving birth and all the things I've already thought about and debated for an eternity. I want to press fast-forward on this speech, because I'm so done thinking about it.

"Annie?"

I sit up straight and nod as if I've been listening attentively.

"I'm not telling you anything new here, am I?"

"No," I admit. "I've thought about all those things. A lot."

She nods and adds a few notations to the form in front of her. "Let me ask you a more difficult question, then," she says. "Is this your decision or your mother's?"

A chunk of ice cracks off my heart, and I see two paths ahead of me. On one, I open up to Janet and tell her everything—all about Madge and my father . . . and even my mother. She'd help me; I can see that. I could tell her about Scott and the girls at school. About how scared I am and how I'm not sure that I'm making the right decision. She'd smile at me and refuse to let me go through with this abortion. Then she'd bring in Madge and lay into her about ruining young girls' lives and taking away their choices.

On the other path, I'd tell her that I've made up my mind and that I'm confident in my decision. That way, I could be free of all of this. I wouldn't have to take on the responsibility of being a teenage mother, throwing away college and my future. I wouldn't have to endure the stares and the whispers and the jokes. And I wouldn't have to explain to my child why her father never visits and why I'm so young compared with the other girls' mothers.

I must have been sitting there thinking about her question for a while, because Janet suddenly puts her pen down and starts to get up. She's going to get Madge, I realize in a panic. The biggest decision of my entire life is in front of me, and there's no *time*.

I don't want Madge in here. I don't want to talk about this anymore. So I say it. "It's my choice."

Janet's hands go to her hips, and she looks at me for a long time while I study the cuticles on my thumbnails.

When she sits down again, her voice is soft. "This is a permanent choice. There's no going back. Which is not to say it's not the right choice for you. It very well might be. But only *you* can decide that. So I'm going to ask you a very important question, and I want you to answer it honestly."

I look up at her.

"Do you have any doubts about this choice, or have you made up your mind?"

I start crying. I can't help it. Because there's only one way out of this mess, and it's not *fair* that the decision comes down to me. I'm not the only one who brought me to this awful moment. So why am I the one who has to shoulder all the weight of this decision?

I could tell her all that. I could tell her I'm not sure yet and need more time.

But I don't. "I wish things were different. But I've made up my mind."

She nods, all business, and writes something on my paper before asking me to take a seat back in the waiting room.

I sit three chairs down from Madge and refuse to look at her. She doesn't even care. She just shrugs and pulls out a book.

How can she sit there and fucking read? We're about to take a life, and she's reading a shitty romance novel like it's nothing.

I can't look at her anymore, so I look around the waiting room instead. There are three other girls here, and I wonder about their stories. They're all young, though none as young as I am. Two of them look about seventeen or eighteen, and the other is probably in her early twenties. The girl in her twenties is alone, and I feel a pang of jealousy. I already know that I'll be walking around with the memory of today for the rest of my life, and I wish that Madge weren't a part of it.

I check out the mothers of the other two girls. They're so different. The one beside the blond girl is holding her hand, and that breaks my heart into a million pieces. They're leaning into each other, and the mom never takes her eyes off her daughter's tear-stained face. I wonder what they talked about on the way here. I wonder if they made this decision together.

The other girl's mother sits rigidly in her seat. She reminds me of Madge. There's no handholding or reassuring pats on the leg with this woman. She never once looks at the shamed-looking girl curled into a ball beside her. She stares straight ahead, and I can feel the anger rolling off of her.

I wonder what Madge and I look like to them. Do they feel sorry for me because she's all I have left in the mother department? I want to announce to the whole waiting room that she's not related to me. That I didn't come from inside this cold woman. *She's just my stepmother!* I want to shout.

A woman in a white coat appears at the door on the far end of the room. She looks down at the charts in her hands, and my heart freezes. *Not yet.* "Amy and . . . Nicole." She looks up and smiles while the two younger girls get up. The blond one's mother stands up with her and gives her a long hug. They rock from side to side while she whispers something in her daughter's ear.

I make eye contact with the other girl, and something passes between us. We're both crying. Her mother doesn't get up or even look at her. I know exactly how this girl feels.

I'm still thinking of her when the nurse comes back and calls my name. She shows me to a little closet closed off by a curtain and asks me to get changed and then sit on a chair in the hallway.

I stow my clothes in one of the cupboards in the little room and then tug at my shirt to make it longer. When they asked for a long T-shirt, I didn't really think about why. Now I find that it's my only coverage. I had to take off even my underwear.

I perch tentatively on the chair, pulling my shirt under me to act as a barrier between the seat and my body. I don't want to touch anything in here. Everything feels dirty.

I look around for another door. Some way to sneak out the back of this building and hide.

But then a nurse taps me on the shoulder and gestures to a dark room. I follow her and climb onto the table, starting to panic. I'm not ready to do this. I turn to the nurse and open my mouth to ask for help when a doctor rushes noisily in.

He peers at a piece of paper on the table and then smiles widely at me. "Annabel? My name is Dr. Duncan." He snaps on a pair of latex gloves and takes a seat beside me.

"This is how things will work. I'm going to use this machine to get a look at the fetus and see where it's positioned. I'll then take some measurements to determine how far along you are. You're welcome to watch the screen or look away if you prefer. Some women find it helps them to accept the loss if they've seen the fetus."

It's all so official. So scientific. I start to calm down a little.

The nurse positions my feet in the stirrups at the end of the table and pulls my T-shirt up. Embarrassed, I look away from my naked body and will them to hurry.

The doctor squirts cold gel on my belly and pushes a white plastic probe hard against my skin. The screen beside me flickers to life, and I see wavy lines and shapes that mean nothing to me. I feel like I'm watching from across the room.

I hear a series of clicks, and then a line appears on the screen. It spans the distance of a little bean shape in the center. I stop breathing and look closer.

"That's the fetus," he says. "And that is its heart beating. It looks to be about nine weeks." He makes a few notations on the paper and then snaps off the monitor. The nurse wipes my belly with a tissue and they scurry around arranging tools.

No one notices that I'm no longer a living person. Something in me died when I saw that little heart beating. But rather than jump up and take it all back, I just lie there and let the scene unfold. And when it's all over and they're congratulating me on how well I did, I feel empty. I wish they could give me a pill that would erase my memory of today. Some drug that could make this terrible feeling go away.

They take me to a little rest area where there's juice and cookies. Like we're a bunch of kindergartners on a break. I sit in a recliner, feeling dizzy and nauseated. Nurses start buzzing around me, taking my blood pressure and monitoring my temperature, but I barely notice them. I'm holed up somewhere deep inside myself.

There are other girls here too, but I'm not curious anymore. There's a low moaning coming from somewhere to my right, and the sound of someone trying to stifle her sobs, but I don't care. I don't want to know their stories or think about their lives. I'm full of my own shame. I haven't got room for theirs.

After a trip to the bathroom and the paralyzing sight of blood, I'm given a pad and shown back to the little closet that holds my clothes. They look like they belong to someone else. I don't even know the girl who wore them here. She's gone.

I stumble into the waiting room, feeling like I'm sleepwalking. Madge looks up at me and hurriedly packs up her bag. She takes me by the arm to lead me out of the clinic, but I yank my arm away and look at her with dead eyes. We ride home in silence. She doesn't speak at all until we hit the driveway.

"I don't think I need to tell you that it would be better for you if your father didn't hear about this."

She's so pathetic to me in that moment. I just walk away. After everything I've been through, all she's worried about is covering her own ass. I almost want to tell my dad, just to watch her burn.

She follows me to my room and watches while I climb into bed. "The doctor says you'll only be sore for a few hours. You should be out of bed and back to your old self by the time your father gets home." Then she shuts the door and leaves me.

I can't sleep. I burrow deeper under my covers and press my forehead against the mattress, trying to force the memories out of my head.

I've been trying to fall asleep for what seems like hours, but every time I close my eyes, I see snatches of the day.

I need my music.

I'm reaching for my iPod when Madge opens my door and walks in, uninvited.

"Your father is home," she says, clapping her hands, as if I'm a dog she's calling to attention. "You need to get up for dinner."

I stare at her, surprised by how different she looks. Madge has always been the enemy. I've been fighting her every single day for as long as I've known her. But in this moment, I look at her and she means absolutely nothing at all.

There's a flicker of something behind her eyes. Fear, maybe. Or doubt. I'm not sure, and I don't care. It's like my mind was a fist clenched around my hatred of Madge, and now I've released my grip and let go. Just like that. Not caring is such a relief that I lie back down and luxuriate in it.

"Anne," she hisses, closing the door partway. "Get up. You don't want your dad asking questions, do you?"

I look her straight in the eyes as I put my earphones in. Then I crank my music, turn over, and tune her out.

✳ ✳ ✳

I wake up to my dad's kiss on my forehead. "Hey, Button," he says when my eyes flutter open. "Madeleine says you're not feeling well again."

"I'm okay," I mutter, sitting up. I feel groggy and stiff. I'm confused, and I'm not sure if it's night or day. Why am I in bed? Then it all rushes back to me with a force that leaves me gasping for air. I look at my dad and burn with shame.

"You've been sick a lot lately. I think it's time to schedule a checkup with the doctor. I don't want you to miss any more school." He sits on the edge of my bed and I feel panic stirring in my chest. No doctors. Just the thought of it makes my heart pound.

"I'm fine. Just tired tonight," I assure him. "I'll be at school to-morrow, don't worry." I cringe at the thought of going back. My dad knows about the first week I was away, but he has no idea that all last week I doubled back home in the mornings and hid in my room all day. I've been erasing the messages from the school's attendance line.

His eyes wander away from me and he looks around my room. "It's been a while since I've spent any time in here," he muses, get-ting up to take a look around. "You haven't fully unpacked yet, I see." He gestures to a stack of boxes in the corner of my room.

I shrug, embarrassed. "I don't even know what's in those boxes."

"It's funny, isn't it? . . . When we were packing, everything seemed so important. But now that we're here, there are boxes and boxes of things we haven't even touched."

It feels weird to have Dad look around my room like this. Scary. There's so much of my life I keep hidden from him that it's terrify-ing to have him show an interest.

"Still, it would be good for you to get more settled here. Put some of your drawings up on the walls, make this room yours." He comes closer to my bed to check out the one thing I've pinned up. The *Alice in Wonderland* quote Jess gave me: "I can't go back to yesterday because I was a different person then." I can barely breathe as he reads it. It feels like a million years ago that I spent that afternoon in Jessie's room.

He smiles sadly at the quote. "Very true." He looks at me over the top of his glasses, as though seeing me for the first time. "Is there anything you'd like to talk about?"

Instinctively, I reach for my necklace, and my whole body goes cold.

It isn't there.

What the . . .

Dad keeps talking, but I can't hear him over the roaring in my ears. *What happened to my necklace?* I close my eyes and try to *think*. I know I put it on this morning. I remember debating it. I didn't want my mom involved in the whole mess, but I needed a piece of her there with me. Regret eats away at my insides.

"Honey? Are you okay?"

"I don't . . . I don't feel very well." I lie down on the bed and run my hands down the sheets, praying that my fingers will catch on the chain of my necklace.

Dad comes over and feels my forehead. "You don't have a fever, but you're very pale." He pulls up the covers. "Get some rest, Button. We'll chat more later." He kisses my forehead and slips out of the room.

The second the door clicks shut, I leap out of bed and tear off the sheets. I search them like a madwoman, feeling every inch of the fabric. I rip off my clothes and search them, too. Then I rifle through the bag I took to the clinic, hunting through every pocket and trying to convince myself that I took off the necklace for safe-keeping and just don't remember it. I search the folds of the T-shirt I wore and then sneak downstairs to search my sneakers and jacket. Nothing.

Back in my room, I go over every square inch of carpet and all around the bed at least five times. Then it's back downstairs, retracing my steps. The necklace isn't on the stairs or in the front hall. It's not on the porch or on the sidewalk or even in the grass. It's not in the driveway or in the car.

The car is where Madge finds me. I'm running my hands frantically over and under the seats, whispering prayers and promises to God if he'll just let me find the necklace. I'll snap out of this. I'll change my ways. I'll make myself perfect and stop pouting and just concentrate on being a good daughter and friend and student and person. Just please, please, *please* let me find the necklace.

But I don't find it.

I can't sleep. I can't think. The clinic won't open again until tomorrow. What if it's not there? What if I've lost it forever? I can't imagine ever looking my dad in the eyes and telling him that I lost Mom's necklace. It's all he had left of my mother, and he gave it to me. He trusted me with her most valuable possession, and I lost it. Not just lost it, but lost it while at an abortion clinic killing the baby I should never have been pregnant with. He'll never forgive me. Why should he? I'll never forgive myself.

Jessie

I pushed my way through the hallway, searching for Charlie. He's been waiting for me by my locker every day this week, but it feels too good to be true, and my heart skitters each morning until I catch sight of him.

The crowd parted and there he was, leaning back against my locker door. When he caught sight of me, a smile lit up his face and my knees went weak with the sheer unexpected joy of having someone so happy to see me.

"Hey," he said, pushing off my locker and handing me his phone. "How's your morning?"

I looked at the screen, open to a list of movie times. "What's this?"

"Be my date. This Friday night. You can pick any movie you like—girly, action, horror, you name it."

I bit my lip and handed him back the phone. "Would you be upset if we didn't go to the movies?"

He blinked in surprise and took a step back. "No. Uh, that's okay, I guess. I just thought . . ."

"Wait until you hear my suggestion before you say it's okay." I laughed. "Because this might well be the lamest thing you've ever heard."

"Lay it on me."

"So, my family has this tradition . . ." I put my hands over my face, suddenly mortified that I was actually doing this. "It's called Avery Family Games Night, and it's way more dorky than you can even imagine. There are tacos and board games, and even sombreros." My face blazed with embarrassment.

"Are you asking me to come to Avery Family Games Night?"

"Um . . . yes?"

He enveloped me in a hug, his laughter vibrating against my chest. "I'd love to," he rumbled. He pulled back and looked into my eyes, and I'd have melted into a puddle on the floor if he hadn't been holding me up.

Oh my God, he's going to kiss me, I thought, just as Kevin walked up and broke the spell by smacking Charlie on the back of the head. "There are impressionable children around," he quipped. "Put that shit away."

Charlie laughed and fist bumped Kevin while I shot him a murderous look. I was about to make a sarcastic comment about how he was just jealous when I caught sight of a familiar-looking figure dressed all in black.

Annie.

After more than two weeks away, there she was, looking like a completely different person.

Charlie noticed the look on my face and followed my gaze to

where Annie was slinking down the hallway, her head bowed and her hair hanging limply over her face.

It was as if years had passed instead of weeks. She was back to her all-black uniform from the beginning of the year—but with a twist. The beginning-of-school Annie had glowed in a rebellious and slightly dangerous way. This Annie was like a shadow. She was pale and vacant, with no fire in her.

"Isn't that your friend?" Charlie asked quietly.

I nodded, my stomach twisting. How could I let myself be so happy while Annie was suffering?

I waited till Kevin made his way to class, then told Charlie, "I've been emailing her every day for the last week. I told her not to worry about Courtney and Scott and everyone else—that I'd be here for her no matter what. But she never emailed me back. She's so mad at me, and I don't know how to fix it."

"I don't think it's you at all," he said gently. "I'm sure she's upset about the rumors. Give her some time, and just be there for her."

I nodded, looking back down the hallway where Annie had disappeared. "I hope you're right."

By lunchtime I felt like the world had flipped on its axis and dropped Annie and me in the wrong spots. There I was, surrounded by friends, while Annie sat alone in a far corner of the cafeteria, her nose buried in a book.

No matter how hard I tried to focus on the conversation around me, I couldn't seem to shake the pull coming from Annie. I knew what it felt like to be that girl sitting alone. I knew what it felt like to be the one without a friend in the world . . .

I picked at my lunch and debated what to do. I was sure Annie must have read my emails, and I was petrified that she somehow knew I'd messaged Scott. I looked at Charlie and Jody, and I felt like throwing up, remembering what I'd done. What would they think of me if they found out?

"You okay?" Jody asked, swatting at Kevin's hand as he stole a fry off my plate.

I shrugged and tried to smile. "Sort of."

She looked over at Annie and then back at me. "Go get her."

That's what I like about Jody. I don't have to say a word for her to know exactly what I'm thinking.

I got up shakily and made my way to where Annie was sitting. As I passed by Courtney's table, I felt her eyes on me and remembered how, in seventh grade, she'd threatened that anyone who spoke to me would become an immediate social outcast.

I hurried over to Annie's table and stood awkwardly, waiting for her to notice me. I cleared my throat, but she didn't look up. "Um . . . Annie?" I gave a little wave that finally caught her attention. She sighed and pulled out her earphones. I could hear the music thrumming through them from across the table.

"What?" The hostility in her voice made me jump. I shifted from one foot to the other and looked back at Charlie for courage.

"I . . . um . . . I just wanted to say hi. And see if you want to sit with us?" My voice went up annoyingly at the end of my sentence, making me sound like a scared little kid.

Annie stared me down for a moment before looking scornfully over at my friends. "No."

"Wh-what?"

She narrowed her black-rimmed eyes and put her earphones back in, tuning me out. Then she picked up her book and pretended I wasn't even there.

Hot tears threatened to spill out of my eyes, and I turned and headed out of the cafeteria before Annie could see.

As I passed by their table, I heard Courtney sing out, "Poor Jess. Even the socially diseased won't talk to her."

Annie

I am disgusting.

I always kind of suspected I was fucked up in the head. I mean, I'd be coming by it honestly, with my mom dying and Madeleine the super bitch invading my life. But this is really and truly messed up. I *know* that.

I'm sitting in the cafeteria hiding behind a book and pretending not to watch Scott hang all over Courtney. They walked in here holding hands and she's now sitting on his lap, feeding him fries off her plate. And it shouldn't matter to me at all.

I shouldn't feel like this. Like my heart is being ripped out of my chest. Not after everything that's happened.

I stare in sick fascination as he loops an arm around her waist the way he used to do with me. She's smiling at him so hard my cheeks hurt just watching it. I can see every feeling I've ever had for him written all over her face, and it hurts so much I can barely breathe.

And suddenly two things are crystal clear to me.

One: Everyone's lives have gone on. While I was locked up indoors, hiding under my covers and wishing I was dead, everyone else's life rolled merrily along. My old friends weren't worried about me. They weren't even thinking about me. Even Jess is sitting with a whole new crowd, smiling and laughing. No one has even noticed that I've become no one.

And two: I am well-and-truly messed up.

When I look at Scott and Courtney, I should feel angry. I should hate them both for what they've done to me. I shouldn't feel what I do feel—which is sad and regretful and jealous. *I* should be the girl under his arm. *I* should be at that cafeteria table, smiling up at him. He told me he loved me. How could he have his arm around someone else?

I've read all the novels and seen all the shows that tell me how I *should* feel, if I was a healthy and whole person. I should be standing tall and knowing I'm better than they are. I should feel happy I'm not the one sitting at that table with him, falling for his lies. I *know* I should gather my dignity around me and move on. But here's the thing . . . I haven't got any dignity left. And I'm not healthy. Or whole.

"Get up!"

I groan and roll over. I am so not in the mood for this.

"I just got off the phone with your history teacher," Madge announces, whipping the covers off of me and throwing them on the ground. "You're lucky I hadn't left for work yet. Her next step was to try your father at the office."

My whole body aches.

"You need to pull yourself together, Anne. This is getting out of control."

I sit up and rub my eyes, my fingers coming away black from the makeup I didn't bother to take off last night. I know I should feel some sense of urgency, but mostly I just feel annoyed. I was planning on staying home today, and there's no way Madge will let me get away with that now.

"What did you tell her?"

"That we're aware you're having difficulties and we're handling it. I covered for you *this* time, Anne. You've got to drop this whole depressed teenager thing, though, and pull yourself together, or there'll be more phone calls and meetings. Do you want your father getting involved? Is that what you want?"

I shrug and lie back down. I don't care anymore. Everything is shit already.

"No way!" she shouts. "Get out of that bed right now. I stuck my neck out for you. I took you to that godawful clinic and fixed everything for you, and this is the way you repay me?"

"*Repay* you?" I can't believe I'm hearing this right. "You pushed me into the worst day of my life before I was ready, and you want me to *repay* you? This is all your fault!"

I'm awake now, anger coursing through my body. I can feel it all the way to my fingers and toes. It feels strangely good. Like I'm *alive*.

Madge rolls her eyes. "Don't you dare try to pin this all on me. I'm not the one who got pregnant at fifteen. You got *yourself* in trouble. If you want to be mad at someone, be mad at yourself."

"Don't you think I am?" I shout, the words exploding out of

me before I can stop them. "Don't you think I hate myself for what happened?"

Madge falters a bit, gripping my bed frame for support. "Anne," she says softly.

But it's too much to bear. I don't want her pity, and it's too late for her to show compassion. The time for kindness was when I was limping home from the clinic. Not now. Not when I've had to beg for it.

"It *is* your fault that you pushed me into that abortion," I shout at her. "I wasn't *ready,* Madeleine. I needed time to figure things out. But like everything else, you just pushed and pushed to get your own way. You went barreling ahead and booked the appointment and loaded me into your car like I was nothing. Like I was a problem to be fixed. You've *never* seen me as a person. I'm just the shit you got stuck with when you married my dad."

"What did you want me to do? I can't win with you. It doesn't matter what I do. When I try to help you, I'm interfering, and when I leave you alone, I'm ignoring you. I was trying to *help,* Anne. I was trying to be a stepmother to you. Sophie told me how girls were tormenting you at school and that you were all alone with no one to help you. Do you really think I wanted to be calling and faxing abortion clinics, for Christ's sake? No! I stepped up because you needed an adult in your corner and I wanted to be that person for you."

"No," I said, shaking my head. "You said it yourself. You only helped me because you think I'm a screwup and you don't want my mistakes ruining everything. You've hated me since the day you met me, so don't try to pretend you were helping me out of the goodness of your heart."

"Is that really what you think? That I hate you? Because I see things differently."

"I'm sure you do. And let me guess: I'm in the wrong."

She groans and pulls at her hair. "You're maddening, you know that? And the crazy part of it is that you remind me of me. You're stubborn and confrontational, and you don't let anyone push you around."

I clench my jaw and stare at the ceiling. *I am nothing like her.*

Madge rubs her hands over her face. "Whether you want me in your life or not, Anne, I'm here. And I'm not going anywhere. I care about your father and this family, and—I've got a news flash for you—I care about you, too. So even though this is going to make you hate me even more than you already do, I'm making sure you get yourself out of this bed and off to school today. Not because I'm a bitch, but because it's what's best for you."

She looks at her watch. "You have exactly twenty minutes to get ready for school, and I'll give you a ride. Any later than that, and I'll phone your dad to come pick you up. I'm done with worrying about whether he'll find out about all this. If you want to tell him, then come out with it and tell him. Don't lounge around in bed like a coward waiting for him to stumble upon the truth himself."

She picks my covers up off the floor and drops them onto my bed.

"I'll walk," I tell her. I don't want to be stuck in that SUV with her again.

"Fine. And I'll phone the school to make sure you get there."

"Fine."

"Fine."

✱ ✱ ✱

She can force me to go to school, I decide, but she can't force me to attend classes. I ditch second period and hide out in a stairwell, blaring my music in an attempt to keep Madge's words out of my head. She's not allowed to be reasonable right now. I want to *fight*. I want to yell and scream. Why can't she just stick to her role as the wicked stepmother, and I'll stick to mine as the fucked-up step-daughter?

With my music blaring, I don't even hear Jess sneaking up until she sits down right across from me and tugs my earphones out of my ears.

What the hell? Why won't everyone just leave me alone?

"I want to talk," she declares. "I know something's wrong, and I want to help you."

What a joke. I look at her, with her preppy clothes and painted fingernails, and I suddenly feel a thousand years old. What would an overgrown child like Jess know about my problems? Her biggest worry is whether she'll get an A or a B on her next test.

"Go away, Jess. I don't want to talk to you."

"I'm not leaving. You need help, Annie. I'm really scared for you."

"*Scared* for me? Don't insult me. You just can't stand to be on the outside of anything. You want to play the big hero swooping in to save me, but you never even bothered to find out what's wrong."

"We both made mistakes," she says evenly. "But I'm here now. You're my friend and I want to help you."

"You're not my friend." My voice is an icy knife. "When I told Courtney about your anxiety, I did it to *help* you. I did it because I *cared*. You turned your back on me when I needed you the most. That's not friendship. Do you really expect me to believe that you of all people can't see how bad things are for me right now?"

Jessie goes quiet. She bows her head, and big tears drop into her lap.

"You gave up the right to say you care," I say, reveling in the sensation of finally letting all my anger loose. "You gave up the right to talk about me like you know me when you turned your back on me and spent your days laughing with your new friends. You're not helping me, so just leave me alone."

She looks up then, fire in her eyes. "I didn't think you *needed* my help, Annie. I didn't think all . . . *this* . . . would happen. This isn't you! How can you just put your head down and give up? You're supposed to *fight!* You're not supposed to let Courtney win."

"You think all this is about *Courtney?* Jesus, Jess. You don't know anything. You never did."

"I know that girls like you don't just roll over and take crap from girls like Courtney."

I shake my head at her stupidity. "That's the most fucked-up thing I've ever heard. *Girls like me.* You just want me to fight your battles from years ago, don't you?" I ask, realization dawning. "I'm not a plot device in the story of your life, Jessie. I'm a *person*. And I'm just as fucked up . . . no, make that *more* fucked up than you or anyone else. There's no such thing as *girls like me*. That's a fantasy."

Her eyes are wide. "I don't want you to fight my battles. I want you to fight *yours*. And you're right that I don't know what you've got going on. *Because you won't tell me.* How am I supposed to be there for you when you won't let me in?"

I shrug and shake my head at her. "It's too late, Jess. I don't *want* to talk about this with you. I don't *want* to let you in. Go back to your friends and leave me alone."

Jessie

"You're gonna say yes, right? Say yes."

I smiled and shook my head at Charlie. He was being ridiculous. "I don't dance."

"I'll teach you."

"I thought we were cool hipster rebels who don't buy into the trappings of conventional teenage life."

"We'll be ironic about it," he said with a wicked gleam in his eye. "We'll expose the ridiculousness of the teen dance trope by playing it out to its fullest. I'm thinking corsage, photos in your living room, first kiss on the dance floor. The whole nine yards."

He gave me his best pleading look but then pulled back abruptly and looked over my shoulder.

I followed his gaze to see what had wiped the smile off his face.

It was Courtney and Scott. Making a scene in front of Annie's table.

"C'mon," Charlie said gently, pulling at my sleeve. "You don't want to see this."

I shook him off and watched as Courtney set her tray down on Annie's table with a clatter. Annie just held her book up higher in front of her face, ignoring Courtney the way she does every day. Today, though, Courtney would not be put off.

"Who's prettier?" she asked Scott loudly. "Me or your ex-girl-friend?"

I could see Annie's book wobble a bit, but she pretended she couldn't hear.

Scott looked queasy. "C'mon, Court, cut it out." He pulled on her arm, trying to end the scene.

"No." Courtney pouted. "I really want to know. You think I'm prettier than her, right?"

"You're beautiful. Now let's go."

Courtney leaned over and yanked the book out of Annie's hands. "I need your help, Annie," she sang. "I want to get Scott something *really special.* You know what he likes, right?"

I watched Annie raise her eyes to meet Courtney's, and I searched her face for any signs of fire. *Come on, Annie,* I willed her. *Fight.*

But Annie just looked back and forth between Courtney and Scott. She was hoping Scott would call Courtney off, I could tell.

"Nothing?" Courtney asked, sidling up to Scott. "I guess she doesn't know you as well as I do." She grabbed a fistful of Scott's shirt and pulled him in for a kiss. And not just any kiss. This one involved tongue, full body contact, and, I'm pretty sure, was worthy of an R rating. Everyone in the cafeteria was staring at them. Including Annie.

And that was it. I lost it.

One minute I was in my cafeteria chair, watching my best friend be humiliated, and the next I had Courtney's golden ponytail gripped in my hand.

I hauled her off of Scott, a red haze clouding my vision.

"What the *fuck?*" Courtney yelled, stumbling backwards and banging against the table.

She whirled around and burst into cruel laughter when she saw who her attacker was.

"Isn't this *precious,*" she said, standing up and brushing herself off. "Little Lezzie has come to protect her one true love." Courtney looked from side to side dramatically, as though she was about to impart a secret. "I hate to be the one to tell you this, Lez, but I'm pretty sure your slutty little friend is into *boys.*"

By the time she finished spitting out her insults, Courtney was bearing down on me, her nose inches from mine. I should have been *terrified.*

But I wasn't.

All of a sudden Courtney seemed small to me. Small and mean.

I drew myself up to my full height and looked her straight in the eyes. "*You're* calling Annie a slut? That's hilarious. What, did you wait like ten minutes before screwing her ex-boyfriend? Seems pretty slutty to me."

"Oh please," Courtney said. "Scott came to *me*. He wanted to date someone *normal.*" She looked over her shoulder at Scott for backup, but he'd retreated to the jocks' table and was cowering among his teammates.

It made me laugh.

"It's pretty *convenient*, isn't it?" I asked loudly, looking around the cafeteria. All eyes were on me, and for once I was glad for it. "A bunch of rumors start up about Annie, making Scott break up with her, and then . . . poof. There you are, swooping in to snatch him up. It's enough to make people wonder . . ."

Chatter broke out all around us, and I could see people tapping away on their phones. The rumor mill was in full swing, and for once, Courtney wasn't wielding its power.

"You little bitch," she said, shoving me backwards as phone cameras clicked all around us.

Something exploded inside me. I was so *done* with being pushed around. My hands gripped into tight fists as years of frustration came bursting out of me. I heard someone shouting at us to *break it up,* but it was too late to stop, and my fist smashed into Courtney's nose just before rough hands pulled me away.

I looked back as the vice principal, Mr. Anderson, marched me from the cafeteria. Courtney was doubled over, with a teacher beside her, and Annie was still sitting in her chair, looking as shocked as I felt.

At least the deadness in her eyes was gone, I thought with a manic giggle.

"This is *not* funny," Mr. Anderson told me, propelling me toward the office. "You're looking at a suspension here."

I tried, unsuccessfully, to wipe the smile off my face while I rolled the idea of a suspension around in my head.

Totally worth it.

Annie

I'm sketching the look that was on Jessie's face at the moment her fist made contact with Courtney's nose, when Jess walks into my room.

I'm so shocked to see her that I don't say anything at first. I didn't invite her, and it feels like a violation for her to just show up like this.

"What do you want?" I say in a voice that lets her know just how unwelcome she is.

She blinks in surprise. "I . . . I thought you'd be happy to see me." She edges closer to my bed, and I close my sketchbook before she can see what I'm drawing. I'm not sure what it says about either one of us that the first time I've managed to capture her in a sketch was immediately after she clobbered Courtney.

"Why? Because you *came to my rescue* today? Am I supposed to fall all over myself thanking you now?"

"No," she says quietly. "But I thought we could talk."

"Trust me. You don't want to talk to me."

"You can't be serious," she says, glaring at me. "What more, *exactly*, do I need to do to prove my friendship?"

"I don't *want* you to prove your friendship. I *want* you to go away."

She shakes her head angrily and storms toward the door. "You're unbelievable."

I knew it, I think. *I knew she'd leave.*

Just before she steps over the threshold into the hallway, though, she whirls around and marches back into my room. "You know what? *Fuck* that!"

I startle, and a nervous laugh escapes me. Jess never swears. "Did you just say *fuck that?*"

"Yeah. Fuck that. And fuck you, Annie. Do you know what a big deal it was for me to stand up to Courtney? I did that for *you.*" A tear escapes her right eye and tracks down her face. "Do you have any idea how much I wish I'd had someone to stand up for me all those years ago? How much it would have meant for me to have anyone—anyone—stand beside me? I wanted to be that person for you, you ungrateful bitch."

Her chest is heaving and her cheeks are flushed, and I'm so scared I'm afraid to breathe. I swallow hard and then ask, "Why?"

"Why?"

"Why me? Was it really for me? Or was it for you?"

Her face melts into a sad smile. "Is that what you think? That I just wanted to get revenge on Courtney?"

I shrug.

"Trust me when I tell you that the last thing I ever wanted to do was stand up in a crowded cafeteria and have it out with Courtney.

I was peeing my pants the whole time!" A giggle escapes her, and she slaps her hand over her mouth as if to hold it in.

"You're crazy," I tell her, trying to hold a straight face. I don't even recognize this girl who swears and yells at me and punches Courtney in the nose. There's a laugh welling up inside me, but when it comes out, it's a sob instead.

I don't know what to do with all this *feeling*.

Jess takes a step toward me, and I put up my hand to stop her. "Thank you for today," I choke out. "Really. But I don't deserve it."

"What are you talking about?" she says gently. "You're my friend."

"Trust me. You don't want to be my friend. If you knew everything I've done. Everything I've screwed up. You'd go running."

"You're wrong."

I laugh a bitter little laugh. "You don't know."

"Try me," she says, folding her arms over her chest. "There's nothing you can say that will change how I feel about you."

She's so naive, standing there. I can't help myself. I open my mouth, and it all comes out. I tell her about how alone I am here at home and how much I hate Madeleine and Sophie. I tell her about the abortion and how I could have stopped it and didn't. I tell her how I spat on the memory of my mom by destroying a life when that was the most precious thing of all. And I tell her how I lost my mom's necklace and was too chicken to go back and look for it.

It all comes spilling out, pooling on the floor between us. All the ugliness and all the shame. I let it puddle in the space between us, sure that it will give her the push she needs to walk away. Sure that she will see me for who I really am and recognize that I'm not the person she thinks.

Jess stands there while I let it all out. She sees it all.

And then she walks right through that sea of ugliness like it's not even there, and envelops me in a hug.

Jessie

Annie pulled away at first, but I held on anyway. She stiffened and laughed uncomfortably, but I held on. I held on until she gave in to the hug, and I kept holding on when she started to cry.

I felt it pouring out of her—all the pain and shame and sadness.

"I had no idea," I told her as she sobbed against my shoulder. "I'm so, so sorry."

She shook her head, pulling back to look at me.

"I'm sorry you had to do all that alone. I'm sorry I wasn't there for you."

She shifted and sat cross-legged on her bed. "You don't think I'm a bad person?"

Something about the way she looked at me broke my heart in two. She looked so uncertain. So full of doubt. "I think you're an outstanding person. And a brave one, too."

She shook her head, as if I'd missed the point. "You're lying, then. Because I'm not brave at all. If I was brave, I wouldn't have let all this happen."

"Bullshit," I told her, reveling in my new, badass way of swearing. "Being brave doesn't mean nothing bad happens to you. Bad things happen no matter what. Being brave is how you handle those things. How you keep going and trying and being yourself."

"*You're* the brave one," she told me, bumping her shoulder against mine. "You really ripped Courtney a new one today."

I laughed. "I *was* pretty awesome, wasn't I?"

"Did you get in trouble?"

"Three-day suspension," I admitted. "And a warning. Courtney and I aren't allowed to talk to each other. You can imagine how broken up I am by that."

"Holy *shit!* Did your parents freak? How are you here and not grounded for eternity?"

I shrugged. "I told them the truth — that my best friend was being bullied and I stood up for her. When Mom found out it was Courtney, she nearly did a cartwheel."

"Well, you found your inner bitch today, that's for sure. Remind me never to piss you off."

"You know what they say," I deadpanned. "Bitches get stuff *done.*"

Annie sputtered. "Put that up on your geek wall!"

I laughed till I snorted, which made both of us laugh harder.

When we finally came up for air, an idea started to take shape in my mind. "Speaking of getting stuff done," I said, "get ready. We're going out."

Annie shook her head. "No way. I'm exhausted. Let's just hang out here."

"No. I mean, we have somewhere very specific we need to go." I pushed her into her bathroom and then pulled out my phone to do some research.

By the time Annie came out, there was a taxi waiting out front. "What the hell, Jess?" she said. "I'm really not up for an adventure right now."

"Tough," I told her, loving the shocked look on her face. "Just trust me."

I had the taxi drop by my house, where my mom was waiting with the money I'd asked to borrow for the fare. I jumped out and grabbed it from her before sprinting back to the cab. "Are you going to tell me what's going on?" she called after me.

"Nope," I said, watching the shock register on her face. "You're just going to have to trust me."

Back in the cab, I gave the address of the building and crossed my fingers that this would all work out.

Annie

The taxi pulls up outside a building I never wanted to see again.

I'm suddenly so mad at Jess, I could cry.

"Why?" I ask her in disbelief. "Why would you do this to me?"

She looks shaken for a moment, but then puts her hand on my arm to steady me. "We're going to get your mom's necklace back."

I feel like throwing up. I love her and hate her, and I feel like I don't know how to get out of this car. What if it's not there? I can't walk through those doors for nothing.

"I'll be right beside you," she says, leaning over and popping the door open. "Let's go."

Inside the waiting room, my legs start to shake. I never imagined coming back here in a million years. Thankfully, the room is empty. I couldn't handle seeing anyone waiting for an appointment.

Jess leads me over to the receptionist, and I notice with some relief that it's a different one from the day I was here. I'm terrified of anyone recognizing me.

"Do you have an appointment?" the receptionist asks, looking from Jess to me and back again.

I open my mouth to speak, but nothing comes out.

"I called earlier," Jess says. "About the necklace."

The receptionist perks up, and my heart starts to beat fast. "Just a moment," she says, getting up and scooting out of view.

I look at Jess, tears brimming in my eyes. "They have it?"

She nods, and bumps her hip against mine.

The receptionist comes back into view, looking excited. "Janet will be out in a moment." She gestures at the chairs in the waiting room, but I'm too excited to sit down.

The door on the far side of the waiting room opens, and I recognize the social worker from the day of my . . . procedure.

She must recognize me, too, because she walks right up and shakes my hand. "We've been hoping someone would come back for this," she says, patting the pocket of her jacket. "It seems very special."

I nod, my mouth going dry.

"Just to be sure you're the right owner," she says apologetically, "would you mind describing the necklace?"

"Um, sure," I squeak out. "It's a single diamond. On a white gold chain."

"We have a winner!" Janet booms, producing the necklace from her pocket and handing it to me.

I fall to my knees, I'm so relieved and grateful. I look at Jessie, tears streaming down my face. "You found it."

Janet looks at Jessie and then at me. "I don't remember your name, I'm sorry. But I do remember speaking with you." She looks at her watch. "I don't have another appointment for forty-five minutes, and I'd love to see how you're doing. Why don't you come back to my office for a bit?"

"My name's Annie," I say, looking over at Jessie. "And thanks, but I think we should probably be going."

Jessie looks at the social worker and then over at the waiting area. "Actually," she says, "I haven't read that issue of *Us Weekly* yet. I'm cool waiting."

I look at Janet and shrug. Might as well.

I follow her out of the waiting room, turning to look at Jess before I step through the door.

She gives me a wobbly smile, and I stumble a bit as I recognize the expression on her face. She's *proud*. Jess is proud of me.

Jessie

"C'mon c'mon c'mon," Annie urges, pulling me through the halls. It's my first day back from suspension. With the weekend falling in the middle of my time off, it's been almost a week since I've been at school. So much has changed that my head is spinning. Changed in a good way, that is.

Annie met me at my locker this morning, dressed in a kilt, crop top, suspenders, and combat boots. It's part of her new *artistic experiment,* she informed me. She's now taking classic looks and deconstructing them by adding unexpected touches. "You should see what I have planned for tomorrow," she said, arching her left eyebrow. "Think zombie stewardess."

Unfortunately for Annie, Vice Principal Anderson is not well versed in the arts. He caught sight of her on the way to first period and forced her to zip a hooded sweatshirt over her belly-baring top. At first Annie refused, ranting about the school stifling creativity. When faced with the choice between going home to change and donning the sweatshirt, she finally relented.

"I can't miss lunch," she said, poking me in the ribs. "There's a big surprise."

We reach the cafeteria, and Annie peeks in and waits for a thumbs-up from Jody before pulling me through the doors. Jody, bless her, stepped right up in my absence. She recruited Annie to our table and made her one of the gang. They texted me over lunch every day, giving me the blow-by-blow of what was happening at school.

That's how I found out that even though Courtney's nose was only slightly swollen the day after our fight, by Monday she had two black eyes and a bandage over her nose. Word on the street is, she used our fight as an excuse to get a nose job, claiming I'd broken hers and it had to be reset.

My knees wobble as we enter the cafeteria. People have been looking at me all day, whispering to one another in the halls, and nodding at me in silent recognition. Still, I'm not prepared for the way that heads snap in my direction the minute we walk through the cafeteria doors. I might as well be wearing a sign: *I'm the girl who decked Courtney Williams.* I put my head down to hide my smile and follow Annie as she weaves through the tables.

When we reach the back of the room, I look up to see Jody and Charlie standing in front of our table, blocking it from view. Jody vibrates with excitement, hopping up and down and clapping her hands. In contrast, Charlie slumps awkwardly, smiling up at me from under his floppy hair. The sight of him nearly sends me into cardiac arrest. Whoever coined the phrase *Distance makes the heart grow fonder* was definitely onto something. It takes everything I have not to leap into his arms.

"Welcome back!" Jody squeals, yanking Charlie to the side to reveal their surprise. Her eyes bulge as she catches sight of Kevin helping himself to a forkful of cake from the center of the table.

"Shit," he mumbles as Jody rounds on him.

She's about to tear into him when Annie starts laughing so hard she snorts. "Don't encourage him!" Jody protests, her face flaming. "I wanted everything to be perfect."

"It *is* perfect," I tell her, taking it all in. There are balloons and streamers and little bits of confetti sprinkled all over the table. The best part, though, is the cake. It's decorated like a jail cell, with gray icing bars and the words *Welcome back, Slugger* scrawled in red.

I grab a plastic fork off the table and take a heaping bite of cake, earning a fist bump from Kevin and a groan from Jody.

"I have plates," she wails as Annie and Charlie join us. Her shoulders slump as we destroy the cake one delicious bite at a time.

"You're a bunch of barbarians," she says grimly.

Kevin slides a fork over to her. "You know you want to."

She heaves a sigh and slides into the chair beside me. "You're a bad influence, Avery. First violence and now the corruption of youth."

Charlie winks at me and slides a wrapped package across the table.

"Presents too? God, I missed you guys."

Charlie and Annie exchange a conspiratorial smile, and I raise my eyebrows in suspicion. I unwrap the gift cautiously and find a pair of boxing gloves, which I stash under the table as the cafeteria monitor wanders by. "You guys are gonna get me suspended again," I warn.

We're polishing off the last of the cake when Courtney walks by with Scott stumbling after her. I stiffen, bracing myself for a confrontation, but she walks right past, as if we don't exist, and finds her way to her table, where a group of minions receive her like royalty.

Some things never change, I guess. And I'm surprised by how little it bothers me. For the first time ever, Courtney doesn't feel like the enemy. She's just a girl I don't particularly like.

Annie's phone chimes on the table, and she looks at it scornfully.

"He's been texting me like crazy," she says, flashing me the screen. Scott.

I blink at her in surprise. "Are you texting him back?"

"Only to torture him," she says mischievously, standing up and unzipping her sweatshirt before giving a theatrical stretch that manages to show off her killer abs.

I sneak a look at Scott and see that he's practically drooling on his cafeteria tray.

"You're evil," I tell her, impressed.

Her phone chimes again, and she shakes her head in disbelief. "He seriously thinks I'll take him back."

Not in a million years, she taps out on the phone, and then turns it off and stashes it in her bag. "He's not worth the time," she tells me. "This is a special day."

I laugh and bump my shoulder against hers. "I have a surprise for you, too." I reach for my bag slowly, drawing out the suspense, and watch as Annie bounces in her seat, excited.

I pull out a stapled packet of typed pages and present them to her with a flourish. "Ta-*da!*"

"Seriously? I bring you a party and you bring me . . . your homework?"

"Not exactly," I say, laughing. "But kinda. Remember that god-awful story I wrote for Miss Donaghue last semester?"

Annie rolls her eyes at me. "You mean the one she told you was *full of potential?*"

"Yeah. That one. I have a confession to make. I was really upset when she hated the ending."

"You don't say."

I smack her with the papers. "I'm being serious here." I laugh. "Back then, I couldn't imagine any other outcome. I got stuck on one idea and couldn't see past it."

Annie gives me a rueful smile. "I can identify with that. So what changed?"

I shrug. "I'm not sure exactly." I look around the table, thinking of everything that's happened this year. "It was so strange, the way the story came together," I tell her. "It's like . . . once I stopped trying to force things to happen the way I thought they should, everything sort of fell into place."

"I like that," Annie says, taking my story and hugging it to her chest. "I can't wait to see how it ends."

Acknowledgments

I'm sitting at my desk, surrounded by crumpled-up papers, trying to find the words to express how very thankful I am. Beyond all my wildest dreams, *How It Ends* has been transformed from a file on my computer to the book you now hold in your hands, and I owe an enormous debt of gratitude to so many people for making this dream come true.

I want to thank my remarkable agent, Mackenzie Brady, who saw a spark of potential in an earlier draft of this story, and who helped me nurture that spark into something more. Mackenzie is everything you would want an agent to be—brilliant, intuitive, savvy, tenacious, patient, and kind. She works tirelessly to protect the interests of her authors, and I am thankful for her every single day.

Mackenzie works as part of a team at New Leaf Literary & Media—and what an incredible team it is! The day my name went up on the Authors page of New Leaf's website is one of my proudest, and I still can't believe I'm fortunate enough to be represented by what is hands-down the best agency out there. Thank you, Joanna Volpe (who knows the answers to all the questions), Pouya Shahbazian, Kathleen Ortiz, Suzie Townsend, Dave Caccavo, Danielle

Barthel, Jaida Temperly, Jackie Lindert, Jess Dallow, and Chris McEwen for all your hard work.

I want to thank my editor, Sarah Landis, and the entire team at Houghton Mifflin Harcourt. I will never forget the first time I spoke with Sarah — she talked about my characters like she knew and loved them, and I couldn't wait to get started working with her. She is a truly phenomenal editor, and I have grown as a writer under her expert guidance. Her insights have taken this book to a whole new level, and there aren't enough words to express how grateful I am.

The more I learn about the world of publishing, the more I appreciate just how many people bring their expertise to each project. The team at Houghton Mifflin Harcourt is beyond compare, and I am thankful for all of their contributions — editors, copyeditors, proofreaders, production and design teams, cover designers (especially the talented Cara Llewellyn, who created my stunning cover), marketing and publicity, sales . . . the list goes on and on. Thank you all.

Thank you to my amazing support group of friends and fellow writers. Especially to Heather and Suzette, who always believed and who celebrated every step along with me, and to Janet Taylor, my fellow HMH author and debut buddy. I can't tell you how many times I leaned on Janet for support. She is one wise and talented lady. To all our fellow Sweet Sixteens: It is an honor to be debuting alongside talent like yours. I am grateful for your friendship and support, and I wish you all the success in the world.

To all the students who have let me into their lives and shared their stories with me over the years: *thank you*. You have taught me more than I could ever hope to have taught you, and you inspire me beyond words. I especially want to recognize Sydney Morris, who passed away before she could see this book in print. I miss you, Syd.

I want to thank my parents, who inspired my love of reading, and who never said no when I asked for another book. They have always encouraged me to dream big and aim high, and they made me believe I could do anything I set my mind to. Thank you also to my brother and sister, Chris and Brianne, for their humor, their friendship, and their support.

The path to publication has been a long one, and my husband, Ernie Lo, has walked it beside me. We've laughed, cried, celebrated, and commiserated. He has picked me up, cheered me on, and kept me on task ("Get off the Internet and back to work!"). Thank you for believing in me. I love you to the moon and back.

And to my children — Ethan and Mackenzie. You are smart, you are talented, and you are loved. Dream big and follow your hearts. There is no limit to what you can do.